ADDICTED

Lies

WARNING

This book contains sexually explicit scenes and adult language and may be considered offensive to some readers. This book is intended for adults ONLY. Please store your books wisely, where they cannot be accessed by under-aged readers.

BLURB

He gets addicted to things to easily...and I'm no exception.

Ford Ivanov follows the rules.

I was born to break them.

A single scandalous moment turns into a year of lies, stolen kisses behind closed doors, and whispered promises in the night.

Sneaking around with my brother's friend is forbidden. Because where I come from, love isn't just dangerous. It's deadly. The lies are unraveling. And in a world where love is a weakness, we're about to find out just how strong we really are.

*Why don't you close those other books like a good girl
and come and join me sweetheart.
Sincerely, your book husband.*

ONE
BILLIE

HE'S ACROSS FROM ME, the one who always stares and rarely speaks but will happily take any of the candies I have on me—sometimes without so much as a "thank you." I never know what he's thinking, though the others around him are slightly easier to read—in an unhinged way—since I grew up with them.

I know all of these men as well as anyone who's related or married to them. The one I'm closest with, who just so happens to be the bane and cause of my non-existent love life, is my brother, Dutton. He has issues with men being around me in any context. If a man talks to me, by the next day, he's actively avoiding walking within my vicinity. If someone asks me on a date, they're suddenly nursing a ghastly wound. If someone touches me… Well, there have been instances which they don't reappear. At all.

He's even advised the two men currently escorting me out of my cousin's home that if they touch me, he'll kill them. And they're *friends*. So, yeah, I'm royally fucked. He treats me like a child, and my father seems to have no issues with it, going so far as to encourage the barbaric behavior. I'm glad for once he's preoccupied in Italy for work while I'm home from college for a few weeks.

"Okay, little tornado, I think it's time we send you back to your palace where you're nice and snug and where no one can touch you," Hawke jokes as he throws an arm around my shoulder and pulls me in. I glare at him because I know ordinarily he doesn't make a habit of touching me, although he does it on purpose sometimes in order to antagonize my brother.

Hawke is the bulkier of the twins, spending way too much time hitting the gym and less on his intellect. The guy's a moron, but maybe I'm biased. Ford's body is leaner, but there's something about him that just sucks me in, like a mysterious vortex. I've always been curious to see what I might find if I could peel back his layers. Both of them are heavily tattooed and give off a dangerous vibe, so much so that most people stay clear of them.

"No, I want to go out," I say, stomping my foot. I've already had a few drinks, and I'm not ready to go home yet.

Ford looks up from his phone for what seems like the first time since being here. His dark brown, almost black eyes seem to stare straight through me, and it's unsettling. "We're not taking you out. Are you trying to get us killed?"

Hawke laughs. "Come on, little tornado wants to have some fun before big bro comes and spoils it all."

"I never invited you," I say to Ford as he intently watches me fish a lollipop out of my handbag. I can sense the shift in his mood the moment I do. It's almost like rewarding a dog. He'll really do anything for sweets. "But say if I were to tag along with you two, I'm sure a few hours might be okay, right?"

He stares at the lollipop in my hand as I step closer to him with a knowing smile. The deadly atmosphere doesn't change around him, but I already know he's a goner. These two men are lethal, but not to me. They both work for my cousin, Eli, who is now the head of the Monti family, but I've never once feared them, especially when I'm offering candy.

"You think a lollipop can bribe me?" Ford asks.

"You've never turned down any of the sweets I've offered you," I say as I pop a hand on my hip. "I've been super stressed at college. Please let me just have this one night while Dutton is out of town."

Ford looks at me—really looks at me—as if it's the first time he's seeing me. I puff out my chest, trying to make myself look bigger next to his six-foot-two height. His large, callused hand wraps around the lollipop. "Do you have more of those in your bag?"

Little does he know I always carry a packet around with me. At first, they were my favorite snacks when I was studying, but I always carry a bag now when I'm hanging with the twins because I find it amusing that such a scary guy enjoys sucking on lollipops. "More than you can ever imagine," I reply with a smile. "So, where are we going, boys?"

"Boxers." Hawke laughs as he slings his arm over my shoulder again and leads me toward the car. I sit in the back seat as Ford drives silently, lollipop hanging out of his mouth. I really can't believe it's that easy to convince a guy like him to agree to my bidding.

I look down at my phone and message the guy I've been texting with since returning to Manhattan. I only want one thing: Fun.

When I glance up, I notice Ford looking at me in the rearview mirror as his brother flips through songs.

"Have you asked for permission?" Ford asks, obviously having watched me this entire time on my phone.

I pocket my cell as I tell him, "I don't need to. Dutton may think he's in charge of me, but he's not. He's my brother, not my father." I flick my hair over my shoulder. Even my father's not that meddling. My brother is just overbearing and protective. I'm almost twenty-three, for fuck's sake. I can do what I want.

Hawke passes me a bottle from the front. I frown at it and look at the label. Whiskey. Can't say I've ever really liked the stuff, but I defiantly take a swig. Fuck these guys. I'm sick of people thinking I'm this dainty little princess.

I choke on the harsh burn but take a second sip for extra measure.

Hawke applauds, actually fucking claps like a clown. "Little tornado is going to make a mess tonight."

I roll my eyes as I pass the bottle back to him. I might think he's a dumbass, but I really like Hawke; he's never treated me any differently because of my brother's influence. And I like the nickname little tornado. He always calls me that because I'm so easily wound up—mostly because of my brother.

I remember the first time I met the twins; it was years ago now. While Dutton and Eli have been friends with them for much longer, I was banned from hanging around his friends even though I saw them all the time. It was only when I turned eighteen and begged to go to the adult parties, that I started meeting people. My parents gave me a pretty sheltered life. Considering our high-profile family, I was sent to private school, and despite how my brother was, I never went behind my parents' back, never snuck out—never had the need to.

Now, it feels like a bright new world has opened up to me. And even though I'm rarely involved in anything the family does, my brother absolutely hates it and tries to shield me from it. I'm kind of addicted to it, though. So, anytime I come home from college, I love to see what everyone is doing.

By the time we arrive at the club, it's fair to say I'm drunk. Hawke jumps out of the car, immediately clasping hands with the bouncer. I look down at my phone, waiting for a response from the guy who is most likely going to be a disappointing fuck tonight, but at least it's something. I haven't received anything back.

I sigh, and as I go to open my door, Ford opens it for me. I adjust my green bodycon dress as I step out. He's dressed in black jeans and a black long-sleeve shirt that's pushed up his arms, exposing a few of his tattoos. I can't help but look at them and wonder how he does them himself. I've never seen him do it, but I heard that's what he does—tattoo people. And it's especially hard not to notice the one across his throat that reads *Bad to the Bone*. I'd probably laugh if he wasn't so ridiculously hot, in an I-definitely-should-not-touch-this-man kind of way.

I pass Ford the almost empty bottle of whiskey. "Lighten up, Ford. You might actually have fun tonight." He frowns at the bottle as I walk past him.

I've never asked Hawke why his brother always seems like he has a stick up his ass. Frankly, Hawke is probably the only fun one out of the bunch. The rest of our friends and family always seem to have a frown marring their features, like they just sucked on a lemon.

It doesn't surprise me when I look over my shoulder and notice Ford putting the bottle on the floor of the car, untouched. Instead, he's sucking on the second lollipop I gave him, the little white stick hanging out of his mouth as he glares at any man who looks at me.

For fuck's sake, it's like having my brother here.

Hawke throws an arm around my shoulders to pull me inside with him as if giving me a personal tour. Once we're inside the club, the flashing lights and pounding music call to me, and the alcohol adds a pleasant buzz. I fucking love dancing, though it might not be the same without the girls. And I sure as shit can't see either of these two being the dancing type.

Hawke leads us to a seating area, Ford begrudgingly following behind. I wonder if he even likes this type of scene, and if not, why does he come? In fact, I have no idea what his idea of fun is. I never see him drink or party. I wonder if the only thing he enjoys is hurting people.

Probably.

He certainly oozes that type of energy.

Hawke's arm drops from my shoulders as a waitress starts pouring us drinks without even asking what we want. Obviously these two are regulars. I wonder if my brother frequents this place with them. Then again, I always see them working for Eli, so I suppose this just proves that he does let them have nights off.

Hawke throws back one drink and then two. I follow his lead, gasping at the potent shit. Ford simply takes a seat and pulls out his phone. It reminds me to do the same. Still no message.

What the fuck, dude? Do you want to get laid or not?

Two women approach us and then drape themselves all over Hawke. He's what we like to call a ladies' man. He likes to fuck. A lot. Every time I see him, he's with a different woman. These two climb all over his lap, and another comes along and sits next to Ford. I sigh. Is everyone getting laid tonight but me?

I let out a quiet huff. It's just so easy for these fuckers. I feel my temper spike. Although the woman beside Ford is talking to him, he makes no effort to entertain her. In fact, he looks up at me briefly, almost expectantly. He then removes the stick of his lollipop and places it on the edge of an ashtray. I roll my eyes as I dig another one out of my bag and hand it to him. This guy really has an addiction to sweets.

I look down at my phone again, and my eyebrows furrow. The contact number and all of my previous text messages to the guy I was supposed to be seeing tonight vanished. *What the fuck?*

My hands bunch into fists as an unbearable amount of fury fills my veins. This has Dutton written all over it. Did he seriously hack my phone just to delete my only means of communication with this guy? I internally scream. Fuck these guys and this place. I'm sick of not being in control of my own life.

I grab my drink as I stand. I need to fucking dance and find someone to eat me out in the next ten minutes, or I'm going home so I can scream and cry into my pillow. And I know which I'd rather be doing.

My name is called out from somewhere behind me, but I ignore it. Pushing through the crowd, I'm bumped and danced up on. I scan the dance floor, searching for my victim. Surely, there's one fucking hot guy in this club. Standing in the middle of the crowded floor, I throw back my drink.

"Billie, should you be walking off on your own?" I turn to find Ford behind me. My gaze drops to the drink he's holding. I don't know why this fucker even pretends; it's obvious he doesn't drink. I pluck the glass from his hand and down the contents. He frowns as I hand it back to him. "Rough night?" he asks.

I eye him and shake my head, reminding myself that it's not fair to take my frustration at my over-bearing brother out on Ford, but my God, I'm about to lose my shit if I don't dance, cry, or fuck it out.

I ignore him as I continue through the crowd, hoping I'll lose him, but it doesn't do much considering he's taller than almost everyone in here, and people make sure to give him a wide berth as he steps through the crowd.

"Billie." I shoot him my best eye roll over my shoulder as he follows me. "Fucking hell, woman, your brother told me to keep an eye on you, and here you are running off."

I turn toward him and snap, "Fuck Dutton and fuck you!" He looks indifferent, almost like a fucking robot. My God, what do I have to do to shake a guy like this? I turn back in the direction I was heading and continue weaving through the mass of bodies. I can feel him following me.

Gah, why won't he just give up?

I stop suddenly, and his chest hits my back. His hands wrap around my waist, and we both tense at the contact. His grip is tight, and I feel like I'm on fire. He's looming over me, and I can sense his intense stare on me. We're stuck, unable to move, as people around us drink, dance, and drunkenly scream the lyrics of the song currently blasting through the sound system. He doesn't release me, and I don't move away, and I wonder why.

"I thought you'd be scared to touch me," I shout over the noise as if that is deterrent enough. My brother has chopped off men's hands before for being so bold.

"I'm not afraid to touch you." His voice elicits goose bumps to erupt over my skin, and my spine goes stiff. A heated pounding begins in my core, and for the first time, I *feel* him.

We stand there like that until the song changes. That's when I finally turn around to face him, his touch falling away, and I instantly feel the loss.

"My brother would kill you for touching me," I remind him. He knows it well enough, as I'm sure he's taken part in dealing out those ridiculous consequences.

"I know." He says it as if he doesn't care. Maybe he doesn't. I don't know.

His dark brown, almost black, eyes consume me. And for all his lack of expression, I can sense his desire. Even while he's sucking on that fucking lollipop.

This is dangerous, Billie.

Walk away, Billie.

I don't want to listen to reason, but I'm so used to people being hurt from just getting my number that I realize I like him enough that I don't want to see him hurt.

"I should leave," I tell him before I can stop myself from taking a step forward. Our chests brush, but he doesn't step back.

What the fuck am I doing?

Me and my reckless brain decided it was best to leave.

And yet I can't look away. I want the heat of his body on mine.

His dark gaze pins me in place as he leers down at me. Ford, like his brother, has high cheekbones and great lips. Both of them are attractive. There is no denying that. But where Hawke is loud and obnoxious, Ford is quiet and reserved.

Or so I thought.

"You're playing a dangerous game, Billie." My name rolls off his tongue, but he doesn't step back or make any type of move.

"Am I?" I ask. His tongue darts out, and it slides over his teeth as his gaze locks on mine.

Ford is a very restrained person, unlike his brother, who acts on all his impulses.

And maybe it's my devilish curiosity to see what he might look like when he loses his shit.

Maybe I want to be the reason he does.

I'm sure he probably lets loose occasionally; he can't be a calm and collected person all the time in this life we live. Even I know that, and my parents tried to shield me from most of it.

"Why haven't you kissed me yet?" I ask. It could be the alcohol talking. Or maybe it's just me. I don't know. Maybe it's a bit of both.

"Kiss you?" he asks around the lollipop as his gaze drops to my lips. It stays there for a second too long before moving back to my eyes. "That won't happen," he says matter-of-factly, but then he leans down, his mouth close to mine. I close my eyes. And I wait. I want this man to kiss me.

I want it like I want my next breath.

I want to be breathless from his touch.

"We're leaving. Get moving," he whispers into my ear.

My eyelids burst open, and disappointment and embarrassment flood me. I stare at him in shock as he backs away from me. He reaches for my hand, clasping it in his before he starts dragging me toward the door. He pulls out his phone, puts it to his ear, and says a few words, most likely telling Hawke we're leaving.

What the actual fuck just happened?!

Did I just get rejected?

I'm reeling from what just happened, and it's not until the cool air hits me and we're almost at the car that I yank my hand out of his. "I'll find my own way home, thanks," I say as I turn to walk away.

"Billie. Stop," he commands from behind me, but I fucking refuse. Whatever the fuck was happening in there, I must've been out of my goddamned mind.

"Stop," he repeats as he grabs my hand. I try to yank it back but can't fight against his strength, so I turn around and swing my other hand at his face. He barely dodges, looking surprised that I tried to slap him.

Tears spring to my eyes. And maybe it's because I've been drinking, or maybe it's because I've yet again been reminded how controlling my brother is. But I won't be fucking humiliated by an asshole who barely speaks.

"What's the problem? Is your dick so small you can't use it? Or do you think you're too good for me?"

"Too good for you?" He frowns.

"It's not the small dick comment you're going to correct?" I growl, infuriated. He genuinely looks baffled. I let out an irritated sigh. "Do you know how frustrating it is to not have any control over your own life? All I want to do is fuck, like a normal college student, but noooooo, Billie has to remain celibate or some shit."

"I don't know if this has to do with me or not," he says, confused. And this only infuriates me more. Yes, I'm winding up for a tantrum. Yes, I'm taking my frustration out on him. Yes, I have a temper. But fuck him. Fuck my brother. And fuck the world.

"You said you weren't afraid to touch me. So why don't you put your money where your mouth is and put your mouth between my legs."

He tilts his head, looking as if he's fighting an internal battle, but he also appears predatory.

"You don't want this," he states. And I think he's talking more to himself than me. I pull my hand free and open the door to the back seat. Luckily for us, he parked on the side street, and no one is around.

Climbing in, I find him still standing on the street, watching me.

"How about you let me make my own decisions? Either you put that mouth to good use, or I'm going to fuck myself in the back of your car."

I'm out of my fucking mind, but I don't care anymore. Maybe it's the liquid courage. Maybe it's because I don't think he'll actually do it. Or maybe because it's so fucking forbidden, and I never thought of it before, that I want it so badly.

Taking a deep breath, I lift my dress over my head. The moment the garment is off my body, his gaze flicks to my bare tits, and he steps closer to the open door so no one can see inside the car.

"You're grinding on my last fucking nerve, Chaos." I like the gravel in his voice. A tic jumps in his jaw, and it fills me with satisfaction. The realization that he's not immune to my looks or body. And that he might not be as uninterested as I first thought.

"It's just sex, Ford. Get in the car," I say as I crawl to the other side of the seat, purposely arching my back to give a good show of my G-string.

He runs his hand through his dark hair as he curses under his breath. He looks around, and then he focuses back on me.

"Now," I growl.

"Fucking hell, Chaos, do you want to kill me?" he asks around the lollipop, and when he sucks, I notice the way his cheeks hollow.

"As long as I come, I don't care how you die," I retort.

That's all it takes for him to slide into the back seat to join me. He slams the door behind him, and then I straddle his lap. His hands find their way to my ass.

I can tell he's hesitant; his cock, however, is not. Leaning down with a smirk, I whisper against his ear, "Now, I'm really fucking horny. Do you think you can assist me in taking care of that?"

One hand slides from my ass to stop between my legs. He pushes my G-string to the side and circles a finger around my entrance before pushing it inside.

"Yeah, Chaos. I think I can," he says around his lollipop. I struggle not to look away from the intensity of his gaze, but I get distracted the moment I unbutton his shirt and pull it open. He's fucking beautiful and more muscled than I'd expected. I knew he was fit, but fuck me... this should be illegal.

My hands glide down his bare chest as I trail the masterpiece of tattoos down to his stomach.

"I want to know how you taste," he says, and I watch, transfixed, as he pulls out his lollipop and moves it toward my pussy.

I'm shocked. Is that even okay? Like, is it hygienic? The corner of his mouth pulls up, and I realize he's challenging me. He won't do anything I'm not willing to do, and considering how boldly I tried to seduce him, I find myself nodding my agreement.

I've never had sensational sex, nor have I experimented much, but I have the keen sense that I've never tried to handle a man like Ford before.

He removes his hand from between my legs and then rubs the lollipop against my folds. I suck in a breath as we stare at one another.

Then I feel it slip inside of me. It's not as thick as his fingers, but the thought of what it is... excites me. Especially with the way his gaze drinks me in. And I notice how hard his cock is pushing against his pants. Dear lord, this man is barely touching me, and I'm getting off.

I lift up on my knees, giving him better access, and nod to his jeans. He doesn't waste any time as he undoes his pants and frees his cock, looking at me as if wondering what I might do. I rock back and forth on the lollipop as I stare at his large, veiny cock, and the ink that surrounds it. And I gulp when I notice the piercing. Fuck, will he fit inside me? I'm hesitant to touch it. And when I finally do, I pull back almost immediately, but he takes my hand and puts it directly on his dick.

"Never hold back," he whispers as he removes the lollipop from my pussy and puts it back in his mouth. I stare, bewitched by the man I never noticed in this way before, and surprised that we haven't gone down this path sooner. Because I know he's about to ruin me for any other man.

I wrap my hand around his shaft and stroke it, my nail catching the piercing at the end every time. He removes the lollipop with a *pop* and smirks as he shoves three fingers inside me and leans back.

"You're so fucking sweet, Chaos."

I've never seen this man smirk, and with it, I realize how royally fucked I am. I thought I'd lured him into this car, but maybe it was the other way around. I feel like I'm in his clutches and under his control.

He leans forward and sucks on my nipple before biting it. Hard. I squeal, surprised by it, but my pussy floods at the sensation. I'm breathing heavily, shocked at how into this I am.

What Ford and I are doing is very wrong.

We should not be in the back of a car together, taking from each other's bodies, knowing who our families are.

But I can't help myself.

And Ford? Well, he doesn't care what anyone thinks.

But after, I'll have to swear him to secrecy so that no one finds out about this.

Little do I know that this one night will lead to heartbreak and secrets.

Pretending we aren't fucking each other every chance we get like it's a newfound addiction.

One neither of us are able to break.

Not until we break each other.

TWO
FORD

Nine months ago

SHE'S BACK.

I always know when she's back because the minute I walk into my house after a night working with Eli and my brother, I can smell her baking before I even catch sight of her. She's always baking something sweet in my kitchen, a soothing habit she picked up from her mother, apparently.

The moment she learned how to break into my home, I decided to give her a key. I'm not opposed to her breaking in, but when she's home on school breaks, it just gives us easier access to what we both want—to fuck.

That first night months ago sparked something neither of us can pull away from.

Her brother is away on another business trip in Italy, which means there will most likely be a lot of fucking. When he's home, it becomes a little trickier to sneak around. Not that I'm scared of Dutton, although I know he'll try to kill me if he so much as thinks I've laid a hand on his precious little sister. But, frankly, I don't give a shit.

No one has any idea about us, and I plan to keep it that way. I love having her as my dirty little secret. Like an addiction and a fix, I get to keep to myself.

It was her idea to keep it a secret. When I suggested telling her brother, she basically screamed at me and demanded that I never tell him. Lucky for her, keeping my mouth shut is my *only* redeeming quality. So I've become her dirty little secret in return.

We've been together three more times since the first night we hooked up. The first time, she'd drunkenly broke into my home. I don't even know how she got my address, but I'm glad I immediately recognized her because I was ready to kill the fucker who thought it was wise to break in. Which is really the main reason I gave her the key.

She complained about being starving, and with the few ingredients I had in the cupboard, she baked a cake, which was kind of impressive since I don't keep a lot of stuff on hand. Two days later, ingredients were delivered to my door for the next time she arrived to bake. I'm certainly not complaining because I fucking love her baked goods.

I go to my room before heading to the kitchen to greet her. I walk into the bathroom and peel my black shirt off. It might have some blood stains on it from handling business tonight. I check my face and arms for blood spatter, then basically swap my dirty black pants and shirt for a similar outfit.

Though Billie was raised with a ruthless brother and father, she isn't a part of this world. She's like a sheltered princess. It's kind of crazy considering her mother was also a mafia heiress. But who am I to judge? If I had kids, I'm sure I wouldn't want them raised in this world.

I'm certain she hasn't even noticed I'm in the house as I walk down the hallway and then lean against the entryway into the kitchen. She's transfixed on icing the cake, rocking her hips back and forth to some ear-splitting music.

And yet I can't help but cross my arms over my chest and smirk at the sight. It's a novelty, really. She's the first person I've ever seen bake anything. My biological mother could hardly put food in our mouths because she was so fucked up on drugs, and our adoptive mother, Anya Ivanov, would somehow turn the smooth-edged utensil used to ice a cake into a weapon. Anya is crafty as fuck when it comes to killing someone, but she's definitely not a baker.

I wouldn't let just anyone in my home. In fact, my brother is the only other person who has a key and has been in here. But ever since I met her when she was twelve and I was fifteen, Billie has always had this ability to include and welcome herself into any situation or group. It's been almost eleven years since then, and in many ways, it hasn't changed.

"I didn't know you'd be in town this week," I say.

Billie jumps back, clutching her chest. "Oh, for the love of fuck, Ford, announce yourself when you're here."

"In my own home?"

She glares at me, and I don't think she realizes she has flour across her cheek. Instead of a smart-ass retort, she breaks out into the brightest fucking smile. "Hello to you." She nods to the cake on the counter. "Dutton's not in town, and I'm bored. I figure you'd have the cure to that. So, while I waited, I baked you a honey cake. I know how much you love them."

I do. I really fucking love her honey cakes. I step toward her and crowd her from behind, placing one hand on her hip. My cock is already twitching at the promise of being inside her. My other hand reaches for the icing.

She slaps my hand away. "You savage! Let me cut a piece for you."

My grip tightens on her hip as I pull her ass against my cock. "I'm an impatient man, Billie, especially when it comes to sweets." She chuckles as she cuts a piece of the cake, purposely rubbing her ass against my now fully-erect cock. This fucking woman is my addiction. I only get sporadic hits of her, which makes me more voracious every time.

She allows me to grab the piece she cut, and she laughs as crumbs drop all over the floor. "How do you manage to stay so fit when you have such a sweet tooth?"

"I like to fuck," I tell her around a mouthful, and the humor in her expression dies. I wonder if she's thinking about all the other women I could potentially be fucking. Putting her out of her misery, I add, *"You."*

She releases a breath, and I don't think she even knows she was holding it.

I didn't think after the first time I had her that I wouldn't want to touch another woman again. It's not that women haven't offered me companionship, but it feels so meaningless to me. I get off on the buildup of not having Billie all the time and waiting for my next fix. The rush of fucking her and pleasing her in ways I know no other man can or has.

We don't message or have deep conversations; we keep it strictly what it is—fucking.

So I'm more than happy to continue what we're doing together because we both understand that this can't and won't be more. We are just two people from the same world who enjoy each other's company and bodies. And, fuck, do I love her body. It's like she was perfectly carved by a master artist. I love to run my tongue over every inch of her, tasting her.

Her skin is smooth, her floral perfume is sweet, and she's everything I'm not. She's a ray of fucking sunshine, and I'm attracted to it like a moth to a flame. And I have to remind myself not to break her for it. Someone like me lives in the shadows, and I think that's exactly why she keeps coming back. That and any other man who tries to touch her is usually not smart enough to avoid her brother's attention and ends up...out of commission.

Hell, I've helped him deal out clear messages to two men in the last six months. If only he knew I was actually the one fucking his sister.

My cock is getting harder just thinking about it, but when she turns, and her lips are inches from mine, I have to restrain myself. Kissing is something I don't do. I'm not the dating or boyfriend type, and she doesn't come here for romance.

"Billie," I growl as I finish polishing off the slice of honey cake and then step back. As I do, I start unbuttoning my shirt. She watches me hungrily, her perfect little apron covering her clothes so they don't get dirty. But I plan to get her very fucking dirty. "Put the icer down."

"No." She smiles as she continues to watch me.

"Such a naughty girl." And she is in her own way. But if she knew my depravities—the things I really want from her—I'm certain she'd run the other fucking way. And I haven't quite had my fill of her yet, so I don't want to scare her off.

I want to tell her to hit me, but I'm certain my sweet Billie wouldn't be into violence as we fuck. I like that she has a bit of backbone and is demanding in what she wants, but that and what I'm into are entirely different things.

I throw my shirt to the floor, wondering why I even put it on in the first place. She watches every single move I make, a smile on her perfect fucking lips. I remove my pants and free my straining cock. She gulps as I fist it. She's always been mesmerized by my piercing, and I love that she can't look away.

She's wearing a little skirt under that apron, and she's barefoot. There's not a speck of makeup on her perfect face, and her hair is pinned up as it usually is when she's baking. She raises the spatula to her lips and licks the icing off it.

My cock gets even harder as I watch her.

"My perfect little secret," I whisper. Reaching behind her, I dip my fingers into the icing and step back. Spreading the icing on my cock, I nod to it. "I think it's time you cleaned it up."

She wastes no time dropping to her knees. The spatula in her hand clatters to the floor, and she crawls forward, opens her mouth, and takes my cock between her lips.

Each time we're together, I want and need more of her. I wonder if that will ever stop. When she's not with me, I dream of fucking her, and when she is with me, I do fuck her. She's literally my perfect little fucking secret, and I hope no one ever discovers us because I'm not sure how I'll give up this new addiction.

THREE
FORD

Sɪx ᴍᴏɴᴛʜs ago

BILLIE and I actively avoid one another as we mingle with family and friends in Dutton's backyard to celebrate his girlfriend's son's sixth birthday. If you'd told me a year ago that Eli Monti, my boss, and head of the Italian mafia in New York, would fall in love and get married but that his equally unhinged cousin, Dutton, would be smitten with a woman, I might've actually laughed.

But they're both lovesick fools. It's not that I can't tolerate love. I just find the notion of it unsettling. It means things are changing. And I don't particularly like change. Especially when, in the past, it always meant that Hawke and I were first to be discarded.

Not that I think Eli will throw us to the wayside; we're too damn efficient. But if those two are somehow finding what I didn't think was possible for any of us... Well, then fuck. It's definitely going to be just me and Hawke again. Because I'm not interested in that level of commitment, and Hawke can't keep his dick in his pants for longer than two seconds, let alone be faithful to one woman.

"Fuck off, Hawke!" I hear Billie yell.

"Shh, we're at a party for kids, little tornado," he teases as he holds something too high for her to reach. She looks around and notices her parents shaking their heads in disapproval. My brother has always had a playful relationship with Billie. If anything, I'm certain Dutton thinks Hawke might try to fuck Billie. If only he knew he was suspicious of the wrong twin.

Either way, I'm not a fan of watching them together.

"It's a lot, isn't it?" Ivy asks, coming to stand beside me. Her short blonde hair is smoothed back, and her blue eyes are fixed on the others, playing over what I now notice is a small gift. Most likely, Hawke is trying to steal the gift Billie brought for Bentley because he didn't think to bring one.

"Hasn't it always been?" I ask rhetorically. I like Ivy Walker, but I wouldn't trust her as far as I can throw her. I say that about most people. It's mostly because of the way she keeps to herself. She's a bit of a mystery, even though I've known her for years. She's close with Billie and my cousin, Hope Ivanov.

"It's even more when my father's here," she says with a smirk, watching Will Walker talk to Billie's parents, Honey and Dawson Taylor. Alina, Will's wife, stands silently next to him, looking amused. Will has the ability to piss everyone off, and yet, somehow, everyone still likes him. That's exactly why I'm suspicious of Ivy. She's a prankster, in a weird, twisted way that only she seems to find humorous. Though, I do enjoy it when we play chess.

I glance back in the direction of Hawke and Billie. My eye twitches at the way she clings to his arm, trying to use it for leverage to jump higher.

I turn and head toward the house.

I need something sweet.

Now that a kid lives in Dutton's home, there are more treats available, which is fucking fantastic for me.

I'm searching through the pantry when Billie walks in. She leans against the counter, pours a glass of water, and hands it to me. She then pours herself a glass of vodka and orange juice. A long time ago, she picked up on the fact that I don't drink alcohol and that I only pretend to do so when around others. Not because I give a shit about what they think, but because there are certain things I don't want people to notice about me. So I try to throw them off the scent.

"Are you not going to talk to me at all?" she asks, placing the small box between us. "This might be what you're looking for."

My gaze dips but not to the gift. She's wearing a low-cut shirt that's showing off her perfect breasts. A small, heart-shaped gold pendant hangs at her throat, and I stare at it, trying to focus on anything other than devouring her with my gaze.

I want her.

I want my next hit.

I want to eat her pussy on this counter and smack her black and blue for ignoring me all day. And it doesn't make any fucking sense because she hasn't done anything wrong.

"I want to fuck you. Now," I tell her.

She sucks in a sharp breath and looks over her shoulder as if someone might hear. They can't; they're all the way out the back.

"We can't do that here," she whispers. And that's exactly why I try my hardest to stay away; I struggle to control my impulse to grab her.

To break her.

To devour her.

To brand her.

"Here, this might tide you over. Sorry, the box is broken a little because of your brother, but I baked you some cookies. Eat them in private in the bathroom or something." She laughs as she slides the box toward me.

I go to take the box, my hand covering hers. The feel of her smooth, cool skin against my hot, callused palm breaks my resolve. I yank her toward me and cup her pussy, holding the box in my other hand.

"I want to eat this," I growl, and a small moan escapes her lips. "I want to taste your sweet cunt right now."

Her lips part and then close. "Not here," she replies, sounding unsure.

I step into her space, pressing against her so she can feel my hard cock against her stomach. I just can't control myself around this woman. It doesn't make any fucking sense.

"Kiss me?" she asks.

My eyebrows drop.

"Kiss you?"

"Yes, Mr. Badass. Ever done it before?" She waggles her eyebrows in amusement as she looks into my eyes. I don't fucking kiss. Ever. But if it's all the crumbs she'll give me right now, I'll fucking take it. "We can't fuck here, but I might be open to—"

I crush my lips against hers, taking whatever she'll give me. Whatever will tide me over until the next time I can get my hit.

She seems startled at first, but her tongue finds a rhythm against mine, then submits to the way I devour her. I place the cookies down and cup her cheeks, consuming her. Scared that if I let myself get used to this, I won't be able to stop.

A soft whimper escapes her, and she tugs at my belt greedily. I begin to lift her shirt off. All of her. I need all of it. Every last bit she's willing to give me.

Something crashes, and Billie shoves me away.

"What the fuck?" Hawke says in disbelief. "What are you doing?"

Billie pulls her shirt back down, and I reach out to help because I don't want anyone else to see her like that.

Especially my brother.

Then, a predator steps into the room, and I'm immediately ready to fight.

"What the fuck?" Dutton snaps. Hawke's staring at him in shock. Dutton barges past Hawke and shoves me away from his sister. I don't even think I'd try to fight him. I'd probably let him pound me into the ground, knowing Billie would hate me if I hurt her prim and proper brother. Who, by the way, I actually like.

I don't even feel guilty.

"Dutton! It's not what it looks like!" Billie yells. "I had a bug on me!"

Dutton pauses, glancing between me and Hawke as we silently communicate in the way twins sometimes can.

The thing about my brother and me is we'd lie for one another.

Die for one another.

Kill for one another.

But right now, I'm silently communicating that I'll handle this.

"Is that true?" Dutton demands, not at all believing Billie's explanation. And if he were to take one look at my cock pressing against my jeans, it would tell him that's the biggest fucking lie. But he's seeing red. I've seen what Dutton does when he's in these moods, and I'm waiting for the punishment.

I go to speak, but Hawke beats me to it. "It was pretty fucking big, but don't tell Eli I'm scared of them or anything."

Dutton's eye twitches as he looks around as if

searching for the imaginary bug. He can't seriously be falling for this. Then again, why would he have any reason not to trust us? We've always had his and Eli's backs.

I feel a sense of guilt because, yet again, I can't refrain from my impulses. Billie's so terrified she doesn't even look my way. And I realize then that it might be shameful for her to be seen with me. She is, after all, basically a princess. I'm no more than a street rat who was polished into a killer.

"And why were all three of you in here anyway?" Dutton asks, and I can tell he's trying to calm himself down.

Billie rolls her eyes. "You can't seriously be pissed right now? And we came in to get the cake."

"The cake's out there," he says suspiciously, staring her down.

Whatever she sees in his expression makes her pause, but only for a moment before she starts arguing.

"Hello? Did you forget I enjoy baking? Did you really think we'd only bring one variety of cake?" Her tone is sassy, yet I can sense the hint of nervousness in it. "Gosh, you're so insufferable. I need to find Hope and Ivy to get away from all this testosterone." She huffs as she heads for the door. "Besides, shouldn't you be getting your shit together?" she asks with an arched eyebrow.

Dutton swallows, and realization dawns on his expression. I notice him looking at the stack of plates on the counter, and I hand them to him. He nods but seems unsure as he stares at my brother and me.

Then he takes his leave.

I don't feel any particular way about it. But I'm certain that whatever Billie and I had is now over. It was bound to come to an end one day, but my hands ball into fists as I grapple with accepting it.

The moment Dutton closes the door behind him, Hawke shoves me against the pantry door, fisting my shirt. "Are you fucking kidding me?"

I don't do anything to resist him. I know I deserve punishment for touching her. I just didn't expect to get hooked on her in the process.

"Say something. Are you serious right now? I thought I had a problem when it came to women, but you've chosen the one woman in this entire fucking world who is off-limits. What the fuck are you thinking?"

I shrug.

Hawke shoves me and takes a step back. "Fuck, Ford." He runs his hand through his jet-black hair. "When did it start?"

I curl my hand around the box of cookies. "About six months ago." His jaw drops. "It's nothing serious."

"How the fuck have you kept this from Dutton?" he demands.

"She only comes around when he's out of town. Besides, he was never looking. He's been preoccupied with his own shit." I jut my chin in the direction where I can hear everyone clapping.

Hawke peers out the window and then throws his hands up in the air. "Dutton's down on one fucking knee. What the fuck is happening around this place? First Eli and now Dutton." He turns on me. "Don't start getting ideas. It's you and me. You know we're incapable of that shit." He grabs the back of my head and brings our foreheads together. "If Eli finds out, think about how this might affect him."

My fingers curl into my palm. Does Hawke think I haven't considered that? That I don't know the chaos it might cause? I've devoted myself to Eli and the Italian mafia. And that reminder makes it that much harder. "I just couldn't help myself."

Hawke sighs as if he understands. "If it's just sex, find someone else. It ends here and now, okay?"

I nod. Killing is the only thing I'm good at. The only thing I'm useful for. And Hawke fucking loves it. We'd survive if Eli decided to cast us off due to my indiscretion. We've always been survivors. Hell, we could probably take over our mother's business. But I don't want to be the reason for any of that. I don't want to let down Hawke again because of my impulses.

"Understood," I say, and he lets out a breath and straightens. He then notices the box in my hand and points to it.

"She baked me cookies," I admit.

He rolls his eyes and snatches the box from me. "You're not eating her fucking baked goods if it's only sex."

Within seconds, I have him pinned against the pantry, his shirt fisted in my grip. "You can comment about my shitty choices, but you don't get to dictate when I can and can't eat my cookies."

He's pissed, and despite being bigger than me, I've always been faster than him. Although we've never truly gone blow for blow, we both know it'd be pretty fucking even. And the one thing he knows not to fuck with me over is my sweets, more specifically, one's she baked for me.

"For fuck's sake, why do I only get anything out of you when it comes to food?" he growls and hands the box back to me. I back up, my temper quickly receding as my stomach simmers contently.

"I'm going to congratulate the happy couple. And I mean it—you two are done," he says.

I run a hand through my hair, knowing too well he's right. We got off by sheer chance this time, but it was too fucking close. I'd become reckless. I open the box and then bite into the first cookie, immediately satisfied by the sugar hit.

And I'm not at all surprised when my phone buzzes with an unknown number.

Unknown Number: *I'm sorry I freaked out. But we have to stop. I'm sorry.*

My jaw clenches, and I have no right to be annoyed by it. It was only ever sex.

I just didn't think it would impact me like this.

FOUR

BILLIE

Two months ago

IT'S our Sunday family dinner, and I have a pleasant buzz going after downing my first drink until Hawke and Ford walk in.

I haven't seen Ford since that day at Dutton's house. After Bentley's birthday party and Dutton proposing to Posie, I've tried my hardest to fly under the radar. This is the first time I've been home in months, and I didn't realize my mother had extended the invitation to so many. But it shouldn't come as a surprise.

It might not be so distracting if Hope and Ivy had come back to Manhattan as well. They're both busy with their own studies, and Hope is at a showing of her sculptures in Russia. The girl is crushing it for only being twenty-two. I'm almost two years older, and still unsure if the degree I'm going to school for even makes my heart sing.

I didn't start college until I was twenty because I wasn't sure it was the correct path for me, so I traveled instead. My family was supportive of my choice, but I realized the expectations placed on Dutton weren't the same as me. Then again, Dutton defined his own path and self-expectations as to how he'd contribute to the family.

Sometimes I feel guilty for not doing the same, even though our parents reminded us time and time again we could choose whatever path we wanted. And I'm still not entirely sure if accounting is what I want. Sometimes, I think I'd prefer baking, like my mother, since I'm good at it, but even then, I don't know if it excites me as much as it does her.

"Earth to little tornado." Hawke snaps his fingers in front of me, and I blink back into focus.

"Did you only come for the food?" I ask him and daringly look over his shoulder at his brother. Fuck, he looks good. He always does. And he still hasn't looked up from his phone since arriving. But that's not surprising in the slightest.

Everyone's already done eating and is now lounging around in conversation. Dutton and Posie are quietly talking to my parents, Alina and Will, about the upcoming wedding. And no offense to my brother, but I don't want to be a part of any conversation when he turns into a groomzilla, which is how I wound up in the same room as these two.

But we were friends before, so I shake off the imposing tension.

"Don't I always come for the food?" Hawke says sheepishly. It goes without saying that Ford comes for the sweets.

I'm grateful he hasn't brought up what he walked in on in Dutton's kitchen and that he doesn't act any differently toward me because of it.

"Do either of you want a drink?" I offer and place a tray of cookies down on the table in the middle of one of our living spaces. The deep, comfortable sofas and rich wooden tones make the room warm and inviting. I love my parents' home. Down the hall is my room—my sanctuary when I'm home from college—which, might I add, no boy has ever entered because of a certain overprotective brother.

Ford immediately kicks off the wall, where he was casually leaning, to make a beeline to the cookies. He finally glances at me, and I feel the air leave my lungs as those almost black eyes take me in. He's silent as he grabs a cookie off the tray. And then two more before he retakes his spot, holding up the wall and staring at his phone.

He's always on his phone.

What is he doing on there?

Is he messaging someone?

A phone rings, and Hawke smiles as he looks down at his screen. "If you'll excuse me, I need your bathroom for a moment."

I frown. "What's that supposed to mean?"

"He's been having phone sex with some chick," Ford says around a cookie.

I stare after Hawke. He really is a manwhore with no shame. I tuck a piece of my long hair behind my ear. Fuck, being in the same room as Ford creates a palpable tension. We never spoke about what happened, and he never replied to my text.

Not that I expected him to.

"You can sit, Chaos. I don't bite," he says, still not looking up from his phone.

It irritates me that he won't even look at me. "I don't have to worry about you biting when you're glued to your phone."

His finger pauses on the screen, and he raises his head. He finishes the cookie and pockets the phone.

Suddenly, my clothes feel too tight. *Fuck.* I haven't been touched in so long, and Ford's gaze alone is always punishing in the way it sees into me. In the memories that flood back to the surface, promising my body pleasure like it's never known.

"Don't look at me like that if you don't expect me to have you crawling to your bedroom so I can spank that tight ass you've been swaying all night."

My jaw drops, and I look away, crossing my arms over my chest. "You seem awfully chatty when you're talking dirty."

"I'm only speaking the truth. And I can tell when you're thinking it, too."

"How?!" I whisper shout, making sure no one in the other room can hear us. I hear Posie giggle, and I know that more than likely, my brother's going to drag her into a dark corner. They do that a lot at events—suddenly leave and come back looking like a rumpled mess.

It pisses me off so much how my brother has double standards. He can do it but won't let me.

"Nothing I'm about to say is sweet. So don't ask questions you're not willing to answer for yourself."

I swallow. Ford's always been so fucking intense. Even as he leans against the wall next to a blue vase with colorful flowers, he seems to suck it into his orbit like he does with me.

Everything feels hazy as I gravitate toward his provocation like it's a fucking dare.

I take a step forward.

And then another.

I'm certain everyone still sees me as the baby sister or like a child. But not Ford. He's the only person who sees me as a woman.

I'm standing in front of him now. "How?" I repeat.

The asshole has the audacity to smirk, and I hate the fact that I ended things between us, but I'm right back where we started. It's too dangerous. But I can't fucking help myself.

He tilts his head slightly, more predator than man, as he reaches out and brushes the back of his knuckles against my cheek.

I suck in a sharp breath, and without him so much as doing anything, heat floods my core. It's so immediate, so forceful in his presence.

It's entirely unfair.

"From the way your body reacts to me. Your eyes go hooded. A slight pink flushes your cheeks, and your shoulders slightly hunch as if purposefully readying yourself to defy or challenge me, even though you always submit. But only when you think you're in control."

"I do not submit," I snap.

He raises an eyebrow. "Are you so sure?"

His hand turns, and his palm cups my cheek. It's not tender. It can't be in the fierce way he stares at me as if restraining himself with all his might. But my body screams for him to finish what he started. And from all the times before, I know exactly how he brings my body and senses to life. He offers me an experience no one ever has.

I'm certain I'm out of my fucking mind as I whisper, "Did you drive here?"

His eyes somehow go darker as if he understands my insinuation. "You're dancing with fire, Chaos. You know I can't restrain myself around you." It goes unsaid that I know if I ask him, he won't deny me. He never has. Not since that first time I lured him into his car. And I'm sure it'll be no different now.

More heat floods my core, and my pussy is fucking pounding, begging, and praying to dance on his cock. To revel in the release I'm certain only he can provide.

Ford is dangerous.

Whatever this is between us is dangerous.

Even if it's only sex, I can't seem to control myself.

And if my brother finds out, he'll kill him. And maybe me in the process.

Yet I can't help myself from whispering, "Then don't hold back. I'll meet you outside in two minutes." I step out of his grip. His fingers curl, and I can see his internal struggle, which gives me a sense of smug satisfaction. He might say I submit only when I think I'm in control, but the reality is, he's no different—this thing between us is a living entity that neither of us can seem to ignore. That's a scary thing, but it's the truth.

"You said we were over," he says pointedly.

"And now I'm saying we're back on." Because I have fucking needs, and I know this man can meet them.

I make my way to the car first, a shot of adrenaline pumping through my veins because it's literally too close to home. Dutton and my parents are inside. But I know with Posie preoccupying my brother, I have a good chance of getting away unnoticed. I'm an opportunist, if nothing else. And even if I wanted to stop myself, I'm not entirely sure I could, especially when temptation comes in such a ridiculously attractive package.

It's cool outside as I wait beside his car, but I'm grateful for it as my palms have started to sweat. The thought of being caught is as terrifying as it is exhilarating. I don't want us to be caught—or almost caught again—but I just can't help myself.

He doesn't even wait the full two minutes before he crosses across the grass to the front courtyard, where guests park.

The moment he unlocks the doors, we waste no time sliding into the back seat. I shove him back, and he smirks, raising his hands and letting me have my way with him. I often think it's because Ford restrains himself around me. That he still hasn't let me see the true version of him and the needs he has. But I selfishly love how much he's willing to give to me. How much he allows me to explore.

"You didn't even give me a treat today," he reprimands as I straddle his lap and undo his belt.

"Consider me the treat," I hiss back, and he chuckles. My hands shake as I paw at his cock.

"So desperate, Chaos." He chuckles, and it's the most beautiful sound because Ford rarely chuckles. He shifts slightly, his hands running over my bare legs and under my skirt. I take in a breath as he dips his hand between us, and his eyes grow darker. "You're already wet for me."

"So soak me up," I daringly challenge. A small

animalistic growl escapes him, and it's what I like about Ford—he's primal. And I like taming the beast. But I know that when we're together, he tries to be on his best behavior. But being curious about what else could be between us would make this about more than sex. And we are absolutely not going down that path.

I hiss as he inserts a finger inside me, and a small moan escapes me when he starts thrusting it in and out. Oh, fuck me, how I've missed this man's gifted hands. His cock springs free from his pants, and I swallow, almost salivating as I stare at it.

"Spit on my cock, Chaos."

He inserts another finger, and I moan as I collect the saliva in my mouth and slowly let the large drop of spit fall onto his cock. Fuck this man and his beauty. I wrap my hand around his shaft and begin stroking. "Harder. You won't hurt me," he growls, and I'm certain nothing could hurt this man. He grimaces as I pull back and forth on the shaft, almost violently.

"Take your shirt off," he instructs.

I giggle. Not because I like admitting Ford's right about anything, but he might be about one thing. Initially, I might think I'm in control, but it's only within a few minutes that he's taken complete control, even though I'm the one in the position of power. And

I don't mind it at all. In fact, I'm giddy with what he might ask for next.

I take my shirt off, moaning as I continue to ride his callused fingers. Fuck me, this man is everything. He's giving me the perfect buildup to the release I need.

Something catches my attention as I toss my shirt onto the seat beside us—a face peering in at us through the window.

I scream, and Ford's hand immediately whips up to cover my mouth as he looks over his shoulder while protecting me with his body.

Posie.

Fuck.

We scramble to make ourselves decent. Once my shirt's on, I throw open the door and find Posie casually walking to my brother's car, which is two behind Ford's.

A wave of relief washes through me when I see my brother's not with her.

"Posie." I try to keep my tone even as I run my fingers through my hair to tame it.

She turns around nonchalantly as if there's nothing to see here. But we both know the truth. "Billie," she says casually.

"Don't tell him. Please." And Posie knows exactly

who I'm talking about. The one person who can't find out about this—my brother. I know it's a big ask, wanting her to lie to her fiancé, but I'm willing to get on my hands and knees and beg if necessary. And besides, it's not lying. It's just pretending she didn't see any of this.

Ford steps out of the car, adjusting his jeans and shirt.

I can see the reluctance in Posie's expression as she looks between the two of us. Its most likely because we're the most mismatched pair anyone could think of. My heart is pounding because, fuck me, we couldn't be any worse with this sneaking around shit.

"Posie, please. You know Dutton will kill him."

Ford goes to step behind me as if to reassure me he'll be okay, but I shake my head at him and point at the door. I know Ford can hold his own. But this involves more than just us. It could ruin Ford's job as Eli's second as well.

Ford's expression shifts, the cocky smirk, and erotic growls of before gone. It's replaced with a cool expression that not a lot of people can read. But I know he's hesitant in letting me deal with this. He dealt with Hawke last time. Now, it's my turn to deal with Posie. But, fuck me, we couldn't be any worse at hiding this even if we tried.

I'm startled as he steps closer and rubs his thumb against my lips, slowly and sensually. It feels like a caress as much as it does him, wiping away the last remains of our moment together. I must've smudged my lipstick. He, however, looks immaculate since he had longer to adjust himself inside the car.

"Go," I whisper. He hesitates but does as he's told, and I'm relieved that in whatever wild understanding we have, Ford will listen to my commands. Sometimes.

Posie steps closer to me, and I hold my breath as her hand grips my arm. I'm confused, but I understand it's her way of comforting me. But I also want to cry because I really don't want Dutton to find out. I was stupid. I was reckless. I shouldn't have asked Ford to meet me in his car.

"If you don't want Ford to die, please don't say anything," I whisper. I know it's a low blow and unfair of me to ask, but I'll do anything to protect this secret.

The front door opens, and I startle when I see Dutton standing there. My heart is pounding as my brother makes his way toward us. Shit, does he already know? I try my best at a smile. He looks confused for a moment, then says to Posie, "You were gone too long."

An involuntary sigh escapes me as Posie's hand drops from my arm. I can't beg or plead my case with her anymore. I have to pray that whatever friendship we've built over the last year is enough to keep this secret between us.

I walk away, fully aware that I'm not welcome by the way my brother's gaze devours Posie, and I'm disheartened to know that, once again, he can have that but won't let me have the same.

What Ford and I have is only about sex, but it doesn't mean that one day I don't want to find someone I can share a bond with, the same type of bond that Dutton and Posie have. But I know my brother will do anything to destroy the potential of that. No one will ever be good enough for him. And before I reach the door to the house, frustrated tears are pricking my eyes.

It's ridiculous and unfair. I'm the daughter of two of the most powerful people in New York. I have mafia blood running through my veins, for fuck's sake. But the two prominent things I've taken from my parents are my father's temper—I'm not good at controlling mine like he, and my brother are, though—and my mother's heart, forever big and wild and curious. And completely at odds with how to handle all of these restrictions.

My nails curl into my palms. I want to obliterate all of the shackles my brother has placed on me. I'm not a fucking princess in a tower.

So why am I crying like one?

My mother notices me in the hallway, and her smile falters. "We're just about to serve some sweets. Honey, is everything okay?"

"Give my portion to Ford," is all I say as I try to hide the bubbling tears as I walk to my room and slam the door.

FIVE

BILLIE

Present Day

"STAY STILL." Ford says from beside me. I awkwardly pin him with a glare from over my shoulder as I lie on my stomach.

"I can't. You're looking directly at my ass, and it's weird." I try to stay as still as possible, but I can't. It's not just because my ass is on display for him, but it's also kind of ticklish in a painful way.

The buzzing sound starts again, and I glance over my shoulder to where one of his hands is wielding the tattoo gun, and the other holds my ass in place. His dark eyes lock onto mine. "If you don't hold still, I'll bite the other cheek." I can't help but smirk at his threat. "Stop it," he growls, knowing full well how much I like his mouth anywhere on me.

I try to distract myself by looking around the room, taking in the darkly painted walls. It's a small room in Ford's home that he uses purely for tattooing. A tray and counter in the corner for his items and ridiculously good designs sketched by Ford hung on the wall. When I inquired about them, he said it was his adoptive mother, Anya, who had them put up for display. Apparently, she thought the room was dreary with bare walls, but part of me wonders if it's because she was proud of his talent and wanted to showcase them. Then again, I don't know if someone like Anya Ivanov has the capacity to be proud or encouraging like a normal parent might. I've never understood the twins' relationship with her and River, but I know undeniably that the twins speak about them with reverence.

My leg twitches a little; I just can't help it, and he sighs, pulling back and placing the tattoo gun next to him. I twist so I have a better view of him. He's wearing a pair of black jeans, and he's bare-chested, which is distracting as all fuck. Tattoos skate up his stomach, but my gaze always lands on the one at his throat. *Bad to the bone.* I always want to make a joke about throwing a bone and having him fetch it, but it feels too dangerous of a joke.

Ford is intentional, even when he seems aloof. He appears disinterested when, in actuality, he's quietly listening. These are the few things I've come to notice about him in the last year. And in truth, it's about all I've been able to uncover about him. I imagine the only person who really knows him is his brother.

But one thing remains the same—since the first time we were together, Ford Ivanov has been the one man I can't take my eyes off of.

He leans forward and presses a kiss to the opposite cheek from the one he's inking, then proceeds to bite it before he straightens back up.

"Ow!" I hiss.

"I warned you," he growls. "Now, stay still."

I let out a *humph* as I lie back down, but I can sense his smirk.

This is the first tattoo that I convinced him to give me. And it took a lot of persuading to get him to agree. He has a fascination with biting my skin. He loves to tell me that I have the most perfect skin he's ever fucking touched, and he wonders why I'd want to permanently mark it in any way. But I want to mark it, and I want him to be the one doing it.

I didn't even ask permission to come over tonight; I just welcomed myself in and baked him a honey cake because it's his favorite as I waited for him.

When he got home, he'd gone straight to his room, and I'm certain that when he does that, it means he's been working for Eli. This time, he showered before he came out to the kitchen, so I know the cleanup must've been bad. It's strange to know I'm sleeping with a killer. Then again, many of the members of my family are killers, so it's not at all surprising that I would gravitate to one. I don't think badly of them, although I know most people probably would. I might have an explosive temper, but not a killer instinct. And I don't look down on them for it. Why would I? I love my family and would do anything for them. And they'd do the same for me.

My relationship with Ford is basically non-existent besides in the sexual context. And only Posie knows about us. Well, and Hawke, but I never cared to ask Ford about the discussion he had with him after the fiasco at Dutton's house. Now I'm just especially careful around him so he doesn't think it's continuing.

Posie hasn't told my brother, which I'm very thankful for because despite Ford and Dutton being friends, my brother would kill him without a second thought. And I quite like what I have going with Ford. In fact, when I came home this time, this was the first place I wanted to return to, mostly because I have needs that haven't been met in a very long time, and he seems to be the only one daring enough to touch me.

We hadn't spoken since we were caught by Posie. We don't text or call, but he didn't seem surprised when he found me in his kitchen tonight.

My leg twitches again, and the buzzing stops. I glance over my shoulder to see him pulling off his gloves. I don't think the tattoo is completely finished, but I slip off the bed, embracing the break. He watches me with those dark eyes, his hands dropping to the sides of the chair, basically inviting me without a word. Another thing I've noticed about Ford is he always lets me initiate or act as if I'm in control. Initially. Or maybe he's trying to restrain himself. Which, fuck that. I want to get off.

"I need to go soon," I whisper. I did organize to meet with Hope and Ivy later. He nods as I slowly straddle him. "You'll miss me, right?"

He doesn't say anything, but I notice the swell of his cock beneath me. I love how responsive his body is to me; it makes me feel desirable.

I flick my honey-blonde hair over my shoulder, and his hand creeps up my back. I feel the moment he wraps my hair around his hand and wrist. He pulls on it, tugging my head back and exposing my neck.

"Give me something to miss," he rumbles as he trails feather-light kisses down my throat and to the tops of my breasts that are exposed by the neckline of my dress. I should be on the bed, letting him finish the tattoo, but I really can't help myself when it comes to him. I greatly underestimated the time it'd take for my first tattoo.

"Ford."

"Hmmm," he hums, the sound vibrating against my neck, and I begin a leisurely grind against his hardening cock.

"I'll be in town more soon," I tell him. I literally have a month left of college, and then I'll graduate. Ivy will be done, too, and we're looking at finding an apartment together.

"Mmhmm" is the only response he gives. We don't really have in-depth conversations, even though I sometimes try to initiate them. Our relationship is strictly sex. And I really, really enjoy it.

He pushes my G-string to the side with the hand not gripped in my hair, and then he slips his fingers through my folds. And before I can stop myself, I'm riding his hand.

He grunts, and I can't help but moan in response.

Ford knows how to play my body, and I fucking love it.

I've had other sexual partners besides Ford, despite my brother's best efforts to stop any man who came near me, but nothing lasted more than a few nights.

Until Ford.

It started off as a way to scratch an itch, and it's morphed into so much more.

Now I don't want any other man to touch me the way he does.

And that's a problem. Because I don't want this to stop. I want to continue when I return to Manhattan full-time.

"You'll be a good girl and stay fucking still once you come, won't you, Chaos?" he whispers into my ear. I nod my head, knowing he means when he gets back to working on my tattoo. "Words. Fucking use them."

I love that I get this side of him. Everyone else gets the quiet version, but I get the dirty-talking, rough Ford. It's my favorite version of him.

"Yes, I'll stay still." Just as the words leave my mouth, he slips a finger inside me.

And that's when we hear it.

"Yo, bitch. Let's go and get fucked up." Hawke's voice echoes through the house, and we both pause, a chill running through me. *You have got to be fucking kidding me!* Why are we interrupted every fucking time?

I go to look over my shoulder, but Ford tugs at my hair. "Finish," he growls, pumping his fingers. His eyes are dark and deadly as we teeter on the edge of being discovered once more.

He means it.

He always does.

So I close my eyes and move my hips, and just as I reach the peak, he kisses my neck.

He never kisses me on my lips.

Only that once, and it makes me work harder against his hand.

This is purely sex, and I'm going to take my pleasure from him every fucking time.

"Fuck," I whimper as I fall over the edge, and stars explode behind my eyelids. I ride the wave, inhaling the smell and powerful presence of him—always at his mercy but realizing I get off more than he does. I reach for his cock that's pressing against his pants, but he releases his hold on my hair and stops me.

"I'm totally going to eat all your cake if you don't stop jerking off in there and hurry the fuck up," Hawke yells.

I growl, infuriated, and he chuckles as he lifts me off him. My legs feel wobbly as my feet touch the floor.

He pulls my dress back down and then adjusts his cock.

"Leave after we do," he says, then slips out the door.

And then he's gone.

SIX
FORD

My brother is clued into a lot of things, but how a freshly baked honey cake made it into my home is not one of them. And it's fair to say that his instinct not to touch the treat Billie baked me likely saved him a beating.

I don't ever intend to share anything about her. Billie Taylor is all fucking mine.

I wish she didn't hold that type of power over me, but the more I see her, the more I let her slip under my skin, and the immediate pleasure of that hit rises to the surface.

"Mother is going to kill you," Hawke says with a mouth full of a protein bar when I step into the kitchen. I have boxes of the shit in my cupboard for when he comes over. He's sweaty, most likely having hit the gym after we were done helping Eli. He sent us home early today because he and his wife Jewel were having a date night, whatever the fuck that's supposed to mean.

I hadn't even realized the time. It feels like time is something that doesn't exist whenever I'm with Billie. Then again, it was the same with all my other previous addictions.

That doesn't sit well with me.

Another addiction.

Another vice.

When we step outside, my brother and I face one another. Silently, we count to three and draw our hands at rock, paper, scissors. I win—which is usually how it goes—and that means I get to drive my car. Hawke does win on occasion, but even then, I end up driving back when he wants to drink.

As we get in the car, I look over my humble home, which offers me everything I need. Hawke's place is flashier and more materialistically impressive, but even with the fortune we're worth, I prefer a smaller space that's more functional. And it's not like I need a lot of things.

A small part of me hopes that Billie sticks around until I get back so I can fuck her senseless—and finish her tattoo. But I'll never ask her to stay. It's not my right. I'll let her use me until she's done with me, and I'll deal with the repercussions after.

But I'm certain she was insinuating she'd be around more because it meant more fucking. Which I have no problem with, but I cut off that conversation, and I don't like to make assumptions. I'm not good for someone like Billie Taylor. Even I fucking know that, so I'll do everything I can to sabotage her forming any attachment to me. But I'm failing miserably as I let her abuse my body time and time again and lose myself completely in her.

"Did you get all clean-shaven for Mom or something?" Hawke asks as he ruffles my hair with a cheesy grin. I shove him back into his seat.

"Fuck off. One of us has to look presentable," I say, but I think the black jeans and black shirt I have on aren't up to the standards of our mother, who loves all things shiny, expensive, and beautiful. But it's certainly better than the sweaty shirt Hawke's wearing.

"Please, I'm the favorite." He huffs without a doubt in his mind.

I don't reply to his statement. We both give her hell in our own ways. But we both know she cares about us exactly the same and punishes us the same.

Anya Ivanov is a woman who hated kids and never wanted them but ended up with two fucking delinquents. We stole from her when we were fifteen. We were nothing but street rats. Our mother had died three years before that because she loved getting high more than she loved her own kids.

But we got by from stealing from the rich. Until we tried breaking into Anya's house. She caught us and held a gun to both of our heads. It was more terrifying than the two dogs we'd sedated only a few minutes before. She scared the shit out of us, that is, until River walked in and asked her to put her guns down.

She looked at us with one perfectly raised brow and said, "Why? If they want to be big boys and steal from me, I'll show them how I handle big boys." She then flicked the safety off the guns.

River looked at us, indulging his wife.

"How old are you two?" he asked us.

We told him we were fifteen.

And that's when our lives changed.

And to be honest, with how well we know her now, we're lucky to be alive.

Our mother is a ruthless, cold-hearted bitch.

She is the fucking best.

And River is the only fatherly figure we've ever known. To be honest, he's probably also more of a motherly figure than Anya. He showed us what it was to be part of a family.

To kill for family.

Anya and River balance each other out. Even if they're both fucked up.

But River seems to have all the patience in the world for Anya's antics, even if it costs him a car or two when she destroys them. In fact, she smashed up one of his cars not even two years ago because *she* forgot their anniversary, and *he* didn't remind her. They're definitely not the ideal couple to base a healthy relationship on, but they're fucking powerful.

When Anya and River first took us in, even though we fought it, we liked the things they provided us with, like a nice school and fancy shoes. The shoes were a big thing for us, considering the shoes we had before we stole from a homeless person.

During the drive to our parents' house, Hawke talks about various topics, not ever really expecting a response. It's how we work. He can't keep his mouth shut, and I'd rather not have to contribute at all.

As I pull up to the house, I spot River waiting on the front patio. We're thirty-six minutes late, and I contemplate breaking one of Hawke's legs so we have a reasonable excuse as to why. Even then, I don't think it'll be enough to soothe our mother's wrath.

Anya hated it at first when we called her "Mother." We did it just to annoy her. But to be honest, no matter how cold and ruthless she is, she's been more of a mother to us than the one who gave us life. And now she won't tolerate it if we call her anything else.

When we step out of the car, our father glares at us disapprovingly. "You're late. Your mother is pissed." He raises a glass of whiskey to his lips, smirking.

"You're only happy because it's not you she's pissed at," Hawke says.

"Is that why you're hiding out here?" I add.

"Damn right." He chuckles. "But someone has to let the dogs out to go to the bathroom." He whistles, and with lightning speed, the two chow chows bolt from the darkness. They're not the same dogs from eleven years ago, but Ivan and Thor are a staple in the family. They greet us happily, tails wagging. I bend over and pat Ivan, him being my favorite of the two, as Thor goes to Hawke.

They appear friendly until the well-trained assholes are commanded to attack or someone breaks in. We'd know because we were made to wear the padded protection gear and run around the fucking backyard when they were being trained. Let's just say dogs are not a deterrent for Hawke and me when breaking into premises.

We follow our father into the house and find our mother pacing the kitchen. She's always been a shit cook, but at least she tries. And she only cooks when we come over, adopting the Taylors' family tradition of dinner once a month to feel "connected." Whatever the fuck that means.

Except in true Anya fashion, once a month was far too long for her not to be in our business, so we're here once a week, as requested.

If we're overseas, we're required to fly home.

We don't miss our weekly visits.

Or else.

"Oh, so you think it's a good idea to roll in late?" Anya snaps at us, a lock of hair escaping her usually perfectly secured bun. She blows at it, irritated. Hawke and I point to one another at the same time. "I don't care whose fault it is. Take a seat. Dinner is ready."

Hawke salutes her, and she says something in Russian, which I know are swear words, as we walk to the table. River's already sitting at the head of the table, looking smug. I swear the fucker actually gets off when we're in trouble, and I sometimes wonder if he cleverly dragged us into this household for his own amusement so he wasn't the only one being punished by his wife's hand.

"What's with the smiling?" Hawke asks. I think, in a lot of ways, Hawke mirrors River, especially in the way he's openly a smartass.

"Your mother makes me happy," River replies. That much we know. This man could literally go out, come home covered in blood, and have the worst day, but when he sees her, everything else is forgotten.

Their love is sickening, considering they have no filter on their still-booming physical attraction despite them both being almost sixty years old. But Anya doesn't look like she's aged a bit since we first moved in. That scorn forever molded into her expression.

I itch to pull out my phone—a habit of mine when in social settings. But considering the last time I did that at the dinner table, Anya stabbed a knife through it, pinning it to the table, and established a "no phones at dinner time" rule, I think better of it.

"What work did you do today?" Anya asks as she carries a plate of chicken into the dining room. It doesn't look fully cooked. But she places it on the table, reaches for a knife, and stabs it. We all stare at her as she attempts to cut it. "Let me guess, top secret because Eli Monti said." Anya doesn't dislike Eli. She actually respects his family. But she hates that we work for someone else.

Our relationship with Eli didn't start out on a good note. One day at school, Eli picked a fight with us, and despite hearing the warnings to stay clear of him, we had no issue hitting back harder. Eli was a finely tuned weapon even then, but we'd grown up fighting for our lives—literally. We were bigger and played dirtier. He was impressed by that, and when he discovered who we were living with, we became friends. We all left the school bloodied, none of us reprimanded for the scuffle, with Dutton shaking his head, disappointed that he didn't get an opportunity to play with his knives.

Eli might've come from money, but he's as fucked up as the rest of us.

That's what we liked about him.

And then, as the years went by, we started fucking around, doing illegal shit with him. You name it, we did it. Even killing with him and for him. Then we became his seconds and Dutton, his silent adviser.

I should feel guilty for fucking Dutton's sister. But I don't.

"Mother." Hawke interrupts the carnage that is Anya Ivanov trying to shred a chicken apart. River's smirking like a dickhead at the still-bleeding chicken. *Jesus.* I'm not a religious man, but that shit ain't right.

I ate before I came. For the simple fact that the food sucks unless she orders in.

But I still attempt to eat it.

"Don't "Mother" me." She stabs the meat again. "You show up late, and now you want to criticize my cooking?" she snarls, despite no one saying anything.

I've never seen someone make such a mess of cutting poultry.

"Red," River says. Her gaze shoots up to him, and she puts down the knife, a forced smile appearing on her lips. "A deal went bad today. You both know how your mother is when things don't go her way." Our father reaches for her hand, and she lets him squeeze it before she pulls it back and looks at the disaster, which is the roasted chicken.

"It's fine. It'll be sorted because our sons will be sorting it." She smiles like that makes her happy, and being the only woman in this house, we sure do love to make her happy. Because when she's upset, we all feel it.

"And who will we be killing tonight?" I ask. It's very rare for our mother to ask for our help and not handle a situation herself. But when she does, I think it's because killing is her love language, which means this time it's personal.

"A man wouldn't sell me a ring I wanted for my collection. He tried to haggle with me." She *humphs*.

My eyebrows furrow. "So why didn't you just kill him?"

She sighs and rolls her eyes, then sits on River's lap. He pulls out his phone, and I imagine it's because he's ordering takeout. "Well, he had his ten-year-old daughter in the room."

Hawke and I are silent for a moment until it dawns on us.

"Wait. Did you not kill him because you didn't want to traumatize his daughter?" Hawke asks, openly in shock.

She curses with a thick Russian accent. "I'm not a complete monster."

"Bullshit!" Hawke says, and I look away, ready for the reprimand to come because Hawke can't keep his mouth shut. But it seems my brother, and I'll be going on a hunt for this fucking ring tonight, and I wonder how many men exactly we're going to have to kill for it.

If the man had any smarts, he would've fled the country by now. But some people tend to underestimate my mother because she's a woman. And they discover their error too late.

HAWKE FASTENS HIS SPIKED GLOVES, and the buzz of energy around him is palpable. I drag my two crow-bars—my preferred choice of weapons—out of the trunk of my car. It's not that we can't use guns or knives; Anya and River trained us extensively with both, but Hawke was accustomed to using his bare hands when we lived on the streets, and I found an affinity for the use of crowbars. I liked the various ways I could use them.

"All of this for a fucking ring," Hawke mumbles with a menacing smirk.

Ironic, considering how much of a big deal she'd apparently made about wearing the one River gave her after their wedding. "What Mother wants, Mother gets," I say, not at all surprised that she's wildly pissed by someone who won't give her something shiny she likes.

From our intel, the man is new in New York's underworld. Anya has had only two business dealings with him, auctioning some of his items on the black market.

He became too cocky, trying to overcharge our mother, but the intel we received from Will Walker showed that he doesn't even have a child, which means he used some poor kid as a decoy and purposefully undermined our mother.

"Hey, I've actually been to this bar before; it's not so bad," Hawke muses as we stand outside the bar in one of the outer suburbs. "I wonder what it will look like coated in red."

"Just don't get blood on my leather seats," I make a point to add because Hawke can get messy once he's in a frenzy.

I don't believe in God, and there certainly isn't room for mercy in what we do. I'd called the cleanup team ahead of time.

"How many do you think will be inside?" Hawke asks giddily as we approach the bar that is a front for the illegal dealings happening inside. Everyone here works for Laurence Tate, which is an unfortunate fact.

"Ten," I guess as I hide my crowbars behind my

back. Hawke begins to whistle a tune as he stuffs his hands in his pockets.

"I'm going to say twenty," Hawke says, and I know it's wishful thinking on his part. My brother and I are the same in that we like to challenge ourselves. Hawke because it feeds his superiority complex. And I love the thrill of putting my life on the line. I love the adrenaline rush. "Don't forget to count how many you kill," he adds because it's always a competition. And I often win simply because Hawke hyper fixates on pummeling each and every one to death or close to it. Whereas I go for precise and debilitating swings.

The security guy steps in front of the door. "You're not invited," he says in a low, menacing tone.

"Oh, that's okay. We often enjoy crashing parties," Hawke says with the biggest fucking smile as he suddenly grabs the guy, who's too slow to pull out his weapon, and throws him into the door. The door bursts open, and I walk in after Hawke.

"Well, well, well. Looks like we have fourteen." Hawke hums approvingly.

"I was closest," I say as I quickly evaluate the scene. Twelve men and two women. Laurence Tate is sitting in the back with a cigar hanging from his mouth in shock. Everyone is frozen in silence before all hell breaks loose.

A woman screams as Hawke takes the right side and I take the left. I waste no time, swinging the crowbar into the security guy's head, knocking him out cold. I use the other crowbar I'm holding to knock a gun pointed at my head out of the man's hand. I plunge the curved end of the crowbar into his stomach, winding him, then smash it across his face, the force of the blow throwing him back against the wall.

Another man grabs one of my crowbars, and I let him as I pull out a gun and shoot him in the head. And when I look up to check on Hawke, I aim for the others who are pointing their guns at him.

Another woman screams, and it's a bloody mess as Hawke headbutts another man and drives his spiked gloves into some guy's face. Blood splatters everywhere.

I catch my second crowbar as it slips from the dead man's hands, holding it by the straight end and swinging it into the back of someone's knee. The guy's leg buckles, and I hook him with the curved end of the crowbar, tugging him close enough that I can bring my foot down on his face—red splashes across my jeans.

A man runs at me with a bat, and I quickly switch my grip on the crowbars so I'm holding them together in both hands like a sword. When he swings the bat at me, I block it with the crowbars, the metal clanging together, sending a vibration down my arms. The guy is stunned for a moment, and I take the opportunity to jab my elbow into his face.

Hawke's maniacal laugh echoes in the room as he grabs Laurence by the dress shirt. "Thought you could try to cheat our mother, huh?" he asks, then headbutts him, blood oozing down his face.

I release one of my crowbars, whipping out my gun and shooting the second to last man standing, who's bleeding but trying to protect his boss. The man keels over a wooden table that was obviously knocked over in the chaos.

My blood is pumping with adrenaline and pounding in my ears as Hawke lets his bloodlust take over. He punches the man again and again.

A sense of calm takes over me as I see the two women huddled in the corner. It washes away the demand for more blood as I pick up my crowbar and slowly walk toward the busted front door. The women seem confused as I point to it.

I know how I must look. I can feel the hot blood on my face and in my hair, staining my clothes and forcing them to cling to my skin. But one thing I will absolutely not do is kill a woman or child.

It's a code I've lived by from the moment I started taking lives. And if it's a weakness, then so be it.

Hawke has stuck by a similar code, but I wonder what will happen when the day comes that Eli gives us the order.

I hope that day never comes.

The women look in Hawke's direction, terrified and shaking. I don't really even see them. The only woman I really notice is Billie, and in their stead, it's her face looking back at me. The monster within me wants to retreat slightly, hide itself from her fucking lively personality.

She might know of my demons and bloodlust, but knowing and being confronted by it are two very different things.

It appears the women choose to risk moving for the door instead of remaining in the same room as Hawke as he beats the man to death.

They slowly approach me, and I look in the other direction.

Our mother would call us weak and deem it a mistake to let witnesses go. But I refuse to kill them. If it's the only rule that makes me feel human, then I'll die because of it.

The first woman sprints out the door, basically leaving her friend behind, but the second lingers for long enough to make me actually look at her.

"Thank you," she whispers.

My eyebrows furrow in confusion because I'm not someone who should be thanked, even if I'm letting them live. I'm anything but a good man. And certainly not one who should be thanked.

"Tell your friend not to speak of this, or I might not be so kind next time," I say emotionlessly, and the fear sparks back to life in her light-brown eyes.

She nods, tears springing to her eyes as she runs out the door.

I assess the carnage as I approach Hawke, who's now shaking Laurence Tate back and forth. "Hey!" He slaps Laurence across the face, but the man doesn't react. "Fuck. I accidentally killed him too soon."

Hawke's gloves are wet and sticky with blood, and it's splattered across his face and clothes, much like my own. I scan the room, looking for cameras and any evidence for the cleanup crew to discard of.

Part of me thinks this is the exact reason Eli elevated us to his seconds. We're ruthless and obedient, much like well-trained dogs. But it's familiar. And it's what we're good at.

"Seven," I say to Hawke, who's coming down from the high.

"Huh?" He blinks rapidly as the more human side of him comes back to the forefront.

"I killed seven, and you only killed five. I win."

Hawke drops the dead man and looks around. He's on his knees, and despite his size, he looks like a child of destruction right now. He runs his bloody glove through his black hair.

"Fucker!" He realizes that I've once again beaten him in body count. I smirk.

"The women?" he asks a little more quietly as he stands.

"I let them go," I confess.

He nods agreeably. Even monsters sometimes have rules.

Hawke fishes around in Laurence's pocket and finds a set of keys. "Right. Let's see what treasure is behind that door." He smiles mischievously just as Eli's cleanup crew arrives.

We step toward the room that better have this fucking ring our mother's fixated on. If not, hell's really going to come down on this city until we find it.

EIGHT
BILLIE

It's been four weeks since I've seen Ford, and I've been craving having his hands on me. The more time I go without him, the edgier I get. It's as if the moment my flight touches down, a spark hits my brain with the promise of pleasure. But it's impossible for us to be together right now, not while so much is happening with me moving back and my brother, the biggest cock block in the world, is still here before he flies to Italy for business.

Ivy and I graduated. We found a three-bedroom apartment that we adore, and my parents helped me move my things in. Naturally, Dutton assessed the property to ensure it met his approval before we signed the lease, and I had him swear he wouldn't buy the entire fucking building so I could at least have some kind of separation from him. I'm certain the only reason he agreed is because I silently begged Posie to intervene. So she swore him to allow me my independence.

I now nervously sit in my aunty Rya's law office, waiting for an interview. Two men are also seated in the reception area, holding folders, and waiting patiently. One has the audacity to give me the once-over and sneer. Fucker.

I rein in my bubbling temper that has me wanting to tell him to shove his ignorance up his ass.

I'm not nervous about the interview itself; it's because I haven't told my aunt that I'm applying to her law firm, and I hope she's not seriously pissed. I want to get this position on my own, and the reality is hers is the most prestigious firm in all of New York.

Rya should be revered as the best criminal lawyer in all of Manhattan, which is ironic since her family is part of the Italian mafia, including my mother, who is her sister. And although for years she's been talking about semi-retirement, it seems she oversees all of the hiring.

"Billie, come through, please," my aunt's assistant calls out. I've seen her before, but was never officially introduced.

I can't help myself as I purposely drop my pen in

front of the man who sneered at me, then bend over, making sure to give him a good cleavage shot. When I glance up, he's staring right down my top. I smirk. *"You fucking wish,"* I mouth, and he immediately turns a dark red.

"How dare y—"

"Is there a problem?" Rya's assistant asks, and he seems mortified. I stand back up and toss my hair over my shoulder.

"No problem. I just dropped my pen. Sorry," I say, then follow her, smirking over my shoulder at the asshole who looks like he's about to explode. I can't help but poke my tongue out, and I swear I see his eyes glaze over. He's totally about to fucking snap.

It puts a pep in my step as I walk into my aunt's office, where I see two men sitting beside her, looking at what I'm assuming is my resume. My aunt looks hot as fuck in a black pantsuit, and her silvery eyes dance with mischief when they meet mine. Though I doubt anyone else would notice it if they didn't know her well enough. Because right now she's strictly business, with her hands clasped in front of her.

Her assistant closes the door behind me, and Rya points to the seat opposite her. "Welcome, Billie. Please, take a seat." I offer a polite smile to them all as I sit and act as if she's not my aunt.

"So, you've applied for one of the open positions here at the firm," one of the men says as he looks up and seems to stare straight into my soul. I understand the tactic—the desire to make me feel uncomfortable. Unfortunately for him, I grew up around people who would literally make him piss himself if he tried that shit on them.

"Yes. You're looking for a junior accountant, and I hope to fill that role," I reply, keeping my back straight and maintaining eye contact. I've been raised in high society. An interview is a breeze, and I already can't wait for my caramel latte as a reward.

"Wonderful. We'll run through some questions."

"Please do," I say with a charming smile, and they proceed to do exactly that.

I flawlessly answer their questions about my studies, my experience, the job I had during college, and my ability to adapt in a fast-moving environment.

They seem impressed by my conduct and answers, and Rya doesn't speak until the end.

She pretends to look at the resume once more. "And you have no other commitments that would prohibit you from completing your tasks here?" She raises a perfectly shaped brow as she waits for me to answer.

I understand it's a question she most likely asks

every interviewee, but I can't help wondering if she's referring to the "family business."

"No, ma'am," I answer politely, and she stares at me as if she isn't sure of my answer. She was referring to the family business, wasn't she?

"Thank you, Miss Taylor. If we decide you're a good fit for the job, you'll receive a call within the next few days," my aunt says as she stands and offers me her hand. It throws me off slightly, but I smile politely and shake each of their hands, thanking them for their time.

One thing I'm certain about when it comes to Rya is that even though we're related, she won't give me the job just because of who I am. I have to earn it. And I like that. I don't want special treatment because of my family name or the fact that my brother would literally pay anyone any amount they asked for in order to give me an opportunity. It's nice and supportive, but it also keeps me from discovering how far I can get on my own. This is why I refuse to let my parents pay any of my bills and I opted to rent my apartment instead of buy.

I didn't originally intend to try to get a job at Rya's firm, but it just so happened to come up when I was looking.

I decide to walk around the city for a bit since it's

been a while since I've aimlessly walked, and I kind of feel like it'll help clear my head.

I chose to come back to Manhattan because I didn't know if I wanted to live anywhere else. Ivy was hell-bent on coming back here. She has dreams of traveling over the next year, but a part of me wants stability after years of the college life. It was fun, but I want something more. I want a sense of direction and purpose. One that's entirely my own and not due to the pressure I feel from my family.

I know that pressure is all in my head, and they're not trying to force anything on me, but my brother's so great in everything he does, and I'm... average at best.

I pause in front of a bridal shop, seeing the dress's reflection cover the clothes I'm wearing. Standing there, I wonder if marriage is something I want. I'm sure it is, but definitely not now. I want to fall crazy in love with someone. I want to be special to someone other than just my family members.

Ford comes to mind, and I want to laugh at the ludicrousness of that thought. It's desperate times if I can't even tell the difference between a fuck buddy situation and the potential of a long-term relationship.

The buzzing of my phone pulls me from my musings, and I fish it out of my pocket. I inhale a sharp breath as my aunt's name appears on the screen.

It's only been an hour since I left her office.

"Surprise, Aunt Rya," I say with a cheeky smirk as I continue walking. I can hear her sighing on the other end of the phone and can imagine her shaking her head.

I love my aunt Rya, especially when she's had a few too many margaritas.

"Do you really want the job, Billie?"

"Yes," I tell her. Because I really do. I want something to work toward and to figure out if this is the right career path for me. I just want the chance to find myself.

"I know what it's like being a woman in our family. I ran from it, but it caught up with me eventually. If you stay, you stay for good this time. You know if you run away again, it will find you."

My eyebrows furrow, and I stop dead in my tracks. "I haven't run away from anything," I say, affronted.

"No? You didn't pick a college in an entirely different country to get away from your brother hovering?"

I tsk, irritated by her keen eye. Then again, that's one of the things that make her a great lawyer. "London isn't that far. And I'll have it known he still hovered, especially when he was conducting business in Italy."

"Yeah, well, your brother is a determined son of a bitch." She laughs. "As your aunt, I'm telling you this is a fantastic opportunity for you, but I want to make sure this is definitely what you want—for you."

"And as my boss?" I push.

She chuckles. "My associates didn't know you're a relative of mine, and they were impressed by how you conducted yourself."

I can't contain a smile from spreading.

"But..."

"But what?" I ask.

"They were concerned once I told them who you were. They're worried that you could use that to your advantage."

"I would never. I want to prove to myself that I can do a good job. I can do this, Rya, if only you give me the opportunity," I say adamantly.

"You and I both know that, Billie, which is why I'd like to officially offer you the job. But never bring anything from our family life to work, do you understand?"

"Yes," I quickly agree. Oh my God! Did I just get the job?

"Good, you start Monday. Check your email. You'll find welcome information, as well as some HR forms that need to be filled out. Welcome to the team," she says, then hangs up.

"I got the job!" I yell excitedly and fist pump the air, scaring a woman walking past me. Fuck yeah! Eat shit, unemployment!

I message my mother to see where she is so I can share the news with her. She's quick to respond, letting me know she's at Dutton's house. I should've known now that she has Bentley as a grandson that she'd be a grandmother hen.

Posie and her son Bentley live with Dutton now. Dutton does everything for her. Saying he's obsessed with her is an understatement. I never thought I would see the day my big brother would be obsessed with a woman, especially with one who has a child. He hates kids. Just not hers.

I call a cab, then message Ivy that I got the job, and it'll require a girls' night out to celebrate.

It doesn't take me long to get to Dutton's. When I knock on the door, Posie opens it with an expectant expression. It's crazy to think she's around the same age as me, and yet we couldn't be more different. I think it's mostly because she has a child, but she treats me more like she's an older sister, and I kind of like it.

"Oh, you look nice. Where are you off to?" she asks with an inquisitive brow.

"I had an interview," I tell her, unable to hide my shit-eating grin as I follow her into the living room. My father is sitting on the floor, playing a board game with Bentley.

"Aunty Billie!" Bentley squeals, then jumps up to give me a hug. I can't help but drop down to one knee for this kid and wrap him in my arms. "Will you come play with us?" he asks, trying to tug me toward where my father is smiling and shaking his head in amusement.

"Soon," I reply, barely managing to get out of his tight grip. "Let me go to the kitchen first, and then I'll be back, okay?"

When I look back at Posie, she's smirking and rolling her eyes. "It's a new board game Dutton bought him. Can you tell?"

I laugh, smelling my mother's baking, before I see her standing in the kitchen. She's making blueberry muffins. Apparently, they're Bentley's new favorite. He goes through phases, and honestly, if I had a baker for a grandma, I'd be going through all the recipes as well.

"How did your interview go?" Mom asks excitedly, and I furrow my eyebrows.

"How do you know about it?" I ask, propping my hand on my hip. "Aunty Rya called you already, didn't she?" Damn. Everything flies through this family so damn quickly.

"She did, and I'm baking you a cake to celebrate." Her eyes shine with pride.

"Billie, sit down and tell me because your aunty Rya never called me," my father says, tapping a spot on the floor next to him. It feels strange being back in this kitchen. The last time I was, I was making out with Ford. And he hasn't touched my lips again since. Well, not the ones on my face, anyway.

"You can play with us too," Bentley coaxes. He's persistent, I'll give him that but then I notice they're halfway through a game.

"Looks like you're kicking Grandpa's bottom anyway, little fella. Keep it going. I might play next round."

"Hey, he is not." My father looks at his cards and then glances at Bentley, who is smiling so wide. Bentley isn't their biological grandchild, but that doesn't mean fuck all. To them, he is theirs.

When Bentley called Dutton Dad for the first time, there were literal tears, and it happened right after my brother proposed to Posie. Bentley's a good kid. And although Dutton never wanted to be a father, he's a surprisingly good one. But he spoils Bentley, and I know this because he spoils me in the same way.

Last week, Dutton attended a father-son night that they put on at Bentley's school, and I wish I were a fly on the wall to see my brother either get sweaty-palmed for the first time in his life or intimidate every teacher there. The latter, I imagine, is more likely. When I laughed at him about the occasion, he threatened to punch me if I didn't shut up. I didn't stop laughing, and there was no consequence.

This family is crazy in its own incredible way. And although I love it, I can't imagine bringing a man around them. My mother would most likely provide a false sense of security by offering him cupcakes, and my father would interrogate him and silently encourage Dutton to kill him. Not that he'd need any encouragement.

So I don't win either way.

Aunty Rya was right about one thing today.

I've considered running away before. Starting a life in a different country again. London was great, but it was fucking cold. And anywhere in Europe still feels too close. If I were to go anywhere, my plan of escape would probably be Australia. But even then, I don't want to get taken out by a snake or fucking spider.

My brother seems easier to deal with than crazy-ass wildlife.

But despite their flaws, I really do love each of them. And I would hate not to see them often.

So here I am, hiding who I'm fucking in hopes no one finds out, and trying to figure out what it is I actually want in life.

"So, my baby girl is now a big accountant," Dad says and pulls me in for a one-armed hug, holding a bunch of cards in his other hand.

"Junior accountant. I have to work my way up," I clarify.

"I'm proud of you either way. You deserve it," he says. "You got your looks and brains from your mother."

My mother rolls her eyes, and I can't help feeling a pang of longing from wanting something that seems so flawless between them. I've never been in a relationship, but from time to time, I think about how nice that type of support and devotion must be. "You do deserve it, sweetie. You even impressed Rya with how good your grades were and the recommendations you got from the accounting firm in London where you worked part-time. We're so proud."

"Thanks." I blush, feeling proud of myself, too. Posie hands me a glass of vodka and soda, and I blow her a kiss —a woman after my own heart. Watch out, Dutton.

Taking it, I sit back and watch my father and Bentley play as Posie asks, "So, what's next, then?"

"Next?" I ask, taking a sip and appreciating the vodka. My Italian grandfather would be rolling in his grave if he knew I preferred vodka over wine.

"Yes, the world is literally your oyster. Are you dating anyone? Do you have plans to travel? You have nothing holding you back. Tell me all your plans so I can live vicariously through you." She smiles. "Not that I don't love my life, but mine was very different raising a child by myself."

I sigh, staring down into the glass. And that's the thing. Everyone wants to know the path I'm on. What I'm working toward. But I don't even know.

"Well, I don't really have any plans," I say with a shrug, and the room goes silent. Then there's that. It just feels like everyone else has their shit sorted out, and I'm just cruising, hoping for the fucking best.

"Billie, I've spoken with your brother. I told him he needs to ease off on interfering with your dating life," Posie carefully says, and I appreciate the fact that she's remained silent about what she saw months ago. However, I am curious about how that conversation with my brother went.

And speak of the devil, and he himself shall arrive.

"Whose dating life?" Dutton's voice booms into the living room.

"Billie's. She has a date next weekend." Posie winks at me when I go to open my mouth to tell him I don't. "And we discussed this. You have to let her date. She needs this. And when she feels like she needs you, she will come to you. Until then, let her date and look after herself." Dutton stares at me, and I avert my gaze. "Right?" Posie asks rhetorically as she places her arms around his neck.

It's not that I haven't had this same argument with my brother a million fucking times. It's that I'm tired of losing my shit every time because he's a brick wall and as stubborn as they come. It's why I've gotten into the habit of sneaking around. It got easier when I found out Ivy could tamper with my phone to counter anyone hacking into it. Namely Dutton. Having a best friend who is a secret hacker is a big bonus.

"Right," he says through gritted teeth, but his glare is warning enough.

I want to laugh at the fact that she's telling him what to do. But I don't because I love that my brother has someone who makes him happy. And I also fucking love that she's totally team Billie.

My parents tell Dutton about my job, and then we spend some time talking about random topics before I decide it's time to leave. Dutton walks me out, stopping me on the porch. Our parents are waiting in their car for me, as they offered me a lift home.

"Just so you know, I'll still kill any man who touches you," he warns, then he turns and walks back inside. A part of me wants to laugh, while another wonders what he'd do if he finds out who I've been fucking.

I ignore the thought as I message Ivy, the buzz of vodka in my veins.

Me: *Hey, girl. I think it's time we go out to celebrate. I'll be home in fifteen. Let's dance the night away.*

I'm awake. It's two in the morning, but I only came home an hour ago from cleaning up some mess for Eli. It's unusual for Billie to text me, let alone call, especially at this time of day.

I answer on the second ring. "Where are you?" I ask.

Her first response is a hiccup. My eyebrows furrow as I look back at the phone. "Calm down, I'm fine," she says drunkenly, then I'm getting a call to FaceTime her. I answer, and her beautiful face appears on the screen. She smiles. "Hey, handsome."

I notice Ivy standing behind her, not looking nearly as drunk as Billie. Then again, Ivy has always been better at handling her alcohol. "Hey, Ford," she says, giving me a quick wave. To Billie, she says, "Now, go away. I need to pee."

"Is she pissing in an alleyway right now?" I growl.

Billie hiccups and smiles. "Yep. We really needed to go."

"You peed in an alleyway, too? Billie, what the fuck? Where are you? Does your brother know you're out?"

"He's not the *bosssofme!*" she slurs, slumping against a brick wall. I feel the vein in my neck throb as I straighten up from my kitchen counter and go to my room to put a shirt on. "Pin me your location right now. And, for fuck's sake, don't move."

She sways, and I get a quick glimpse of the short fucking dress she's wearing. I'm fucking furious that no one is with them right now. It's very rare that Dutton isn't on this shit already. Unless, of course, he's preoccupied with his fiancé.

"Boop!" She giggles as she taps the screen and drops her pin. "You know I was calling you to tell you to take me back to your place," she says smugly as if that's the reason why I'm picking her up. But there's no way I'm having her in this condition.

I'm already in the car, counting my fucking blessings that she's only ten minutes away from me.

Ivy laughs in the background. "As if Dutton would ever let you! You two are funny." She grabs the phone and pushes back her short blonde hair. "But seriously, Ford, can you please come and pick her up so I can go get laid?"

"She's ditching me!" Billie whines. "Ford, I—"

Her phone cuts out. I wait for it to reconnect, but when it doesn't, my heart fucking races. I hit the gas, threading through traffic. Fucking hell, this woman. I swear to God, if anything's happened to them, I'll strangle her myself.

I get that I'm only two years older than her, but it's different for a man to be drunk in an alleyway than for a woman.

Fuck.

I try to call Ivy, but it goes straight to voicemail.

I'm swerving wildly in and out between cars as I try to call Hawke. He doesn't answer, which means he's probably fucking someone right now. I curse.

Five minutes later, I pull over to the curb of the location she sent me. I can't see any sign of either of them. *Fuck.* Red fills my vision as I storm toward the alleyway and round the corner. A wave of relief passes through me as I catch sight of long honey-blonde hair.

Billie is crouched over a box, her ass almost hanging out of her tight pale blue dress. I grind my jaw. How many men saw her ass tonight? What the fuck is

Dutton even doing? He seems to be failing miserably at this overprotective brother bullshit.

Ivy's standing behind Billie, her arms crossed over her chest, and when she notices me, she beams a smile. "You made it!" she screams and throws herself at me, wrapping me in a hug. I catch her hand as she tries to pull my phone from my pocket. She smiles slyly. "I can always steal Hawke's stuff, but I can never manage to get one up on— *hiccup.*" The smell of vodka wafts into my face. "I need your phone to call a cab. Our phones died."

I feel an immediate sense of relief before fury runs through me. I let Ivy take the phone to call a cab, and then I storm over to Billie, furious she put herself in this predicament. But when she looks up at me, she's all innocence, and I hate the way it makes my cock twitch. It's not fucking okay.

I peer down at the box she's so focused on and see there's an all-black kitten with bright green eyes staring up at her. The thing looks fucking creepy. Like its face is too big for its malnourished body.

"Okay. My cab's just pulled up. Bye, you two. Ford, get her home safely. We owe you one!" Ivy waves as she hands over my phone.

"Are you going to be okay?" I grit out, not at all

comfortable with this situation. Christ, is this what all of their nights out in London were like in college?

She smirks. "How chivalrous, Mr. Ivanov. But, yes, his place isn't far from here. Just make sure she gets home, and for God's sake, don't bring that thing into our home. I'm allergic."

She's gone with lightning speed, and I watch as she gets into the cab before I turn back to Billie, who's now sitting—actually sitting—on the fucking filthy ground.

"Get up," I growl as I lift her to her feet. Something as beautiful as her should not be touching something so filthy. It reminds me of the years when I lived on the streets.

She doesn't seem to care as she uses a small leaf to tease the kitten, who seems curious to play with it. "It got left behind," Billie says sadly as she curls into herself. "I wonder where it's mom and siblings are."

A small, unsettled feeling stirs in my chest, and I don't like the way it dredges up memories I'd rather leave buried. Would she take pity on me and Hawke if she knew we were no better than this discarded kitten? Billie knows where we come from, but all our dirty, dark secrets we did to stay alive she doesn't.

She looks up at me then, that brilliant fucking smile unsettling me because I know when she's beaming so brightly like this, she wants something. "Let's keep it."

"Isn't Ivy allergic to cats?"

"Yep," she says, still smiling. It doesn't take me too long to understand her line of thinking.

"I'm not taking that thing back to my house."

She frowns. "Of course not. I'll carry it in." She picks up the box, and the kitten's back straightens, frightened but doesn't attempt to get out. That is, of course, until it's at eye level with me, and the nasty little thing hisses and has the actual balls to flash its tiny little fangs at me.

I frown. "That little fucker probably has rabies."

Billie clicks her tongue. "We all probably have rabies, Ford. Get over it."

I go to counter her logic, but then she looks around as if suddenly realizing something. "Oh shit, I forgot my jacket at the club. It was my favorite one, too. It cost me ten thousand, and that was on sale. Fuck."

I stare at her in bewilderment. "We're not done discussing the cat."

"Of course we are." She rolls her eyes. "You can't let me leave behind a stray kitten, Ford. And besides"— she looks back at it lovingly, and I never thought I'd be jealous of an animal—"it kind of reminds me of you."

I blanch and stare back at the little fucker, who

purrs for her but hisses at me. "I don't see the resemblance."

She giggles. "It's fur is the same color as yours. And it's nice to me and no one else."

I can't help but notice the backhanded compliment. She might be drunk, but her smart little mouth seems to be fine. "I wouldn't say I'm particularly nice to you."

She smirks as she passes me. That fuzzy little fucker hisses, and I can't reprimand him for having keen instincts. I silently fall into step behind her as she coos at the kitten.

When we round the corner, I notice a few people staggering out of the club.

"Is that the club you and Ivy were at?" I ask, and she nods.

I take the lead toward the bouncer, who halts me immediately. Fair, considering I look exactly like the type who shouldn't be let into a club.

Billie pops her head around my shoulder, her thick hair falling over her shoulder. "Hi. I left my coat here. Can I get it?" She bats her lashes at him.

"No can do," the bouncer says, not looking at her.

I grab him by the collar, and his eyes widen with surprise. "She was being polite. I'm not so *nice*."

The kitten hisses behind me again, and Billie

awkwardly pulls at my shoulder. "Ford, it's fine. Not everything has to end in violence."

The bouncer tries to break my grip but can't. Shit fucking bouncer. Another two bouncers come out to assist, but Billie stands in front of them, the box with the kitten in it propped on her hip. "Don't fucking touch him. He's crazy," she warns with a brilliant smile. And I can't help but smirk. Then she turns to me. "Ford, let's take Felix home."

"Felix?" I question. She shoves the bouncer back into the wall.

Billie's already walking toward my car, and I'm grappling between the need to get her jacket or following after her. Her attention span is shorter when she's drunk. She goes to open the door and sets the alarm off. I curse under my breath.

"Ford," she whines, and I rush over to her. Why do I feel like tonight is going to be a nightmare? It's been a very long time since I've seen Billie this drunk. If ever.

"That cat isn't com—"

She drops into the passenger seat, slams the door behind her, then waits patiently for me to join her.

I stare at my car that's basically been hijacked by a very drunk Billie...and Felix the fucking cat.

My teeth grind as I conclude that there is no reasoning with Billie right now. If anything, she'll start kicking and screaming, and I don't have it in me to pry the stray from her hands. It's that fucking cat's lucky night.

When I get in the car, she's already tuned the radio to some classical music, which is very different from the heavy metal I usually listen to when I'm tattooing. When I notice she doesn't have her seat belt on, I reach over to buckle her in. The kitten hisses and swipes at my arm, and I curse.

"Felix, no!" Billie reprimands. "Gosh, he's cute, though, isn't—" She hiccups. "We need to get some cat food on the way home."

I turn to face her. "My home?"

"Well, duh. Felix can't come to mine. Ivy's allergic, remember?" she says as if I'm too slow. My jaw clenches, yet I find myself pulling away from the curb.

"I've never had a pet before," she singsongs, and I side-eye her, still perplexed that she wants this kitten but thinks bringing it to *my* home is the solution.

"I'm more of a dog person," I admit.

She looks at me and then angles her head so her loose curls fall to one side. "I would've thought you were more of a cat person."

"Why?" I'm not sure if I want the answer.

"You're independent, just like a cat, and cats are sneaky, doing their own thing. You do what you want and stick to the shadows." She hiccups again. "Fuck, did we get my coat?" she asks, and I curse under my breath. She's so drunk, and the only reason I didn't bust my way through the club doors is because I was chasing after her.

The cat circles the box a few times and then lies down. I envy how comfortably it sits in her lap and the way she looks at it adoringly.

How the fuck am I so jealous over a cat?

"Does Dutton know you're out?" I ask, my grip tightening on the steering wheel.

She pouts at me. "I'm not just Dutton's little sister, you know." I try not to smirk at her tone. For all her fiery temper, I must confess I find the brattiness in her...cute. She's always trying to step out from her brother's shadow and defying the idea that she's a princess. But she very much acts like a bratty little princess sometimes. "And, yes, sort of. He's busy with Posie tonight. Ivy and I went out to celebrate. I don't need a permission slip."

That's news to me. Dutton monitors her every move, and while he's in town, it heightens the risk of her being found at my house. Then again, I'm sure he'd be appreciative of me collecting her in the state she's in.

So I carefully ask, "What are you celebrating?"

That big smile breaks over her face again. "I got a job as a junior accountant at Aunty Rya's law firm."

I raise my eyebrows in surprise. I'm not shocked Billie was able to find work so quickly. She's bright and personable. She can work a room like it's nobody's business. But I am surprised by the fact that she got a job with Rya Monti. "Congratulations."

Part of me wants to ask what kind of night she had. More specifically, how many men were floating around them? But I suppress my desire for the answer. We're just fucking, and the way she's staring lovingly at that kitten, tonight is not the night.

My phone rings, and Eli's name shows up on the screen. I place my finger to my lips as I answer via the car's Bluetooth. "We have a problem." It's the first thing he says.

"Where?" I ask.

"My bar. Be here in twenty. I'll call Hawke." Eli hangs up.

Billie mouths the word wow then says, "Good to see my cousin is straight to the point as usual." She yawns. The location appears on my screen, and I gauge the time it'll take to drop Billie off and reach him. "Oh, and I got a new apartment. It's really nice. You should visit sometime," she adds as she leans her head against the window.

I side-eye her and watch as she passes out immediately. She looks peaceful.

I consider how easily she spoke with me tonight as if there's no barrier between us. That me picking her up from a drunken night out is as normal as any other night. She comes to my house for sex. That's all it's ever been. But tonight, when her phone cut out, I panicked. And I don't like that lack of control. Billie is not someone I can control; she never has been. She's a free spirit in every sense, besides the overprotectiveness her brother shackles her in.

But a small part of me thinks maybe she's feeling too at ease with me when I'm the last person she should consider a companion of any kind. She has no idea how much better than me she is. The world is at her fingertips, and someone like me will only weigh her down.

Yet I can't help myself from pulling into a service station to purchase cat food, an electrolyte drink, and pain killers because she's going to need them when she wakes. I am at her mercy, beck and call.

When I return to the car, she's snoring. Not elegantly but like a train. The cat's ear twitches and it opens one groggy eye as if wary of me, but then goes back to sleep, just like its savior. That little fucker got comfortable real quick.

I pull into my driveway, turn off the car, and then go around to open her door, catching her head before she falls out. I shake her once. Then twice. Dear God, she sleeps like the dead. I awkwardly lift her out of the car. And although she's passed out and deadweight in my arms, she clings to the box, the kitten hissing at me like a gnarly little fucker.

"I will defang you," I tell him, which surprisingly has him taking a step back in the box.

After I get us inside the house, I carry her to my room and lay her on my bed, tucking her under the blanket. The kitten is beside her, and I'm still majorly pissed he somehow made his way in here. A small part of me considers putting the little fucker on the street where he belongs, but I'd never admit openly that I'm not that much of a monster.

I know what it's like to be abandoned and then to be given a new home and family. I just hope by tomorrow, he flees or Billie decides to find him a proper home.

I take a seat beside her, watching as she sleeps, fixated on her soft features. For all her wit, spite, and fire, Billie is one of the kindest women I've met. It might not be obvious on the surface, but she couldn't be a more polar opposite to my demons.

Demons that I'm about to exploit again after only

working with Eli a few hours ago. Whatever's happened in that time must be bad.

I tuck a piece of Billie's hair behind her ear. It's strange to have her in my bed like this. And I wonder if she'll regret it tomorrow. I need to put distance between us, but I'm not entirely sure I'm capable of doing that. So, at the very least, I need her to understand that this is only sex.

I'm not the hero who saves the day and picks her up when she's drunk. I'm the feral fucking cat hissing in the alleyway. Hunting and always finding my prey. I can't let her be my next target. She can't be my next vice.

TEN
FORD

It's four in the morning when I arrive at Eli's bar, Lucy's, and Hawke pulls in just behind me. Eli's already waiting out front, and his wife, Jewel, is with him. He doesn't often bring her into his business dealings, so I wonder if this interrupted whatever they might've been doing.

I don't ask about the blood seeping through the back of his shirt. Since meeting Jewel, the fucker's had a fixation with her carving into his back and other parts of his body. I don't care about other people's kinks; mine isn't exactly normal either, but he's not even trying to hide it.

"Sorry I missed your call," Hawke says, throwing an arm over my shoulder. He holds up two fingers. "I was entertaining two women and had to wrap it up quickly when Eli called."

Eli nods to us as we approach. "And next time, I'd rather you not answer while you're still fucking," he says, though it's certainly not the first time any of us have called Hawke when he's mid-fuck. He seems to never have the common sense to stop or just not answer.

"It was exciting to hear your two-pump wonder over the phone, though," Jewel teases as we go inside.

Hawke laughs, putting a hand to his chest. "It's called multitasking. What about you? What were you doing?" he asks me.

I ignore him and instead focus on the dead body on the floor beside the bar.

"What happened?" I ask Eli. He's staring at the body of one of his security guys and the empty glass resting near his hand.

"I received a call thirty minutes ago from one of my other security guys. It happened just before last call, and they shut down and hustled everyone out straight after. I'm having someone look into what happened, but I suspect he's been poisoned."

Likely so with the white foam coating his mouth. His eyes are open, and I crouch down to get a better look.

Although poisons aren't my specialty, Anya certainly had us study various ways to kill people. Poison being one of them, and had us microdose as teenagers. Our mother has unorthodox practices, but I'm certain she has her reasons for it. It would appear it might finally come in handy.

"Do you think this was a targeted attack or coincidence?" Jewel asks, and it's refreshing that we don't have to pretend around Eli's wife. She's a hitwoman who is equally as dangerous as any of us.

But we all know we never leave anything to chance.

"Hate to stereotype, but poison is usually a woman's weapon," Hawke says, raising his hands in the air. My brother and his fat mouth. But he's not wrong. "Maybe old mate here pissed her off."

"And why does it have to be a woman?" Jewel asks pointedly.

I step in for my brother because articulating himself objectively has never been his strong suit. "Poison is usually used by someone who doesn't want confrontation, whether that be they're hiding their identity, or they feel weaker if it were to be a physical confrontation. Gender aside, this is a new security guard. He was most likely targeted at the bar after his shift. Those who have been working for Eli for a while know not to drink while they're on the clock."

To Eli, I ask, "Have you looked through the video footage?"

I look up and see Jewel staring at me.

My eyebrows dip. "What?"

"I don't think I've heard you say so much at one time before."

"He's super smart, right?" Hawke adds.

"More like saving your ass from sounding like an asshole," Eli corrects. Not that I think Eli's any better. "But we're going through the footage now, and I'm going over his files to see if it was an attack against him personally or us. I just wanted you to both be made aware so you can keep an eye out. If there's a repeat of this, there might be someone targeting my life."

Jewel clicks her tongue. "What a big fucking surprise there."

"Jealous someone else might beat you to it, wife?" Eli challenges.

She grins, and it's sadistic. "I'll put a bullet in anyone who tries to do that, husband. That's *my* job."

The sexual tension between them is palpable, and I stand. "Hawke and I'll check the footage in your office and make sure this is cleaned up." I look at the body again. Those two are about to rip at one another, and I'm not here for the show.

But more than likely, someone is after Eli. It's not

the first time someone has tried to take out the mafia boss, and it won't be the last. But it's my and Hawke's job to make sure that doesn't fucking happen.

LONG NIGHTS and getting home at unusual times aren't abnormal for me. I don't return until ten in the morning, and a selfish part of me hopes Billie is still here. But the logical part of me that warns me to put distance between us is telling me she won't be. I head to my room first. The bed is made, a few of the painkiller tablets have been taken, and the electrolyte drink is gone.

I lean against the doorframe with my arms folded, picturing her there last night. I wonder what time she snuck out and how much she remembers. I hear a small hiss and turn to my left to see the feral little monster slowly stepping toward me.

I sigh. How the fuck did I end up with this thing?

That's when I notice the note at the end of the bed. I pick it up, recognizing her handwriting.

Make sure to feed Felix.

P.S. I stole one of your shirts after I vomited on myself.

Thanks xx

When did she vomit on herself?

A deep sigh escapes me. This girl may very well be the death of me. I go to the kitchen, and the little monster follows me. I see the cat food on the counter and one of my bowls on the floor, full of water.

I look between the tin and the cat, confused. How much does a kitten even eat?

ELEVEN
BILLIE

I'm NURSING the biggest fucking headache of my life and embracing my mortification. I skipped our hot yoga class this morning, and instead, I'm grumbling my complaint in my living room with the shades closed as I nurse a bowl of popcorn while trying to watch TV. But so far, all I've managed to do is switch through multiple shows, not processing at all what's happening because my thoughts keep drifting to a certain grumpy killer.

I consider texting him to say thank you or sorry or how's Felix, but every time I pick up my phone, I put it back down. Ford and I don't text. It's like a silent rule. I have to remind myself that we're just fucking.

Well, you didn't get any fucking done last night when you passed out in his car and woke up in his bed.

And the cat...

I slap my forehead.

The front door bursts open, and Ivy skips inside, wearing the same clothes she had on last night. "What a fucking night!"

She closes the door behind her and then looks at me. "Oh shit. You look rough."

I've always cursed her for being able to hold her alcohol better than me.

"Is that a barf bucket?" she asks, pointing to the bowl resting on my stomach.

"Popcorn."

"Uh-huh. And how much of that have you actually eaten?" She throws her jacket beside the door. The bitch is a slob, but I love her, and it's not so hard to live with her considering we lived in the same building in London. "Are you going to be okay for the party tonight?"

I groan, wanting to bail on the formal event. I understand that we have to show our faces every now and then at high society functions, but it's just a cover for the truth of what our families actually do. And I'm certain quite a few people are already tapped into what that is.

"I'll be there," I say merrily because I don't want to admit defeat due to a hangover.

Ivy takes the bowl of popcorn and throws a few pieces into her mouth. "That cat's not here, right?"

"No, I took it to Ford's."

She laughs at that. Hard. "You dragged a stray into Ford's house? I can't believe he actually let you."

I groan in response and put my head on her shoulder. "I named it Felix."

She laughs harder. "Ford and Felix. Has a ring to it, no? I can't wait to tell the others."

"Please don't," I say quietly. "I don't want Dutton thinking anything weird just because Ford picked me up."

"Why wouldn't he be grateful that Ford picked you up while you were smashed and then dropped you off safely?"

Except he didn't drop me off at home.

And it's not the first time I've been at his house.

I give her a look, and she sighs. "Then again, your brother is pretty psycho. Always has been," she states, patting my head where it rests in the crook of her neck. Ivy and I have always been close. My mother and Alina are also close, which means we basically grew up as sisters. The difference is she doesn't have an overbearing brother, although Dutton had many times shooed away boys who tried sniffing around her in our younger years.

The doorbell buzzes, and I groan. *Who could be dropping by at this time?*

Ivy laughs. "Don't worry, I'll get it."

"How was your lover boy?" I ask as she goes to the door.

"Oh, you know, another one to cross off the list. He wasn't great, but it was enough to scratch an itch," she says, looking at the security camera. "That's weird. Did you do any online shopping?"

"No." I groan. The last few years, the only time I go on shopping sprees is for my birthday when I'm using my parents' credit cards. Or when Dutton is overbearing and pisses me off, I use his credit card to make up for him cockblocking me and especially on my birthday, because I like to spoil myself. That tab builds up pretty quickly.

Today, however, is not my birthday, and Dutton hasn't pissed me off this week. Yet.

"Are you sure?" she asks, opening the door to a man who kindly greets her with a rack of hanging garment bags.

"I have a delivery for Billie Taylor," the man announces.

Ivy steps to the side, letting the man in, but we're both suspicious. We were raised to sit on the edge of caution considering the world our parents are in, which is also why we're both blackbelts in karate.

The man leaves the rack with the garments behind, and Ivy closes the door behind him. She opens the envelope as I finally stand. She turns the piece of paper back and forth. "No note, just a list of the items and no prices. You been holding out with a secret admirer or something?"

I open the first bag, and my jaw drops. It's my favorite jacket. But not in the same color. I snatch the list out of her hand. It tells me nothing. I know these jackets are easily $15,000 each, and I got mine on sale for $10,000. I open each bag—eight in total—revealing the same jacket in every fucking color.

"Aren't these the same as that one jacket you like so much?" Ivy asks inquisitively. "If you want, I can do some hacking and figure out who sent them."

"No, it's fine." I dismiss her quickly, biting my bottom lip. "Maybe I drunkenly ordered these last night and forgot."

Except I know I didn't.

She laughs hysterically. "Fuck. It's like when we went to Rome, and you accidentally ordered those fifty pizzas to our room instead of five. We were eating pizza for days."

I grumble about her sharp memory.

Holy fuck. Did Ford buy me a jacket in every color because I lost mine?

No.

No?

No.

He wouldn't. We're just fuck buddies, after all.

Right?

TWELVE
BILLIE

I STAND AT THE PARTY, wearing a tight green dress
and a necklace made of small pearls. My hair is twisted
in an elegant updo with a few loose curls around my
face. I laugh and jest with a group of people while
simultaneously taking note of every person who walks
through the door.

The event is for the very wealthy and elite, and our
families come to see and be seen. Even Anya and River
are here, which is rare, simply because Anya doesn't
like people. So if she comes to one of these events,
there's often something in it for her—most likely
jewelry of some kind.

The fact that they're both here also means their
sons might be, too. And since they're often wherever

Eli is, and he and Jewel just arrived, it leads me to believe that Ford is probably somewhere close by.

I'm cautious as to who I talk to. If any unknown man attempts to speak to me, my brother will cross the room within seconds and break their hand. It's something that's happened on more than one occasion. That, and most of the people here, are disingenuous. The number of people who have tried to use me to get in favor with my father or brother is mind-boggling.

My mother also has a distaste for these types of events. I find her across the room, and I admire how beautiful she looks, standing by my father's side, nodding politely at a woman who has been rambling on for the past five minutes.

She told me she was once the perfect example of poise and personality at every event, but after meeting my father, she removed that expectation from herself. However, she still occasionally attends considering that her company caters most of the events.

Alina and Will Walker rescue my mother and father from the conversation they were having as Ivy stops beside me, looking elegant in her long black dress. She hands me a glass of champagne. Nausea swirls in my gut as I'm still not entirely recovered from my hangover.

She scans the room, most likely looking to see if anyone fits her type.

Ivy is selective as to the events she attends, so I ask, "What made you want to come tonight?"

"I had nothing better to do," she replies with an eye roll. She continues talking about finding a hunk tonight, but we both know she isn't going to find one in this pompous circle. My gaze diverts to the door the moment Ford walks in, his brother entering right behind him.

Butterflies take off in my stomach as I watch them. Watch *him*.

He's absolutely stunning when he's dressed in something other than jeans. He's wearing slacks, and he's paired them with a long-sleeved shirt buttoned up high enough to cover his neck tattoo. And he's freshly shaven.

Fuck me.

Bend me over right now and take me.

I inwardly slap myself. Drooling much?

"So I killed him." I whip my attention back to Ivy, who's smiling at me. "You weren't listening to a thing I said, were you?"

"I'm sorry. I thought I saw someone I know," I quickly say, trying to cover the fact that I was staring at Ford. Ivy's perceptive, and the last thing I need is her investigating any further into me and Ford, especially since we've already been caught twice before.

"Well, I would hope so, since your family knows everyone here." I watch as person after person approaches my parents, some just to chat and others to talk business.

I'm not as involved in the darker side of the family businesses as some of my relatives are, but I'm not dumb, and I understand they're all shady as fuck. Even my own father. When my parents sat me down and explained what it was my father does beyond lingerie store franchises and the darker demands of the world, it didn't make me feel any particular way. Even the fact that he runs one of the largest escort businesses and sells virgins at auctions—consensually, of course.

Even though Dutton wanted me to know nothing about the things they do, I'm grateful they sat me down to explain the situation rather than acting like something they're not. And I was happy to discover that though many of their businesses might be illegal, they're very protective of their employees' safety. I'm kind of proud of that because I know there are other illegal—and even legal—businesses where women, especially, don't have that same sense of safety.

From what I've seen, my brother has taken over Dad's business flawlessly, and he's grown it with ease.

And I guess it was always assumed I'd take after my mother, considering how much I enjoy baking. But I'm not sure I want to follow in either of their footsteps. That's the kind of thing you do in families like mine—you take on roles and responsibilities that are handed down to you so your parents can retire and enjoy life. Or you take up a profession that will somehow benefit the family.

Which is how I ended up choosing a career I thought could be used in different ways and not entirely for a shady business. It was a stupid mistake when I picked something to do with money, though. Because even though I might not be physically involved in anything they do, I can now be asked to hide money and move it without being caught. Which, to my family, is just as helpful as putting a bullet in someone's head.

"That guy's cute," Ivy mentions and immediately pulls out her phone. "But let's take a deep dive." She means stalk him. Ivy's father is a tracker—the best one in the world. There is no one that man can't find. And Ivy is just as good, which is a little scary. I remember in high school, I told her about this boy I had a crush on. I hadn't met him in person, just online. She took it upon herself to find him, go through his messages, and basically perform a deep dive on him in a matter of hours, then she requested I block him and never talk to him again.

She doesn't want her family to know how good she is, though, because, like me, she's not sure she wants to follow in either of her parents' line of work. But I wonder if her family already knows, what with her father being able to find out anything. Or maybe he respects her enough to leave her alone. Doubt it. All of these men are controlling and meddling.

She grimaces, and I laugh. "That bad already, huh?"

"I think I should just stop at his Instagram page. And this embarrassment is public." She laughs.

I can't help but glance in Ford's direction again. I need to apologize for last night, and I need to ask about the jackets because I'm certain he's the one who sent them. But I also still have half of a heart tattoo on my ass that he needs to finish.

"Earth to Billie." Ivy's snapping her fingers in front of my face, and it draws me back into the room. "Damn, it's either that hangover hit you harder than I thought, or you're epically distracted."

That's when I notice my mother has joined us, catching the end of the conversation. "Why are you distracted? Is everything all right?" she asks, resting her hand at the small of my back.

I smile. "Yes. I've just been thinking about my first day at my new job on Monday," I lie.

My mother's expression softens. "You're going to kill it." But I can tell Ivy isn't so easily convinced. "And what about you, Ivy? How long will you be here before the next adventure?" my mother asks. Ivy works freelance IT and can do her job remotely.

I zone back out of their discussion and look over to where Eli is having what looks like a hushed conversation with Ford and Hawke. Most likely discussing mafia business.

I stare for God knows how long before Ford's dark eyes finally meet mine. He looks away without giving me any type of reaction, whereas his brother notices and gives me a wave. I wave back, sighing. Not the brother I wanted a warm welcome from, but when has Ford ever been inviting, especially in front of others? If it weren't for his calm demeanor, we most likely would've been caught much sooner, and it was *my* idea to keep us as a secret.

When I return to the conversation, my mother is explaining how to make the maple syrup dumplings she loves. She then glances over to my father and whispers into my ear, "Billie, can you go and see if your father is almost ready? I'm just going to send Ivy this recipe first."

"We've only been here for an hour," I remind her. She smiles politely, like I should know better. If my mother can escape these events, that's exactly what she'll do. I try not to laugh as I make my way over to my father, who is speaking to my uncle, Crue.

Crue stops talking when I reach them. "Billie. I hear you'll be working for my wife's firm."

I give him a hug. Although he's not the affectionate type, he always humors us and at least tries to be nice. But he's as ruthless as they come, and it's obvious where Eli gets it from.

"Hey, Uncle Crue. I start on Monday," I say with a smile.

"I'm surprised you're allowed out without your brother here," he says, and my father chuckles.

I roll my eyes. "Yeah, well, apparently, he and Posie are selecting flowers for the wedding. More specifically, Dutton's choosing and dragging Posie along for the ride."

My father laughs at that.

"Also, Mom wants to leave," I tell Dad.

"Of course she does." He smiles.

I make a point to walk past Eli and Ford, deliberately not looking his way, but I feel when his gaze is on me. So I make my way to the small hallway leading to another two conference rooms and the bathrooms. The first room is empty, so I step into it, holding my breath and hoping I'm not acting foolish. Once I'm in the small room, I notice the two red seats with a coffee table in between them. Still holding my glass of champagne, I take a seat and wait for him.

Hoping that he'll come.

THIRTEEN
FORD

It's hard not to notice Billie and even harder to try to ignore her. That tight green dress is going to be my fucking undoing. I tried multiple times to look away from her and failed miserably. And then the little ball of chaos decides to saunter past, her hips swaying in invitation. I might be conceited, but I can tell she wants my attention, and I'm the fucking fool unable to suppress my desire to run to her when she calls. Now that I know what she tastes like, I can't resist. And last night was peculiar, and I'm hellbent on reiterating what we are to each other, what our bodies can do for each other. But I'm hiding under the reality of just needing my next hit.

Eli is discussing the politics regarding his crew back in Italy, and although I make a point to absorb all knowledge, whether it directly impacts me here in New York or not, I can't focus after watching Billie walk past.

Jewel interrupts Eli by placing her hand on his arm. The moment he's distracted, I use it to my advantage to slip away. I can afford a few minutes. Besides, once they start touching each other, no one else in the world exists. Eli won't even notice my disappearance.

"And where do you think you're going?" My father asks, and I inwardly cringe, as if I'm a teenager about to get up to no good. A lifetime ago, I did a lot of sneaking around, and none of it was ever missed by my adoptive parents.

When I turn, I see it's only River. My mother is talking to her brother, Alek. And it's weird as fuck to see him at a party like this. He can't stand people, and his daughter, Hope, is the same when it comes to big crowds, which is probably why she isn't here. His wife, Lena, is made for it, however. She's a famous singer and is used to the spotlight, but she isn't with him tonight, most likely traveling for her work.

"Away," I say casually. He gives me a knowing look, and I immediately have the urge to defend myself or tell him it's not what it looks like. Because I'm certain, it's definitely not what he's thinking. Before he can say anything else, his attention is drawn to my mother. Anya is eyeing a man with a look in her eyes that indicates she's about to do something at this party that everyone will regret. Except for her.

"Never ceases to amaze me," my father mumbles in awe as he goes to her.

The moment his back is turned, I scan the room to make sure no one else is watching me. My movements usually go unnoticed by most; I purposely make myself as invisible as possible. But my father is attuned to my every move. Fucker.

Hawke is leaning against the bar, talking to a blonde I've never seen before. He briefly glances in Eli's direction, making sure to keep an eye on him. The guy might be constantly thinking with his dick, but he does prioritize Eli's safety above all else.

I slip down the hall Billie went into only a few moments before. There are two rooms and restrooms at the other end, but I come to a stop at the first room. I can feel her before I see her as enter, ensuring no one else notices.

"What took you so long?" she demands, sounding high and mighty as she sits on the leather couch, looking like a queen worthy of a throne in that green dress. That fucking dress that accentuates all of her curves. The strand of pearls around her neck, begging to be broken and scattered on the floor from some breath play.

"Lift your dress and turn around," I command. I'm not fucking around with Billie tonight. She's not drunk now, and I had to show a restraint I've never known by not touching her last night. My body is humming, my cock already rising and begging to be buried deep inside her. It's been fucking months. And the first thing she does when she sees me is brings a fucking cat into my house. She will be punished for it.

"No, hello, how are you, Billie?" she sasses.

"Hello. How are you, Chaos? Now, turn and lift your fucking dress and touch your toes."

She uncrosses her legs and stands. The woman has the audacity to put a hand on her hip.

"How about, no?" My cock hardens at her defiance. I step into her space, but she doesn't even flinch. Not that I've ever given her a reason to.

I lean over and whisper against her ear, "Did you really think you'd get away with last night?"

She stiffens, and I take the glass from her hand and put it down on the table.

"Well, I have a question for you, too," she says, and I smirk as she tries to defy me even now.

"You can ask after my cock's buried deep in that

sweet cunt of yours, and you show me how appreciative you are for last night."

"About last night—" I cut her off by putting my hand around her throat and angling her head to look up at me again. My cock's straining against my pants, and I'm fighting against logic. I know I can't fuck her here. I won't be able to restrain myself if I bury myself in her now, and every time we've fucked at an event, we've been caught.

"Bend over and let me inside you. Tell me how fucking sorry you are," I demand. Because I want her to know what it's like to be teased. I let Billie have control over me and use me for my body as she pleases, but she needs to remember that I'm not some cute puppy to be patted and cooed over. I'll let her use me for my body, but last night was something different entirely. I even acted so stupid that I bought her favorite jacket in every color like a fucking fool. I've never felt the urge to spend money. Not until her... knowing that something is her favorite, I just couldn't resist, and now I feel like a fool for it. As if I have to reiterate for the both of us that this is just sex between us. I'm only here for her to use my body as she pleases. And I know very much that she enjoys the way I force her into submission.

"We shouldn't," she breathlessly whispers but does

as she's told, turning and brushing her ass against my cock. Interesting. The little bundle of chaos does know how to be obedient, though she's still as reckless as I am. Right here and now, I could have her. Fuck, do I want her.

"I need to check the tattoo, so fucking bend over."

But I don't want her to be caught once again because one of us doesn't have any restraint.

She lifts her dress and exposes red lacy underwear. I bite my bottom lip, my knuckles turning white as I try to contain my urges. Fuck me, this perfect ass. I place my hand on one plump cheek and push my bulging cock against her panties. She hisses. Fuck me, I so badly want to free my cock and pound into her.

I can't help but slap her ass. She straightens at the contact, and I grab her by the back of the neck, bending her back over, admiring the view. So fucking perfect.

So fucking everything.

I grit my teeth as I lock my gaze on her tattoo. It's healed nicely but still not finished.

"I said touch your toes," I demand, and I swear the vein in my neck is about to rupture as she sensually runs her hands down her smooth legs and touches the tips of her toes in those sexy heels. I want to drop to my knees and feast on her sweet pussy and ass. Fuck me. I don't know how she's able to get me this amped up without even touching me.

Her breath hitches as I trail my hand over her firm ass, and goose bumps scatter in its wake. I can tell she's anticipating the next slap. My fingers dig into her cheek as I get a better view of her tattoo. The red ink pops nicely against her pale skin.

Fuck, she's beautiful.

Before I can stop myself, I lean over and bite her ass. She yelps but doesn't move. I slap her cunt over her lace panties, and her legs tremble from the impact.

"Are you wet already, Chaos?" I ask, but it comes out as more of a demand. I can feel her soaking through the material, but I want more. I *need* more.

What has this woman done to me?

"Yes," she whispers, and I step back, adjusting my cock in my pants. "You'll finish this off tonight, won't you?" I ask, gripping her by the hair and yanking her head so she's looking at me.

"Tonight?" she asks breathlessly, and I try to rein in my desire to push her down and fuck her into oblivion. I've been restrained around Billie, not wanting her to see how deep my depravity goes, but something changed last night. I don't like this undercurrent of curiosity, and we both need to be reminded of what this is. It's purely sex. And maybe if I handle her the way I like most, she'll run scared and never return. That's what we both need. That's what's best for both of us because this addiction is a disaster waiting to happen. But I don't have it in me to be the one to cut it off.

"Figure it out," I demand as I release her hair, then turn and stride to the door. Before I fuck her into that red couch. "Your tattoo has healed nicely, by the way."

"Wait. Did you do all of that just to check out my tattoo?" she demands from behind me. "Are you fucking kidding me? Finish what you started! Ford, you dickhead! Don't leave me like this!"

I close the door behind me and let out a shaky breath. Jesus Christ, that woman is going to be my undoing unless I'm the one with sense enough not to lose myself in what we have going.

But, fuck, I need her to deal with this soon, I think, looking down at my painfully straining cock.

FOURTEEN
BILLIE

I'M FUCKING FURIOUS. He left me high and dry and
panting. I've got marks on my body from him, and he
didn't even get me off—the nerve of that asshole. I
never actually thought Ford would deny me... ever.
And it's made me furious that he has. So furious that I
snuck out of the apartment at one in the morning in
baggy clothes and a lingerie set underneath that will
bring any man to his knees.

I catch a cab to Ford's house. When the car drops
me off, I hurry to the front door and start banging on it.
I have a key, but he needs to know how fucking angry I
am. My saving grace is that Dutton's on a flight to Italy,
which means I'll have a few days of not having him
breathing down my neck. Since Ivy blocked him from
being able to track my phone, I've noticed a little more

freedom, but I also think that has to do with Posie's influence.

Ford opens the door, wearing nothing but a loose pair of sweatpants.

"You!" I point my finger at him. "How fucking dare you deny me after not fucking me for months."

The fucker has the audacity to fold his arms over his chest, lean against the doorframe, and smirk. I want to wring his fucking neck. How does no one else know he has this asshole side of him?

"Seems like you're shit at apologizing."

"Me? Apologize?!" I shout, a flood of heat pounding in my core. This should not be fucking turning me on. Why does he have to look like that? I catch a glimpse of the sun tattoo on his hand and internally scoff. Ray of fucking sunshine, my ass!

A small meow comes from behind him, and I lean so I can see around him. "Felix!" I scream, delighted, but Ford steps in front of me.

"Get in the house. *Now*."

His dark brown eyes stare down at me, and it's the first time he's ever looked... furious isn't the right word, but there's something else there that I'm not understanding.

I cross my arms over my chest. "Being a bit bossy tonight, aren't you?"

"You came here for a reason, didn't you? And it better not be just because of the fucking cat," he grumbles.

I can feel my cheeks heating and know he's right. A woman has needs, but there's a different energy around Ford tonight. I feel like I'm actually catching the first glimpse of the predator beneath the mask.

My heart kicks up its pace at the way he's looking at me. I want to ask about the jackets. I want to ask about Felix. I want to ask about what happened last night. But all of that can wait because my pussy is begging for the release I've been dreaming of for months.

It doesn't make it any easier to walk past Felix, who doesn't seem too curious about me as he plays with a small mouse-shaped toy. It's then I notice all the toys littering the hallway, and I can't help but smirk at the knowledge that Ford must've bought them for him.

I step into his bedroom, and Ford closes the door behind me. The moment I turn around, his hands are on me. Branding me with a firm grip. His movements are startlingly fast compared to his usual nonchalant attention.

It fills me with feminine pride to know how much he can't keep his hands off me, how quickly his self-control snaps. I feel the same way as my arms wrap around his neck, and I arch into him, letting him devour my throat with kisses as he pulls up my shirt.

This side of Ford is demanding and needy as if his patience has snapped, and it satisfies me in a way I can't express. When he removes my top, he pauses for a moment to stare at the yellow lingerie piece. He licks his lips, and I shuffle out of my pants, revealing the crotchless lace underwear and garter belt.

"Fucking hell, you make me crazy." His callused hands are on me again, but I push him back.

"You need to be naked too," I demand, shoving down his pants and boxers. God, he looked so good today in dress clothes.

Once he's out of his pants, he's back on me. There's no time to prepare as he pushes me onto the bed, crawls over me, then thrusts inside.

"Oh fuck!" I cry out. He pauses for a moment, tentative. I realize then that he's holding back by a thread. "No, it's fine! Keep going!" I insist. And without delay, he starts railing into me. I jolt under him, my hands twisting into his blankets and sheets, unable to keep up with his rhythm. It's outright hard fucking.

His hand clamps down on my mouth, and I bite it, whimpering in pure, painful pleasure.

It's been over a month since we've been together,

and this... It feels like more than I can take. I cry every time his piercing hits my G-spot, the added pressure forcing my eyes to roll into the back of my head as tears streak down my cheeks.

His hand pins my hips into place so I can't move, like a doll being fucked, and it does all types of things to my brain.

It's the most aggressive I've seen him, but fuck, I love it. Being punished through sex might be my new favorite thing. If I knew being a brat would result in this, I might've pissed him off sooner.

"Fuck, I've missed this sweet cunt of yours." Ford curses and my heart falters. I know it's not because of me. I know we use each other for this. It shouldn't affect me the way it does.

Tingles begin to spread throughout my body, and I know I'm so close to crashing over the edge. He's taking everything from me. Like he's ripping the orgasm out of me, and I fucking love it.

I mumble around his hand, trying to speak, that sun tattoo covering my lips. I bite harder.

"Fucking harder!" he demands, and I bite down until I can taste blood.

"Fuck!" he shouts as he thrusts into me one more time. I hit the final peak, breaking into a million pieces, panting, and screaming behind his hand, saliva everywhere. My back arches, but he's holding me firmly in place as he explodes inside me.

Fuck me.

What the actual fuck?

I've never felt more possessively claimed.

Ford's panting over me, those almost black eyes blinking a few times as if he's suddenly back in the room, his animalistic side receding, sated. Now I understand why he walked away earlier tonight. Because if he'd fucked me like he just did... there would've been no way we could have walked out of that room without everyone knowing about us.

I'm breathing heavily, still trying to grapple with what just happened, as he removes his hand from my mouth. A hint of remorse flashes across his expression, and I grab his hand to place it against my cheek.

"You're crying," he says, mortified. "Did I hurt you?"

"What? No," I say quickly. "I'm not as breakable as you think."

Even I don't know why I was crying. It was probably due to the mixture of pleasure and pain. "Ford, that was fucking mind-blowing."

He rolls off me, sitting at the end of the bed, and I perch on my knees next to him. I put my hand on his shoulder. "What's wrong? I fucking loved all of that."

He wipes a hand over his mouth. "I didn't mean to be so rough."

My eyebrows furrow. "Have you been holding back on me all this time?" Because that makes me even more furious.

He glances at me, then quickly averts his gaze, which is answer enough. I feel my temper rising. This is so fucking frustrating.

"I'm not some breakable thing." I get to my feet. "Everyone keeps treating me like a princess, but I'm not!"

"It's not that," he says adamantly.

"Then what, Ford? Because that was the best sex of my life, and you're acting like a frightened child."

"You are breakable, Billie. More than you know." He clenches his hands into fists. "I'm a killer. I know how to kill you a dozen different ways, and you so easily let me take control of your body. You should be more wary of me."

Everything feels heightened and charged, and I'm about to lose my fucking shit. "Are you fucking kidding me? Don't treat me like a child. Of course I know what you do for a living. I was in this fucking world before you were, so don't treat me like I'm uneducated."

"I wasn't insinuating—"

"That what? That I'm not a fucking idiot?"

"I can't control myself around you!" He shoots to his feet, and it startles us both. His chest is rising and falling rapidly. "You don't understand my depravities. Or how addicted I can become."

I'm so fucking angry that my hand is moving before I register what I'm doing.

Slap.

The sound echoes in the room, and my hand print reddens the side of Ford's face, not that it did anything to budge the oaf. I immediately regret striking him, despite how furious I am, but when his eyes meet mine, that look of hunger and need is back.

What the fuck?

Glancing down, I see his cock's getting hard again.

Huh?

"Do it again," he encourages.

"But I—" I stop short because Ford is giving me insight into what he likes and needs, and I'm not sure if he wants this because he thinks he should be punished for something or if it's because he likes it.

"Hit me," he grits out. "Or leave."

I swallow at the challenge. Ford's trying to push me, and it infuriates me. I always thought he was straight forward, but maybe he really is as fucked up as the rest of the men I know. I channel that rage into my hand and slap him again. This time his face does turn to the side, and he grinds his jaw.

He's on me in seconds, and my back hits the bed. A jolt of fear runs through me, until I see his expression. He's not mad. He's turned on, and his cock is pressing firmly against my inner thigh.

"I need you to know I'll never hurt you, Chaos. But I'm not a sweet Prince Charming. I'm struggling to restrain myself around you."

A shaky breath escapes me as I nod. "I know you'll never hurt me. But I need you to teach me what it is you want."

He lets out a dark chuckle, and it's terrifying because I feel like there's a whole lot I don't know about Ford. "You and your body. We'll start with that," he says, leaning down and biting my tit. I hiss at the flash of pain, but the ache it leaves behind goes straight to my pussy. His cock twitches against my thigh, and it becomes clear that Ford *likes* pain.

I reach between us, grip his cock, and pull hard. He hisses again, the muscles in his neck bulging. I guessed right.

"Fuck me, you're so going to leave here black and blue tonight," he promises. I feel like I'm out of my depth, but I'm also curious as to where it might lead me.

"And you want to be marked too, right?" I ask, hoping I don't embarrass myself with the assumption.

His gaze becomes hooded as he answers, "Yes." And he shoves away my hand as he thrusts his cock into me, pushing our cum back inside me.

My eyes immediately roll back into my head, and I'm not sure what I've stumbled into. This isn't anything like the random nights we had while I was in college. This is something darker and entirely untouched. Something to be explored. And I can feel my thirst for him has plummeted into another draining well.

FIFTEEN
BILLIE

Iт's my first day at my new job, and I'm fucking sore and sleep deprived. I knew it'd be a risk having a late night at Ford's, but I didn't anticipate we'd be fucking until five in the morning or that I'd have to sneak back home before Ivy woke up. I don't want anyone else catching wind of this. Part of me knows I should stop, but I can't. Especially after last night. I don't know what the fuck possessed Ford in the early hours of the morning. He was like a feral animal, but I am so here for it.

Have I bitten off more than I can chew, though?

It's like he was challenging me. And he awakened something in me I didn't know was there.

Most of the day is spent on orientation: visiting the different departments, meeting coworkers, going through the onboarding process, and setting up my workspace. I lucked out with a desk by the window. It's got a nice view from the fourteenth floor. And my manager, Tarissa, seems nice enough.

It's not until midday when I'm standing in line for coffee downstairs, that I consider texting him. I tap my phone against my chin. I know I shouldn't. We don't message each other, but what harm could there be if we did? Ivy's blocked my brother from hacking my phone and going through my messages so I could text him, right?

Would texting make things between us feel more serious? But fuck buddies still message, right? I mean, I've had fuck buddies before, but I always made a point not to message with them so Dutton couldn't interfere.

I start typing out a question about Felix, but I realized last night that Ford's kind of jealous of the attention I give the kitten, and it's funny that he hisses at Ford. I made sure to spend as much time as I could with the little fluffball before I left.

And I still didn't have the chance to ask about the jackets. So I text out a message asking about that but then end up deleting it. I kind of want to see his reaction about it in person, because it's very unlike Ford. I remember going back for my jacket and a confrontation at the club when they wouldn't let us back in to get it. Then it's a little hazy after that.

I bite my bottom lip. Did I somehow force him into buying me one of every color?

Definitely not asking about that over text.

I finally settle on one thing I know he won't be able to resist.

> Me: I'm coming over this week. I need you to finish your job on this tattoo. I have to go to the beach.

I collect my coffee and go back to the office. I don't check my phone until I've finished with work, and I release a breath because he did reply, though it was hours later.

> Ford: What has your ass got to do with the beach?

Ford hasn't really shown me he is the jealous type, but I'm curious if he's capable of that emotion. I know we're just fucking, but I want to prod him enough to see the real Ford, the man under the killer that not many people see.

I smile as I reply.

Me: Because my bikinis will show it,
and I want a complete tattoo.

HE REPLIES QUICKER THIS TIME, and I read it
as I'm stepping into my apartment.

Ford: Wear a cover-up. You shouldn't
be showing that ass to anyone
but me.

Me: I'm looking forward to escaping
to my favorite resort in Mexico, where
everyone will see it and I'll be fueled
by margaritas. Jealousy doesn't look
good on you.

I BITE my bottom lip mischievously. It's no secret that
I do, in fact, have a favorite resort in Mexico, and there
are plenty of photos from our girls' trips in the last few
years where we practically lived in our bikinis. Ford
knows this, but it's interesting to see how he reacts.

I hate that waiting for his next response makes me
giddy. The thought of him being jealous causes a
flutter in my chest. And after being completely domi-
nated by him last night, I kind of want to act like a
brat on purpose. Because I want that kind of hard

fucking all over again, even though I'm battered and bruised.

"Oh, thank fuck you're here. You didn't reply to my text," Ivy says as I open the door. I immediately hide my phone, as if she might discover who I'm messaging.

"Sorry, it was hectic at work," I reply as I slip out of my heels. She's wearing a tight black dress, and I smirk. "You have a date tonight?"

"Correction. *We* have a date tonight. If you read your messages, that is. You've got twenty minutes to get ready."

"What?" I ask, surprised. She's combing her hair as she looks in the living room mirror, deciding between different earrings.

"It's a double date. And you can't bail. Dutton's not in town, and when big bro is away, it's time for Billie to play."

I scoff as I set my stuff down. "You know I don't date, Ivy. You've met my brother. Do you want my date killed?"

"Relax. He's not going to get killed. And even if he does, I don't really care because I'm just trying to fuck his friend."

I laugh. "That's fucking horrible."

She shrugs. "Yeah, well, we're far from saints. Put something cute on. His friend saw a photo of you and thinks you're really hot. Shocker. Who wouldn't think that with those bountiful tits of yours."

I roll my eyes. "I don't need that kind of flattery from you, bitch. She who has the curves for days and tits twice my size." It's why she's so popular with the guys.

She smirks and waggles her brows. "Want me to hook up a threesome situation? Or maybe we can swing."

"I love you, but not that much." I laugh as I walk into my room. I check my phone for a reply from Ford, but there's nothing.

I mean, it's stupid, really. I know it is. I shouldn't have any kind of loyalty to Ford because it's just sex.

"Come on, it's not like you're seeing anyone anyway. Who knows, it might be super fun," Ivy says as she barges into my room and begins flicking through my clothes. She pulls out a short skirt and a top that shows my midriff.

I yawn, exhausted from my night of no sleep.

"That new job already working you to the bone, huh?" she asks as she rummages through my jackets. "Well, fuck me. Take your pick of color, girl." She laughs. "I still can't believe you drunk ordered all of these."

Next time I see Ford, I vow I'll ask about them, but

until then, I know if I don't go with Ivy, it'll only raise suspicions. And I really can't have her snooping into me and Ford, because I'll never hear the end of it.

Ford and I aren't even exclusive, and considering how fucking beautiful he is, he'd still be getting propositioned all the time if we were. An irrational pang of jealousy unfurls in my stomach, and I adamantly refuse to go down that route. Ford and I can't be anything more to each other than what we already are.

Neither of us made any promises, and for all I know, he's out there fucking other women without my knowledge. So why should I stop dating just because I can't stop thinking of him?

"Fine, but it has to be a small restaurant, one where no one knows my brother," I tell her.

"Well, that's going to be hard since nearly everyone knows your brother." She laughs. I bite my lip and really hope I don't like this guy because my brother may just kill him.

"IVY TELLS me you haven't been in a serious relationship before," my date, Ryan, says from across the table. I inwardly sigh. There's an energy about this guy I don't like, and I'm too fucking tired to pretend to be nice. I'm already long forgotten in Ivy's peripheral as she sits two tables beside me, excitedly chatting to a guy I've never seen before. We were meant to be next to each other, but there was an issue with tables, and now I don't have her next to me.

Ryan's attractive. I mean, if you passed him on the street, you'd probably take a second look. But he's not my type. Not that I've thought too much about my type before, but it's certainly not the turtleneck-sweater-wearing type. I think my brother would actually laugh at him instead of killing him, and the sheer embarrassment would be enough of a shot to his ego.

"No, have you?" I reply because so far he's only spoken about himself, and we haven't even been here for that long.

He seems bewildered by my dry response. "Wow. You really don't know who I am, do you?"

Immediate revulsion curdles in my stomach with that single statement.

"Nope." I turn to Ivy, but she and her date are making out over the table. Fuck me, that escalated quickly. I look back to Ryan. "Should I?"

"You don't go on social media much, I take it?" he asks.

"No, sorry." Which is a lie. Social media? Who the

fuck is this guy? I reach for my cocktail and then take a sip.

I'm on social media as much as the next person, but I only care to upload photos of my travels and time with my girlfriends. Stalking pinprick assholes like this is not at the top of the list.

"Maybe you should." He winks.

"Yeah, maybe one day." I take another sip.

This guy is boring and dead in the head. How much longer am I expected to sit here?

Is it too early to leave? I glance at my watch. I've only been sitting here for thirty minutes, and I already know this man is some type of model, loves social media, and thinks he's God's gift.

I'm trying not to throw up in my mouth.

"Here, let me show you my most viral video." He opens his phone and clicks a few things before he slides it across the table so I can see a video of him. It's him on a motorcycle, holding a book, shirtless. I want to gag. He's clearly thirst trapping—at least that's what I think it's called—and sure, women love a good-looking guy to look at. But meeting him in person must sure as hell be a letdown. I wonder if all these women in these comments know that each time they comment something about how sexy he is, his head gets bigger and bigger. I bet he doesn't even know how to ride the fucking bike.

"Good, right?" He nods, answering himself.

"If you say so," I drawl, and a yawn escapes.

His gaze shoots up from his phone, where he was scrolling for another video to show me, and his nose scrunches.

"You don't like it?"

"Like what, exactly?" I take another sip of my drink. This might be the fastest way to get me drunk on a date.

How the fuck did I get stuck on a date with a man who needs so much validation? Ivy fucking owes me for this.

I'm not your fucking therapist. If you have issues, hire someone, fuckface.

I smile at him.

He frowns back.

"You're very peculiar," he says, and I shrug in response. "That wasn't a compliment."

"Luckily for the both of us, I don't need validation from strangers."

And let's be real because if someone really hurt my feelings, I'm sure once my family found out, they would be dead anyway.

"I could end your social life," he threatens, clearly pissed that I didn't buy into whatever it is he's selling.

"I could end your life, so let's not throw words out we don't want to play with." I lift my drink and salute him.

He's gobsmacked, his jaw dropping open. Ivy stops at the end of our table then, her pink lipstick smeared and her date smoothing over his hair at the bar as he orders them another drink.

"How's it going over here?" she asks.

"Ready to go?" I ask with a beaming smile.

Dickhead stands, his chair screeching, as he mumbles under his breath and stomps to the bar. A woman approaches him and asks for a photo. He turns back to me with a look that says *see, people know me*. But I just laugh. I can't help it. How can I make this shit up?

His expression darkens, and then he looks away and fake smiles for the photo.

"Let me excuse myself," Ivy says.

"I can walk myself home." It's only ten minutes away, at most.

"Hos before bros," she singsongs as she saunters over to her date. I watch as she flirtatiously leans into him. He looks her up and down, basically devouring her with his gaze. I stare into my cocktail as I play with the glass, thinking about a certain man who looks at me far more violently than that.

I glance out the bay window of the restaurant, and my eyebrows dip. I'm certain that's Ford's car sitting at the curb. I leave the drink behind and head out of the restaurant with my bag. By the time I'm outside, the car is gone.

Maybe it was a similar car to Ford's?

I go to check my messages to see if Ford's replied, but that's when Ivy comes bouncing over. "Oh, that was fun!" She stretches her arms, and we begin our walk to the apartment.

I side-eye her. "Was it? For whom? You set me up with someone who was a total waste of my time and potentially space in society."

She laughs, then cringes as she sees my expression. "Yeah, sorry about that. I just wanted to fuck his friend, and you've used me as a decoy more than once in our friendship." True. I've used her to distract my brother when I'm up to no good, so I can't really be mad.

"How did you even find them?" I ask.

"A dating app. But he asked me to bring a friend for his friend. Guess he won't ask that again." She laughs.

"Yeah, probably not," I agree. "Well, tell me how *your* date went."

She begins to tell me snippets about him. Ivy doesn't take men seriously, or maybe it's that no one can hold her attention for longer than a few days. I imagine this guy will be spat out by the end of the week unless he actually knows how to please her.

A flush of heat rises up the back of my neck as memories of my night with Ford flood my mind. I wonder what Ivy would say if she knew.

When we return to the apartment, I see him. Or, more specifically, his car.

I bite my bottom lip. Having to sneak around means one becomes really good at car sex. And Ford and I are basically pros at this point. I tilt my phone away from Ivy as I text him.

Me: Is stalking on your resume now?

I SHOOT another glance in his direction. He looks down at his phone, and the screen lights up his gorgeous face.

Ford: If it was, I would tell you that your date is already dead. But lucky for you, I think he never wants to see you again.

. . .

I TRY NOT TO LAUGH. I should be concerned that he knows how bad of a date it was, but a thrill jolts through me instead.

I clear my throat as Ivy and I reach the apartment complex entrance. "Hey, I'll be up in a second. Mom's trying to call me, and I just realized I need to grab some tampons from the corner store."

"Oh, you can take one of mine."

"It's fine. I might get a snack as well. I need chocolate to recover from the awful taste that guy left in my mouth."

She laughs again and shrugs. "Sorry, girl. But I appreciate your time sacrifice."

I pretend to call my mother as I walk down the sidewalk. The corner store is literally one block up, but the moment she's inside, I pocket my phone and race across the street. A low hum of anticipation stirs in my stomach.

His window rolls down, and he looks more sinful than he has any right to be. And he also looks like a stalker. "Are you in the habit of following me now?"

"You think it's funny?" he asks, and I can't help but bite my bottom lip. I'm not sure about his response, but maybe he does seem a little jealous.

"So you're not here to have car sex?" I ask, confused. "Then why are you here?"

His hands grip the steering wheel, and that's when I realize that Ford is internally struggling with himself. I notice when the switch happens. I don't know what triggers it or what he's thinking, but I feel the shift in energy around him.

"Go inside before Ivy becomes suspicious."

"Wait. Why are you here? You're not here because my brother told you to watch over me, right?" I fold my arms over my chest, now kind of pissed about the situation. If he isn't here for sex, then why is he here?

"No." He starts the car. "Go upstairs, Billie."

Why can he not look me in the eye now?

What the actual fuck is running through this guy's head? We're just fucking, but he watches me when I'm out on dates?

"I need my tattoo finished," I demand. It's the only reason I can think of that he might see me again because whatever this weird tension is, I'm not having any part of it.

"Not right now," he says calmly as he turns his head toward me, his expression emotionless. I fucking hate it when he looks at me like that. Not now. Not when others aren't around us, and we have nothing to hide. Because Ford has shown me more of himself, and right now, I can tell he's pushing me out.

"Okay. Well, I'll go find someone else to do it, then," I throw back, then walk away.

"If you let another man tattoo your ass, I'll send you his hands as a present!" he yells out after me. I flip him off over my shoulder, intentionally swaying my hips as I walk across the street.

Fuck him. He's so hot and cold.

I won't be told what I can and can't do.

There's also a caveat in everything. He didn't say no to a woman tattooing me...

"Fucking hell, you seem more tense than usual," Hawke remarks from beside me. We're currently at one of the Ivanov auctions. Sent away from Eli, yet again, for one of his "date nights" with Jewel, which is just code now for "I'm going to rail my wife into oblivion."

And the only reason we're running the black market auctions tonight is because Anya, River, Alek, and Lena had to "attend to something." I'm certain it's just an excuse, and it's really our mother getting up to her old tricks, trying to persuade us to take over the auctions for them and truly adopt the Ivanov name.

"When was the last time you got laid?" Hawke asks.

"Shut up," I grit out.

He laughs. "A while, then, I'm assuming. Want to

go beat one off while I wait for everyone to come in?" I cut a deadly glare in his direction. He puts his hands up in defense, still laughing as the final preparations for tonight are completed. A few patrons have already taken their seats, and the stage has been set for the guns that will be displayed and sold tonight.

I stand beside the door as Hawke circles the room. I catch one man staring at me, and he quickly averts his gaze. I'm almost praying someone picks a fight with me tonight.

It's Friday night, and I've barely slept. My mind wanders to what Billie might be doing. Probably getting shit-faced. Our cousin, Hope, is in town for the weekend, so I hope maybe that will rein her in. Hope isn't much for the party life, though she'll grudgingly go out sometimes if she has to.

Billie and I are just fucking. I made a point to fuck her brains out and show her the edges of my depravity, and then the next day, she went on a date with another fucking guy. He's lucky I didn't fucking kill him.

I'm the one trying to push her away and reiterate that it's just sex between us, yet I'm losing sleep over the way I spoke to her. I'm wildly pissed at the thought of her with anyone else. And I haven't heard from her since that night, which is good. It's probably the reality check we both need. She has better sense to keep me at a distance. But even as I'm certain I have to draw a line in the sand for both of us, none of it sits right with me.

I don't know when she became the sole focus of my thoughts or why, when I decided to purposefully act so coldly toward her, I can't just cut and run. I know I'm not good for, her but the moment Ivy mentioned taking her on a double date, I was fucking furious. Not at Billie, but whatever asshole was actually daring enough to try with her.

It's selfish. It makes no sense. I promised myself I was just checking up on her to make sure she was okay, but I'm lying even to myself, and now I don't know how to slow it down. Even if I might feel a certain way about it, I push those thoughts away because, at the end of the day, *I* am not what is best for Billie.

My fingers curl into my palms. It doesn't make it any easier to try and rationalize with me or her what's best for her.

When she came over that night, I couldn't contain myself. I went absolutely feral on her, marking every inch of her as mine, and that terrifies me. The way I get lost in her, needing hit after hit after hit. I can't get her out of my bloodstream, and that's exactly why I followed her on her date. What if next time it is too much for her? I'm the worst type of influence for her and have so much blood on my hands that, at times, when I touch her... it feels like I'm tainting her in the process. Yet I'm failing miserably at stopping it.

"Looks like it's about to start," Hawke notes as he stops at my side. I roll my shoulder because these fucking collared shirts always feel stiff, but our mother insists we look as presentable as possible when we conduct business on her behalf.

Our father always gave us shit for being like little dress-up dolls. I don't give a fuck. It's the perk of getting first choice of the stock we receive that makes all the bullshit worth it.

"Good evening, ladies and gentlemen, and welcome. If you would please begin to settle in, the auctions will start momentarily," the auctioneer announces. The lights dim, silhouetting the people in the crowd. I keep a keen eye on the room, watching for anything out of the ordinary.

Anya and Alek want us to take over. They want us to do this right.

And that's saying a lot, considering my mother and uncle are control freaks.

I recognize most of the attendees since admittance to the auctions are by invitation only. Those invitations are sent only to those who plan to buy. If someone doesn't bid, they don't get a second invitation.

We auction off various items, but guns are our

biggest business. They bring in the most money. Though the sex auctions are a close second, and the Ivanov siblings work closely with Dutton to conduct them after he took over the business from his father.

A few late arrivals enter, shaking my brother's hand before finding their seats. I refuse the greeting, leaving my hands in my pockets.

Fuck, I could go for something sweet right now. My fingers twitch around the lollipop I brought with me, desperate to unwrap it and pop it into my mouth. But Anya would beat my ass if she found out I was eating here.

The familiar face of Waylon Striker appears in the doorway. It's unusual to see the motorcycle club president from Boston not wearing his leathers, but there's a strict dress code here.

Since he and Eli went into business together, the two have been brokering good deals, however, it doesn't mean we entirely trust the biker group. I, personally, don't mind him, but with the shit that happened over killing three of his men, including Posie's ex... Well, it's choppy waters. Especially if one of his members find out we're responsible and come after us.

Whatever. We'll cross that bridge when we come to it.

He shakes Hawke's hand, and he's the only person I bother returning the gesture for.

"Boys." He nods. "I'm surprised to see you somewhere other than at Eli's side."

"He's taking care of 'personal business' at the moment," Hawke tells him, and I shake my head because my brother never knows when to keep his mouth shut.

"You bring anyone else with you?" I ask because every member is welcome to invite one guest, though they have to be registered with us first so we can personally screen them.

"No, I rode in for this and will ride out after."

"Our boy here wouldn't do the wrong thing." Hawke throws an arm over Waylon's shoulders and escorts him to his table. I avoid rolling my eyes. My brother's a psycho, drawing people in with his blinding energy, much like Billie, but then there's also the side of him not many see—the bloody beast behind the smiling man.

I pull out my phone to mindlessly scroll before I even realize I'm doing it. My mother wouldn't be too pleased if she knew I wasn't paying attention to the auction, so I go to put it away, but a message notification grabs my attention. When I open the message from Billie, I see there's a photo of a tattoo parlor with the text.

> Billie: Don't worry about it. I can take care of it myself. I'm all booked in for tomorrow. Hope you've pulled the pole out of your ass. xx

LIKE FUCK.

I'm gripping the phone so tightly I'm certain it's about to splinter into a million pieces. I know Billie's tactics; I've seen her work them on her brother many times before. But I never thought they'd grate on me so easily.

She seriously fucking thinks I'm going to let anyone else ink her skin or finish my job?

It's because she couldn't stay still in the first place that it's not a complete piece.

Hawke returns to my side, and he scans the room before turning to me. "Jesus. Who are we killing?"

"Nobody," I say under my breath. "But I'm suddenly feeling like committing a little arson tonight."

Hawke whistles as the auctioneer kicks things off.

Each attendee's face is highlighted by the screen of their iPad where they place their bids—no one being the wiser as to who is bidding or how much.

It keeps the bids high and keeps the money coming in.

But right now, I don't give a shit about money. I have a personal vendetta against a certain little bundle of chaos who's acting like a brat.

THE TATTOO PARLOR is engulfed in flames as I slam the car door behind me. Hawke whistles in the passenger seat as he admires the blinding flames. "Fuck yeah. It's been a while since we've done this. Brings back memories."

I turn the engine on, smugly satisfied at our handiwork, and that's ridiculously stupid. I'm not better by reacting to her provocation, but she obviously needs to learn a lesson.

"Pearl?" Hawke asks, hope and anticipation stamped on his face. Dutton's Gentlemen's Club has become one of his favorite places to visit.

"Whatever," I grumble, still fucking furious. I can't believe she actually had the guts to book a tattoo appointment with someone else and then act smug about it.

"So, is there a reason why we're so pissed off with

the guy who owns this place?" Hawke questions as I throw the car into gear.

"No particular reason."

"Cool, cool," he replies. "You've been acting strange lately. Are you sure everything's okay?"

I ignore him. Even if I wanted to answer him honestly, I wouldn't even know how to put it into words. I just know I'm furious. Past that, I'm probably being a petty prick, but so fucking be it.

SEVENTEEN

BILLIE

I DON'T EXPECT a message back from Ford, but it still pisses me off when he doesn't take the bait. I pocket my phone again.

"This is the fucking best," Ivy squeals as she sifts through the selection of lingerie. "I want to try these on." She races to the fitting rooms.

No one else is in Honey's, the exclusive lingerie franchise my father started and that both my parents now own. A friend in college once asked me if it was weird to know my parents ran a lingerie shop, and I was baffled as to why they'd even think that. Because it has perks like this—opening the store afterhours and taking whatever we want. It's not considered stealing since my mother handed me the keys and told us to have fun, but whatever.

I'm certain they're happier for us to spend time in here where the security is top of the line than in some shady club. But right now, I could certainly go out for a few drinks and dance the night away.

Ford's pissed me off. Epically. And no matter how much I try to push it away or simmer down, I can't.

Trying to understand the fucker is like trying to break into a vault. And this is the second time he's denied pleasing me, when that's all this is supposed to be—sex.

I take a seat on the sofa beside Hope. "You're not going to try anything on?" I ask her.

She only flew in today, and it's nice having her in town to check out the new apartment. Hope adjusts her glasses that frame her beautiful eyes and complement her naturally vibrant red hair. "Nah, I have a few pieces already."

I sigh and drop my head on her shoulder. Where Ivy is the outgoing party girl, Hope is on the other end of the spectrum. She doesn't like crowds and is awkward in social settings, so she usually keeps to herself. But she has a calming energy around her. It's crazy how successful she is at only twenty-two. And to be honest, I'm a little envious. She's world-renowned for her sculptures, and she seems more put together than me or Ivy.

"How did the last show go?" I ask.

"Sold out" is all she says. Seems about right. She's a woman of few words, taking after her father, Alek Ivanov.

"Oooh, how cute! Damn, I can't wait to be railed in this!" Ivy screams, opening the curtains and sauntering out.

"Damn, girl, your ass!" I snap to attention.

"I know, right?" she says, smacking said ass and then walking back into the fitting room.

Hope shakes her head and then looks down at her phone, sighing. "I was hoping to see Hawke and Ford this weekend, but it looks like they're at Pearl, and I'd rather not go there."

I frown. They're practically cousins, and Hope and Ford seem to enjoy one another's company. But it pisses me off to hear they're at the strip club my brother owns. I know it's unreasonable, and they've gone there plenty of times before. Hell, I go there too. But it's eating me alive not knowing what Ford is doing. Not that he owes me anything.

I throw my head back on the sofa, frustrated that this fucking thing is taking way too much of my energy. Maybe I really do just need to go and fuck someone else to bring me back to reality.

"What did you need to see them for?" I ask.

She casually shrugs. "Just stuff."

I glance at her out of the corner of my eye because I can't help but feel like there's something she's not saying. But that's always been Hope's style—keeping things close to the chest.

"Okay, I'm grabbing all of these. Shall we go home and put facemasks on and watch a horror movie?" Ivy asks.

Hope's eyes glisten with delight. "Really?"

I pull her in for a hug. "Of course. We don't get to see you all the time." Horror movies filled with gore are her favorite. And though I don't share the same sentiment, I can at least keep my stomach for most of them, and Ivy chooses when to be curious but is often scrolling through her phone.

We close up the store, and before we leave, I find myself looking at my phone again. Still no response. I'm not at all surprised because why would he bother messaging me when he's at a strip club doing fuck knows what?

I internally slap myself. Fucking stupid. I don't even care that he's there, so why is it affecting me so much? But it's more the not knowing what's going through his mind that's bothering me. I shouldn't be taking it personally that he's not replying to me since we were never like that before. But it does.

THE NEXT MORNING, my jaw drops when I arrive ten minutes before my appointment only to discover the tattoo parlor has been burned to the ground.

That fucking psycho!

Rage bubbles in my bloodstream.

I'd like to say it could be a coincidence, but I very much doubt that.

I'm fucking furious. If he wants to be controlling like my brother, then so be it. But I'm going to make him wish he never pissed me off.

It's time Ford learned what the wrath of a woman really feels like.

EIGHTEEN
FORD

"Fuck. Another one? Really?" Hawke says, devouring a burger in two bites as he looks over the body. We're on the wharf, between two cargo ships Eli owns. It's where we conduct most of our business, and where we take delivery of our imported stock.

"Move everything out and relocate immediately," Eli's fast to instruct.

"Waylon was in town this week," I mention. "He knows these locations."

Eli thinks this over. "He wouldn't be stupid enough to attack on the same weekend of being here, and besides, it's only one person."

It's pissing down rain, and I'm soaked through. "Think it was the same poison?" Hawke asks after swallowing the last bite of his burger.

"It's hard to tell since the rain's washed everything away, but most likely," I reply.

Fuck. This isn't good. It means someone really is targeting Eli's men. When we watched the surveillance video from his club, the bouncer had spoken to three women at the bar. There was nothing obvious linking any of them to the poisoning, but it doesn't mean it didn't happen. It just means the person was either lucky or acutely aware of the security camera angles. This, however, is too close to home.

"The poison used on the bouncer at the club took about twenty minutes to take effect, and this guy just started his shift, didn't he?" I ask the security guard.

"Yeah. I literally swapped positions with him five minutes before I found him like this. I thought it was weird he hadn't replied to my cross-check message."

Eli tsks under his breath. "We need to figure out where he was before he started his shift."

"It's possible the cargo wasn't the target. So far it's just been your men," I point out, but it's still best to move the product and operation just in case.

The rain picks up, plastering my black hair to my forehead.

"One of us should be with you at all times," I say to Eli.

"Fuck that," Eli growls back. "We're around one another enough as it is."

"That's literally what you pay us for," Hawke adds, rolling his eyes.

"I won't be intimidated by a coward who hides behind poison. Get in touch with Will. Have him back-track this guard's every move over the last few days and note who he's been in contact with. You." He points to the security guard. "Clean up this body. And no one finds out about this, especially not my father."

"Roger that!" Hawke salutes like an asshole, and I nod in acknowledgment. Eli has only officially taken over as head of the Italian mafia in the last year, and he doesn't want his father, Crue, interfering in any of his dealings. Frankly, the guy's a ruthless helicopter parent. Not when it comes to Eli but with regard to the business. And he'll do anything to dip back into the game.

"We're done here." Eli dismisses us. I don't move, and when Eli notices I'm hovering, he frowns. "What is it?"

I clear my throat. "Don't you have anyone who needs to be dealt with? A cleanup, maybe?"

He looks me up and down. "It's usually Hawke who's trying to pick fights."

"I'm not trying to pick a fight, per se. I'm just... trying to blow off some steam."

Hawke chuckles. "Then why don't you fuck someone?"

I'm the face of calm because there's no fucking way I'm letting them sniff out the truth of my frustration. But I can't fuck another woman. I haven't been able to for over a year, not since a certain little chaotic mess coaxed me into the back of my car.

My phone dings with a message alert, and I pull it out of my pocket. My security system has picked up something on the front cameras. My grip tightens on the phone because there's Billie, standing in the pouring rain and setting my front yard on fire with a blowtorch.

That little-

I pocket my phone and take my leave.

Why is it that chaos seems to ensue in every part of my life this woman touches?

Maybe she's pissed about the tattoo shop. I manage to fight a smirk as I get into my car.

The tattoo shop had to go. So I set it alight.

And I will do the same for the next shop she thinks she can go to.

Because that is not happening. She is not letting another man finish my job. I'll get to it when I get to it.

It's not my fault she couldn't sit still long enough for me to finish it in the first place.

But this? This is an entirely different game altogether.

If she wants to play, then we'll play.

But she'll be punished for it in the process.

NINETEEN
BILLIE

"Stupid fucking blowtorch doesn't fucking work with a little bit of rain. You stupid piece of shit." I throw the contraption to the ground and storm over to my rental car. I open the trunk and pull out the shovel and bleach.

I push my soaked hair out of my eyes, then start digging letters into his front lawn. "If the fire won't work, then I'll bleach the fuck out of your grass. Thank you very much, internet."

I'd furiously scrolled through ideas all day while fuming over the stunt he'd pulled. "Have to be a crazy woman to be this dedicated to give you a message like this, but boy, oh boy, do you deserve it, asshole," I say to myself as I continue digging. I'd researched that shoveling the grass and then pouring bleach over it will permanently keep it from regrowing.

I sigh because I loved the idea of the blowtorch—it felt cathartic in a way and would have been poetic justice—but it just wasn't effective due to the rain.

"You're lucky I like the fucking cat, or it would've been your house I tried to burn down," I grumble. I know I'm seeing red. I know there might be consequences. But fuck him. He doesn't own or control me. "Stupid fucking egotistical men, throwing around their big dick energy."

I shovel for an hour, cursing the entire time and constantly wiping the rain out of my eyes. After the digging is done, I pour the bleach across his lawn. By the time I'm finished, I'm exhausted but proud as I lean against the shovel and take a breath, looking over my handy work.

The words "Limp dick asshole" with a heart next to them are carved into his front lawn. I fucking hope every neighbor notices its artistic flare. I take in the darkness of the night, only a few lamp posts shining through the gloom.

"Shitty neighbors anyway," I say out loud. If someone did notice me out here, they probably know better than to make any kind of complaint regarding Ford's home. Despite him living in suburbia, I've never really seen any of his neighbors walk past his house as if they know to avoid it at all costs.

Well, now they're all going to know he's a limp dick asshole.

"Humph." I smile, my mood suddenly so much better. As the rage slowly drains from me, I feel depleted from the rain. I throw the stuff back into the trunk of the car and then use the key he gave me to walk into his home.

"Felix!" I call excitedly as the little kitten bounds down the hallway and meows at me. "Who's a good boy? I bet you're hungry, aren't you!" I coo, picking him up and scratching under his chin. He still looks a little feral, but that's most likely because Ford hasn't even thought to bathe him, and he still doesn't have a collar. "Maybe we should have a shower together before we feed you."

I take him into Ford's room and head straight for the en-suite. I run the water in the sink and wait until it's warm. "I don't even know if I can use human soap on you. Maybe we'll just rinse you with water until we get you something else."

The moment I put Felix under the water, he claws up my arm. I scream, letting go of him immediately, and he jumps toward the doorway, looking over his shoulder and hissing at me before sauntering off.

"Ow. Little fucker." I look at my arm and laugh at the small claw marks. Okay, that's no to baths. I'll let Ford enjoy that himself.

I peel off my loose pants and long shirt, then step into the shower. I let the water run down my back as I consider how crazy this might seem. I'm showering in the bathroom of the guy whose lawn I just destroyed. But I don't give a fuck. I'm proud of it. And the asshole is out at all hours of the night. I doubt he'll even be back tonight. Or, who knows, maybe he's with someone else...

"Shut up," I say to myself, tired of that stupid narrative playing in my head. I mean, I was the one who went on a date, not him.

I enjoy the heat of the water, not having realized how cold I'd become outside. It just shows how determined I was. But now, all the energy is sapped out of me. I use his shampoo and conditioner. I sniff them both. Yep, definitely smells like him—deep and rich. I lather my hair and body, my nostrils flaring at the familiar scent.

I rinse off, then step out and grab a towel. After drying my body, I run the towel over my hair as I walk into his closet to find a shirt. Of course, all of them are black.

The first time I waited for him to come home, I

snooped through his things. It turns out Ford is a very boring person: no vices, secrets, or abnormal discoveries. The most peculiar thing about him is the tattooing.

I put on one of his black shirts that's so big it hangs to my knees, and continue towel drying my hair.

When I step back into the bedroom, I see a shadow leaning against the doorframe, and every hair on my body raises as a cold chill takes over the room.

"Are you ready to be punished, Chaos?"

TWENTY
FORD

I STARE at the bold statement carved into my front lawn. *Limp dick asshole.*

The corner of my mouth twitches. She must've had the determination of a thousand burning suns to dig this into the grass during this torrential rainstorm. But I'm not surprised. When she's on a chaotic rampage, she'll stop at nothing. I've seen it before. But when it's turned on me? Well, I can't help but find it amusing.

The car she drove here is still parked out the front. Saturated from the rain, I step into the house and kick my wet shoes off beside the door. I follow the lingering smell of her scent down the hallway and notice Felix sitting outside my bedroom door, licking himself. He looks kind of wet, and I wonder if he was caught in the rain. I leave the kitchen window open just enough so he can come and go as he pleases. My hope is that one of these days, he'll decide to stay gone permanently, but the fucker keeps coming back to be fed.

I pause in the doorway of my room. Billie is rummaging through the clothes in my closet, and I take a moment to appreciate her. The cocky woman is so bold and defiant that she didn't even flee the scene of the crime.

Billie Taylor has balls. More than most men I know because if they committed the same crime against me, they'd be packing their bags and leaving the country.

Not this woman, though.

She lives for the challenge.

She thrives in creating chaos.

She exits the closet wearing one of my shirts that hides her curves, but I know exactly how she looks beneath the material. She stumbles, startled, putting her hand to her chest when she notices me.

And although she's beautiful and has become my biggest temptation, she's also been a very bad girl.

"Are you ready to be punished, Chaos?"

She pales, and I can tell she's uncertain despite being ballsy enough to stay and wait for my reaction.

Her trepidation quickly fades, replaced by a flush of red as she points her finger at me, furious. "Did you burn down that tattoo studio?"

"Yes," I reply, trying to hide my smirk.

"Why?!" she demands, and I find it so ironic that she comes into my home demanding answers and acting like a fucking saint who's done no wrong.

"They needed a refurb," I tell her, then kick the door closed so the fucking cat doesn't interrupt.

She scoffs with that nose pointed in the air. "That is showing signs of jealousy, Ford. Are you jealous?" She's intentionally pushing my buttons.

Her hair is damp, and she looks like a fucking goddess that was crafted from the rain itself.

I take a step toward her, and her mouth snaps shut.

"No, they needed a refurb," I repeat as her back hits the wall, and I grab her by the throat. It bobs beneath my thumb as I graze her jaw. This poisonous little vice of mine is making me act crazy, making me do things I wouldn't usually do.

Seeing her in my room, wearing my clothes, and smelling like me, has my cock jumping to attention. *Mine. Mine. Mine.*

I can't contain myself around her, and it's a big fucking problem.

She opens her mouth to speak and then shuts it again. It draws my attention, and I trail my thumb along her lips, fascinated. I should walk away from this —from *her*—so she can find herself a better man. But with that thought, my other hand grips her waist possessively. Even when I think it, my body reacts, needing to feed off her.

She opens her mouth again, and I wait for the smart-ass comment, but instead, she asks seductively, "Have you missed me?"

I'm startled by the question. My grip on her waist tightens, and I release my hold on her throat. I twist her around and push her onto the bed face-first. A small squeak escapes her as I crawl on top of her. That perfect ass is pointed to the ceiling as my shirt bunches around her hips. My mood darkens when I notice she's not wearing panties.

She looks over her shoulder as I mount her, pressing my groin against her ass.

I slide my hand over her hip and under the shirt, skating up to her tit and grabbing a handful. Fuck me, this woman makes me crazy.

She moans and presses her bare ass and pussy against my soaking wet pants. "Have you?" she asks, almost a little desperately.

"Yes." She seems surprised by my confession, but I don't give her much time to think about it as I slap her ass. She buckles under the pain, red immediately blooming along her skin and blemishing her ass cheek beneath the half-finished tattoo. "But that doesn't mean you'll go unpunished."

"For the grass?" She grins mischievously.

"No," I growl as I fist her hair and yank her head back. She gasps, and I love the way her body perfectly angles into me. Like my own personal fuck toy that couldn't be more beautifully designed. And she's wearing my fucking shirt, which I very much want to fuck her in.

"Then what?" she whispers. I rub my thumb against her entrance, mesmerized by the pink pussy I've thought about every night since fucking her the first time. I thrust my thumb inside, and she arches, but I tug her head farther back so she can't embrace her own moans.

Punished.

But her punishment is my own undoing because it strains my patience.

"Tell me, did you want him to touch you?" And the question sounds more feral than I anticipated. I insert a second finger, and she pants, her eyes searching mine as if trying to figure out what I'm referring to. Then her gaze clears as she makes the connection—Mr. Sweater Guy, who's so fucking lucky I didn't kill him that night. I remove my fingers and slap her cunt, tearing a scream from her. "I asked you a question."

"No," she's quick to say. I rub my thumb against her entrance again. She's already soaked. I bring it to my lips and suck; the sweetest fucking thing I've ever tasted. She's transfixed as she watches me.

"Did you want him to kiss you?" I ask before sucking harder on my fingers. I go to insert my fingers in that sweet little cunt again until I see the challenge flick through her gaze.

"Yes."

My fingers hover at her entrance, and I pull my hand away completely. I release her hair and get off the bed.

"Liar," I growl. I know she's fucking playing this game as much as I am.

She quickly scurries to her knees, flushed in the face, her damp hair a tangled mess.

I remove the belt from my pants, and she swallows knowingly, expectantly.

"Do you think he would have fucked you like I do?" I ask, trying to restrain the bite in my tone. I fold the belt over.

"No," she breaths out and has the good sense to add, "Because no one will ever fuck me the way you do."

Ain't that the truth. "You'll do well to remember

that. Now, get on all fours on the floor and crawl to me for your punishment."

She swallows, glancing between me and the belt in my hand. But she does as she's told, coming to a stop at my feet. She looks up at me through thick eyelashes, and I adjust my cock. Fuck me, she's so perfect.

"What if I went on another date? Would you follow me again?" she daringly asks. My energy shifts dangerously. This woman continues to provoke me, even when she's in the most vulnerable position.

"I would follow you, and I would watch," I tell her as I trail a finger over her shoulder while I move so I'm positioned between the bed and her ass. She goes to look over her shoulder, but I snap a command. "Stay."

She grumbles with complaint but remains still. If this little temptress wants to fuck with me and play games, then she'll find out the consequence.

"And then I would kill him," I say as I snap the belt on her ass. She yelps, and I'm quick to catch her so she doesn't fall to the floor.

She's breathing hard. Maybe this is the thing that will break her. Maybe this is what will push her to leave.

"Fuck me," she says under her breath, blinking her eyes as if she's been blinded.

I expect her to get up and leave. To never come

back. To put an end to my fixation. But instead, I find myself dropping to my knees behind her. "Are you okay?" I ask, rubbing over the welt on her ass, practically salivating at the blemish on her perfectly smooth skin. I'm tarnishing her one bit at a time.

She looks over her shoulder, and I can tell she's slightly confused. I'm confused, too.

But she bites her bottom lip and pushes her ass against my crotch.

"If you're going to make me crawl, you might as well fuck me like an animal on this floor."

A guttural sound comes from my throat, and it's the last thread to my control snapping. I undo my pants frantically, needing to be inside her. My soaked clothes are sticking to my body, and I push my hair out of my eyes as I slam my cock into her wet pussy.

She grunts and curses as I pound into her. Her head lowers to the floor as she cries out, gasping and begging for more. Fuck me, the things this woman does to me.

"Turn around," I order as I pull out of her and yank my jeans off completely. I sit on the carpet, my cock glistening with her juices. She turns and reaches for my dick, but I grab her by the throat and drag her up to hover over my lap.

I wrap the belt around my throat and tighten it at

the front, then hand her the end. "I want you to milk my cock, Chaos. I want you to take all that pent-up rage and take it out on me. Curse me. Choke me. Own me."

"I—" She seems lost for words as she stares into my eyes, realizing how deadly serious I am. I want her to take that hatred out on me. To feed my demons that tell me she's only using me for my body. To punish me for tarnishing her beautiful skin. But I'm too selfish to step away, and I want to watch her come undone.

This woman is my undoing, and I'm handing her the reins.

Hopefully, the lack of airflow rewires my brain.

Or better yet, maybe she'll walk out the door.

But instead, her perfectly manicured hands wrap around the belt, and she swallows.

"Will you kiss me if I do this?" she asks.

My eyebrows furrow in confusion. *Kiss her?*

She doesn't wait for my answer as she lowers her head to hover her lips over mine. My heart races abnormally, and I fucking hate the way it changes the energy around us. It's not just animalistic. This little vixen somehow brings something out in me that I'm not used to. Tenderness. Connection. A need other than the physical. It's completely opposite to what I'm trying to solidify between us.

Yet, I'm at her mercy, unable to deny her. I'd give it all to her—everything I have—whenever she asks. I'd do anything for her but I'm certain there will be a time when she doesn't want me to, that she'll see the darkness of what's inside. So, I waste no time in giving in to her demand as I crush my lips to hers at the same time I slam her down onto my cock. She screams into my mouth, and I swallow the sound. Bite at her lips and overpower her with need as I devour every whimper and moan. This is who I am. She might try to make this into something sickly sweet but I'm anything but.

She yanks on the belt, and it constricts my airway, but it does nothing to lessen my dedication of feasting on her like a starved man.

Billie bounces up and down on my cock as I palm her ass—that beautiful fucking ass—and slowly move my finger toward her asshole.

She pants and pulls away momentarily. "You don't tell me what to do," she says as she bounces on my cock and kisses me again. She's starving for the pleasure I can give her, yanking at the belt as if it's a new toy. Then she leans back, meeting my gaze, and gives me a look of silent permission. I shove a finger in her ass, mesmerized by the way she arches uncomfortably, and if I were a sane man, I would've lubricated the digit first, but I just can't hold back.

"You'll do as you're told," I rasp, the lack of oxygen feeding my high.

She doesn't know how much control she truly has over me.

Her tongue is fighting against mine as her pace picks up, and I thrust into her, unable to contain myself.

Fuck, she's everything.

"You're so fucking beautiful," I say through the pieces of her wet hair that have mixed with our kisses.

Her golden eyes shine brightly as her pace picks up. Then she leans back, tugging the belt with her. I lean forward, kissing down her neck, worshipping her chest, then cutting off my breath completely so I can bite at her nipples.

So fucking perfect.

My heaven and my hell even with a noose around my neck.

If I could lose myself in her every day, I'd forever be a man on a high.

"Ford!" she cries. "I'm so close."

I lean up for a gasp of air, and I see tears streaming down her beautifully flushed cheeks.

"Slap me," I tell her. "Show me how angry I made you."

She doesn't hesitate this time, slapping me across

the face so hard it's blinding. A jolt runs through my cock, and I jerk inside her. I grab her hips—the only thing keeping me grounded—and she screams, her body contorting when I twist my finger in her ass. She pulls on the belt, restricting my breathing further as I hazily watch her reach the high and come back down.

Her cunt pulses around my cock, milking me, and I can't help but give her what she wants and needs as I kiss her. Slowly and gently this time. Appreciative of her meeting my every demand. She removes the belt from around my neck and then cups my cheeks as she kisses me back.

I don't kiss; it's never felt like there's a purpose, but with Billie, she teaches me things I'm most likely not worthy of. This gentleness, a leisurely pace as if we have all the time in the world to explore one another, like our encounter isn't fleeting. I know I shouldn't feed into her, giving her this, but I can't stop myself. I want to give into her every demand, even if it's damning me in the process. I feel like the more attached I become, the more I'm tainting her. I'm not a good man for her but it's becoming harder to pull away. Even when I do, she does something to demand my attention. The thought of my front lawn brings a smirk to my lips as I kiss her. She's total chaos.

Billie's hips roll slowly back and forth as our

panting falls into sync with one another, and we stare at each other in disbelief. There's something else there in her eyes, and I shy away from it. Knowing that she's too good for me. Acknowledging that I'm still no better than the street rat I was. There's no way I can fulfill the needs of someone like Billie Taylor. I've known from the start I'm temporary, but it's gone on for much longer than I expected and definitely becoming harder to let go.

"No one will ever fuck me like you do," she says on a shaky breath. And it's as good of an apology as either of us can give right now.

I don't understand this game. But what I know for a fact is we'll continue coming back to one another, unable to control ourselves.

And it's so fucking dangerous.

We're both too exhausted to move from where we're lying on our backs, his head on the pillow and mine at the opposite end of the bed. Which is a step up from the floor where we did most of our fucking. But the sheets are now soaked and destroyed from our exertions and his wet clothes.

He palms my inner thigh, thumb skating over my skin. Goose bumps erupt at his touch, and my pussy starts a gentle pounding. I mentally try to snuff it out because there is no way I can possibly move.

Ford is a god in bed. And every time we have sex, it hammers home the fact no other man will ever even come close to what he can offer me.

I stare at the ceiling and swallow hard before I ask, "Why did you never tell me about the things you liked?

I mean, we've been fucking for over a year, and I never knew you were into...this stuff."

"'This stuff'?" He knows exactly what I'm talking about; he's just trying to mock me for saying it out loud.

I've learned a few things about Ford during our time together. One, he's a petty bitch, and two, he's very intentional in how and why he does things. Well, except when his control snaps. But we're alike in that way, I guess.

"The pain, the belt, the slapping, the biting, all of it. Why did you never tell me? I could've..." I lick my lips, searching for the right words. "Tried to cater to your needs earlier."

He removes his hand from my thigh, and I immediately feel the disconnect. Until he sits up and then lies with me so both of our feet are facing the headboard. He's on his side, head propped on his hand, staring down at me. He looks more beast than man right now, a glaze of satisfaction in his dark eyes. His hair is a mess from air drying after the rain. Tattoos mark his beautiful body, and the muscles of his abs and arms are cut to perfection.

"Because I didn't think you could handle it," he confesses.

Ordinarily, I might be mad by the assumption, but I'm too exhausted to fight him. Also, he's not entirely wrong. I might've been intimidated by his demand. I mean, hurting him isn't exactly something I thought I'd be signing up for. But watching the way he gets off on it? The way the control switches between us fluidly in the bedroom? I like it. A lot.

"So why now?" I ask.

He shrugs as he caresses my collarbone with the backs of his fingers. The shirt I was wearing has long since been discarded, thrown to the floor among the mess of his own wet clothes. "Because you needed to see the real me. Well, part of it, at least. To be honest, I thought you might run the other way."

"What do you mean by that?" I ask, too afraid to reach for him because I feel like it might scare him away. Ford and I don't usually do deep talks, but there are so many things about this man that remain a mystery, and I want to know. I want him to let me in, little by little.

He watches me for some time, the space between us seeming to grow wider and wider, and I think it'll swallow me whole before he finally answers. "Because I'm not good for you, Billie. I thought you seeing this side of me might scare you, I'd be lying if I didn't admit I hoped that it would. I can't offer you more than this- my body. This might be exciting for you, but I have no self-control when it comes to you, and I'm scared I'll do something reckless one day because of it."

I bring my hand up to cover his, and his nostrils flare, reacting to the tender touch. I often feel that Ford struggles when I bring any level of softness between us that might be considered normal for others, especially when we kiss.

My eyebrows furrow, and I stare at him, my gaze dipping to the words tattooed on his throat. *Bad to the bone.* I can't help but wonder if it's some kind of self-branding. Ford has always had a quiet confidence and self-assurance about him, but it's moments like this that I see him waver as if he's unsure how to act or what to say around me. Like I'm some little princess who has to be protected... from him.

"I feel the same, you know. I can't keep my hands off you, either. Is that so bad?" I ask quietly. This is the first time he's let me see the way his mind works.

"It's different."

"How?" I push, and his jaw tics like he doesn't like being pressed. I'm certain he'll get up and leave, but instead, he averts his gaze.

"Because I have issues with addiction," he confesses.

My mouth opens and closes. Did I hear him right? "As in, you're using drugs?"

"No." He shakes his head and sits upright.

I follow suit, putting my hand on his leg to stop him from leaving. "Explain it to me."

He looks away as if ashamed, and it's the most vulnerable I've seen this powerful man. Sitting naked in front of me, tempted to tell me tidbits of the life he lives that I've never known.

"Not anymore," he admits. "My biological mother was addicted to crack. She overdosed when we were twelve, so it was just me and Hawke. We stole, cheated, and lied in order to survive. And when we started filling out in size, we'd physically hurt people. We were no better than animals." I try not to react as if any small movement might interfere with every shocking thing he's telling me.

"I was fourteen when I became addicted, swapping out my reality for anything that could numb it. It was Anya and River who helped me get clean. But the impulses are still the same when I become fixated on something. I relapsed once. Now I use other methods to get the high I crave."

With sudden clarity I understand why he doesn't drink. Why he's always on the phone. His need for sugar.

"How did you come to live with Anya and River?" I ask, bewildered, trying to process everything.

He smirks as he recalls the memory. "It was me who convinced Hawke to break into their home one night when we were fifteen. And my stupid miscalculation almost cost us our lives. But they saw something in us. Took us in, cared for us, and sharpened our fangs. I'll forever be grateful to them, and to Eli, for letting us be who we are without judgment and for giving us a purpose."

"You mean killing?" I clarify.

The energy around him shifts and crackles like wild fire, the man gone, nothing but a beast now. "Precisely."

The hairs on my arms raise, and I swallow hard.

I've always known Ford isn't a normal man. But where my brother and father try to hide their savage nature from me, Ford comes entirely unfiltered. And it is terrifying. This man is powerful, with the grace of a predator I'm not even sure he's aware of.

"What does the tattoo on your throat mean?" I ask because I feel like there's more to it.

He stares into my soul, and it makes me shift uncomfortably. As if realizing he's doing it, he blinks a few times and shifts.

"It was the second time I relapsed. I was clean for a few months, then slipped into old patterns. I expected Anya and River to discard me, but they didn't. My father found me high as fuck, pummeling my dealer's ass. The guy had picked a fight with me, and I couldn't stop. I don't think he would've cared if I killed him that day, but he stopped me. It was after that he got me the tattoo gun, to help me focus on something else. The first tattoo I gave myself was this. As a reminder of my roots."

I don't like that tattoo and its purpose there. But I don't voice that. I crawl over him and straddle his lap, wrapping my arms around his neck as if rewarding him for opening up to me. But it's also because I feel like I need to reassure him.

The fucker doesn't even flinch. Like everything he just told me happened to someone else. I know men like him don't feel too deeply or think too much about their emotions or traumas, but I think that's precisely why it's so sad. Because he'll never truly understand that he deserves so much more. But I could never say that to him. I don't speak a language he can relate to because fundamentally, I'm different. I only hover around the edges of his world. That's never been more apparent than it is right now. I always thought Ford was a vault, but this runs far deeper then I realized.

Eventually, he gets uncomfortable with my affection, his entire body going rigid. But he doesn't try to pry me off him.

"Have you ever let anyone else tattoo you?" I ask.

"No."

His cock is hardening under me, and I smirk. I love how responsive his body is to mine. He might consider it as a problematic addiction, but I don't think it's that bad at all, especially when my body is demanding the same thing despite how battered and bruised it is.

I press a gentle kiss to his cheek, silently thanking him, for ever so slightly opening up to me. Ford might not think we're compatible or he's incapable of affection, but bit by bit, he's opening up to me, and I'm becoming more curious about this man that I thought I knew but am realizing someone as strong as even Ford has been let down and hurt. He might speak about it all with ease but surely it impacts him in some way. So, I decide to speak in a language that he does understand.

"Tell me what you want me to do right now," I say, encouraging his most primal needs as a reward for telling me something I know for certain not many people would know.

His gaze becomes hooded, and a low growl escapes him.

Ford Ivanov is definitely not a normal man.

I'm certain he's more beast.

But if being addicted to one another is wrong, I don't want to be right.

TWENTY-TWO
FORD

She's sound asleep when I hear footsteps outside the bedroom door. I know who it is without having to see them. So I pull the covers up over her and then step into the hall.

"Fucking hell, man, put on some clothes," Hawke says, rubbing his eyes, then peering over my shoulder as I close the door. He smirks mischievously. "Who is it?"

"No one." The lie feels natural coming from my lips. No one needs to know about Billie and me. We fucked up a few times already, and I'm not going to let it happen again.

"No one. But she's asleep in there, I take it?" He whistles. "You let a woman sleep over? In your bed?" He raises a brow and continues, "Does it have something to do with the message carved into your lawn?"

He can't even keep the laugh in. "Because, honestly, whoever did that has fucking balls of steel. I like it."

"I pissed the neighbors off."

He scoffs, knowing too well that I'm lying again. He heads back down the hall, saying over his shoulder, "Better not be who I think it is."

I grind my jaw, tentative about Hawkes timing of always appearing when Billie is here or maybe it's by chance since she's here more frequently. He warned me from seeing her ever again, and I didn't specifically promise him shit. But I know if he finds out about her, he'll try to take matters into his own hand by warning her away, and that makes me prematurely want to beat the shit out of my brother because I don't want him anywhere near her.

It makes me recede into myself because it has always been me and Hawke through thick and thin. The thought of me prioritizing anything over being honest with him is...unsettling.

Hawke stops dead in his tracks. "What the fuck is that? You raising dirty little raccoons now?"

Felix pads up to him, and I grind my teeth as the little fucker meows at Hawke and rubs against his leg. The little shit has the audacity to start purring.

"Something like that."

Hawke picks him up. And Felix looks even smaller

when held in Hawke's giant hands. He rubs Felix under the chin, and I'm furious with their immediate bond. "It's all skin and bones. Are you even feeding it properly? You barely know how to look after yourself."

I lean against the wall. "I don't need to hear that coming from you."

He smirks and then looks me dead in the eyes. We have the exact same dark eyes. "Well, I'm glad you finally found your fucking solution. You've been acting weird, man. It's about time you took my advice."

"Hell will freeze over on the day I take advice from you."

He chuckles as he enters the spare room with Felix in his hands and shuts the door behind him. I sigh, exhausted. I should've known after the way I was acting that Hawke would check up on me. Not that either of us would ever admit that we care.

Hawke has his own place, but sometimes our demons get the best of us, and we can't sleep. I've stayed up for nights on end sometimes. When Hawke has those nights, he'll stay here. It also has a lot to do with the fact that Hawke doesn't do well being alone. And I get it. But being alone is my preference. Turning, I head back into my bedroom to find Billie awake and sitting up, no sheet covering her perfect tits.

"Does he know?" she whispers.

"No." I never told her about the conversation I had with Hawke that day he found us in Dutton's kitchen. And I'll never admit that he tried to force me to promise to stop seeing her. "Go back to sleep. He won't wake for a good twelve hours." I don't usually invite her to stay the night, but with Dutton out of town, I feel like, for some reason, I might sleep better, like I need her too.

I climb in next to her, and she lies back down on her side, facing me. "Do you fuck anyone else here?" she asks. Which means she overheard the conversation.

"No." I hear a soft sigh leave her lips. "Does that bother you? Do you want me to be fucking other women?"

"No." She's quick to reply, then immediately lowers her voice. "It's just... What are we, exactly?"

My eyebrows dip in confusion. I know what she's asking. But if she thinks we can be anything more than what we are, she's living in a fairy tale. Tonight should've deterred her from those thoughts. I confessed my demons and ugliness so she'd have more reasons to run the other fucking way and kill this off for the both of us, because I'm incapable of doing it.

I realize that if anything, I'm running away, and I'm okay with that. I don't deserve someone like Billie Taylor, especially when she's adamant that I remain as the man that sticks to being her dirty little secret. I even lied to my brother to respect her wishes. I don't resent her for it but there can be nothing for us past this point. She needs to find someone who can offer her a stable relationship, someone whose not prone to violence or addictions and have a white picket fence lifestyle. I stand for everything that is opposite to that so I harden my jaw as I once again purposefully push her away because maybe this time she'll finally have the strength to step away. Because I certainly don't have it. I already tried that once and it lead us right here in the now.

"We are nothing but two bodies who like to touch each other," I say matter-of-factly.

I can see the immediate hurt in her expression, and I fucking hate myself for being the one to put it there. But I can't let her get attached to me. I'm a sinking rock. She needs stability and a man who can give her what she wants. That's not me.

"And that's all?" she asks incredulously.

"Yes."

She nods once, and I can see the hurt shift into anger. Billie turns away from me and gives me her back.

Silence fills the room for another few minutes before she pushes the covers back and stands.

"I need to go." She goes to the bathroom and puts on her wet clothes. I consider offering her something of mine to wear, but I have the good sense to keep my mouth shut.

She avoids my gaze until she's fully dressed and untucks her hair from the hoodie so it falls down her back. "Will your brother see me?"

"No, he'll be asleep now." Hawke's a heavy sleeper and is out cold within minutes of his head hitting the pillow.

"Good." And then she slips out the door without so much as a goodbye.

I know I'm an asshole for what I said.

But I also know I wouldn't have said it if I didn't care.

And that's a fucking problem.

TWENTY-THREE
BILLIE

"You've been awfully quiet lately. Why?" Ivy says from beside me as we sit in the back of a cab on the way to my brother's club, Pearl. We've been there a few times before, and it's because Posie invited us that we're going tonight. I'm hoping to drag her out afterward if my brother lets her out of his sight for more than two seconds. But I know she doesn't enjoy going out too much because she prefers being home with her son, so this might be the compromise.

"Huh?" I turn to face her.

Ivy sighs, exasperated. "There you go again, off with the fairies. Everything okay? Is it the new job?"

"No, everything's fine. Just tired lately, that's all." I shoot her a small smile. "Did you end up seeing that guy from our double date again? And by the way, I am never doing that with you again."

She starts laughing and nodding her head. We haven't seen much of one another this week because our schedules haven't lined up, and I'm grateful she wasn't home when I returned to the apartment last weekend after spending time at Ford's. I went home that night and had a hot bath, my mind running over a million thoughts. And I've tried since to forget about it. To forget about *him*. To reshape my expectation that sex is all we'll ever be. And it's fucking hard.

Hope is traveling again but is due to return soon, which will be nice. It's good to have our trio complete. I don't think Hope was built for the spotlight like her mother. She definitely acts more like her father with her quiet, solitary ways. I'm certain she takes the time coming back home to recharge.

"Yep. I went over to his place last weekend. They live together, too. Anyway, after we fucked, which was shit, I might add, his friend, the one you went out with, asked if he could join us. My guess is this is something they do often. It was so obvious." She nonchalantly shrugs. "And I figured, what the fuck? So I fucked them both. Didn't improve much, but oh well. Eiffel Tower ticked off the list."

I can't help but laugh at her ability to always embrace her nature and have the best fucking time doing it. Maybe I need to do the same thing: branch out to other guys beyond just Ford. I'm certain no one will live up to him, though.

If I want anything more than just sex, I have to let Ford go before I get hurt. Because I was hurt the other night and furious at myself for feeling anything more for him when it was me who set our boundaries to begin with. And I still haven't completely digested the news about his vices and addictions. What does that even mean to be addicted to someone?

But a flush runs down my neck as I think about our time together, the way we can't keep our hands off one another. And that paints a very clear picture of what that addiction might look like. I cut those thoughts and memories off. God, I need to stop this. It's too consuming.

"You really fucked both of them?" I ask, then laugh at her smug expression.

"Yep. Would not recommend," she states, flicking her hair over her shoulder. "Or maybe next time I just need to find two guys who actually know what they're doing. And who think more about the woman than themselves. Besides, I had to wait for like two hours until he could get it back up. I don't have the patience to wait around like that." She laughs.

I laugh, feeling light and free for the first time in ages. I'm so grateful for Ivy. She does what she wants, when she wants, and isn't restricted in the same ways as me because of my asshole brother. "Well, someone has to do it because I certainly wasn't going to fuck him. That guy was a dickhead."

"Look, I wasn't going to either, but I was bored." She smirks, readjusting her heels.

"Oh, boredom. Now that's a worry."

"Shut up." She bumps my shoulder with hers. "Do you think there will be any hot guys there, or will it be the usual group?"

"I'm not sure. Posie just said they were closing the venue down for the night to throw a surprise party for the manager or something. Apparently, Posie really likes her and didn't have to twist Dutton's arm much. So it's a free-for-all."

"Noted. So no hot guys and most likely the usual suspects. I hope the twins are there, at least. They're always a bit of fun."

I raise my eyebrows. "It's desperate times if you're depending on the twins for entertainment."

"Oh, come on now. Hawke's always down to party,

and Ford is comical in his serious, stoic way, with his ability to ignore everyone and stare at his phone the entire time. I always wonder what he's doing on that thing."

I go quiet because I wonder that, too. He said he's addicted, and his phone seems to be another vice, but I can't imagine him to be the type to scroll through social media.

"Oh well. Even if there were hot guys, it's not like your brother will let you around anyone, so it means ample opportunities for me." She laughs.

We arrive at Pearl a little late and adjust our dresses when we step out of the cab. Posie themed the party as a red-carpet event, and it's not like our family doesn't have plenty of gowns and suits to choose from. I feel like any time we do anything together as a large group, we're always dressed up. Sometimes I just want to show up in a pair of jeans and call it a day. But I know this is fun for Posie, and that makes me excited as well.

I'm wearing a red dress with a plunging neckline that drapes low at the back and has a slit up to my thigh. I don't always love getting dressed up, but I love this dress. My hair is curled and blown out, falling over my shoulders.

Ivy and I have already posted our obligatory pic,

and we couldn't look more different; me in my daring red dress, and her in a knee-length, high neck pink dress.

When we step inside the club, I spot Posie straight away, mingling with the dancers. Every time I've come into my brother's strip club, there has been a naked dancer on stage. Tonight, there is a dancer but she's fully clothed, though she's clearly drunk and having the best time of her life as another two girls applaud her. I'm envious of how they ooze beauty and sensuality. There's no way in hell my brother would permit me to do anything like this. He'd most likely burn down any club I even attempted to dance at, even if just for fun.

The moment Posie spots us, she rushes over and grabs our hands. "You came! Come on, let's have some drinks." Before I can even say hello she's dragging us to the bar. Okay, the girl is ready for a party night.

She orders a round of some cocktail she swears by. Everything is free tonight, and two waitresses circle the room offering drinks. I see a lot of men in suits, which tells me that, although my brother approved the party, he's still mixing business with pleasure, which isn't a surprise.

"Hello, Daddy," Ivy purrs as she scans the room.

I laugh. "Calm down. We've only been here for two seconds."

"And I already know what I like." She chuckles as she accepts the drink and brings it to her lips.

"I'm living through you, girls," Posie says with a laugh.

"Says the almost-married woman," I retort with an arched eyebrow. The wedding is only a few weeks away, and I've already started making jokes that Dutton is going bald from being a groomzilla. He's not, but it's still hilarious.

Posie's cheeks brighten, and I see the natural glow she has whenever my brother is mentioned. She certainly puts him in his place and challenges him, but she also loves him unconditionally. "I have a surprise for you. There's someone here I want you to meet." I gape at her in surprise and Ivy gasps.

"Don't tell me Posie got big brother Dutton's permission for Billie to actually talk to a real boy?" Ivy jokes.

"Shut up," I growl.

"Yes, he knows. And I've warned him to be on his best behavior and to leave the judging of who you date up to you."

My eyebrows spike in shock. "What did you have to bribe him with for that outcome?"

She chuckles and gives me a very obvious expression.

"Pussy power, right?" Ivy says.

Posie nods. "Yes. Sex." She waggles her brows, then turns me around and points to a man standing next to my brother. "That's him, and your brother doesn't hate him, which is a plus. He is a powerful man, which I know your family respects. He owns a large marketing company but specializes in smear campaigns." I shoot her a puzzled look. "Oh yes. One smear campaign can start at $170,000. Granted, people in Hollywood usually hire him, but I know Crue has worked with him before when he wanted to take over a big chain restaurant." She shrugs. "He's young, only in his late twenties, and single."

"While you meet new Daddy Smear, I'm going to circle the room," Ivy says, then she's gone. I admire her for her confidence. And I'm not surprised when she approaches the women on the poles and asks one of them to teach her some things.

Posie pulls at my arm, leading us in the direction of where the men are talking. My brother's wide shoulders are blocking the view of the third person in the group. Posie comes to a stop beside Dutton and then introduces me to the handsome guy in the cream suit.

But it's not him my heart falters over. Because the third man is...

Ford.

I fix my attention on the newcomer, smiling at him, and hating myself for immediately comparing him to Ford.

He doesn't get to have that type of power over me.

It's just sex, Billie. Get a grip on yourself.

"Matthew, this is Billie, Dutton's sister. She's the one I was telling you about," Posie says. The tension around the group thickens, mostly coming from my brother, and I despise the fact that Ford can act so casually. It really shows how little I must actually mean to him. I know he can't do or say anything, especially in front of my brother, but I expected some kind of reaction.

It's just sex. I have to remind myself again of that.

Matthew's gaze locks on me, and I immediately know he's interested, which is flattering. I try to block out the tatted, leanly muscled man standing just a few inches from me as Matthew offers his hand. I give him mine, and he shakes it gently.

"Lovely to meet you. I've had mixed messages on whether I should actually talk to you or not," he jokes, eyeing my brother, whose jaw is clenched tight. The fact that Dutton hasn't stabbed him yet is a promising yet strange progression.

Posie threads her arm around Dutton's elbow with a smile. "I'll handle him. You two talk. Have fun." She makes as if to lead Dutton away but then pauses and looks at Ford, who doesn't seem to be moving. Posie shoots a glance between us like she's wondering if we're still seeing one another. She wouldn't be wrong in that assumption. "Ford, come and entertain Dutton with me."

Matthew drops my hand and politely smiles at Ford as he reluctantly joins the others.

"I'm not a child," I hear my brother grit as he's basically dragged away by the woman half his size.

I can't help but glance at Ford. His focus isn't on me, though—it's on Matthew. And Matthew's attention is on me, not at all picking up the tension.

"So, I hear you're a brilliant accountant," Matthew starts, and I have the impression he's very charismatic, most likely the reason he's been so successful in his career so far. I try my hardest to ignore the sensation of being watched. I don't know if it's my brother or Ford, but I know who I want it to be, and I hate that I give him that power.

"We are nothing but two bodies who like to touch each other."

Yeah, go fuck yourself, Ford.

"I wouldn't say brilliant, but I'm getting there." I try to sound modest, which is very unlike me. But it's best to be humble around strangers, especially if Posie handpicked this guy for me.

Matthew leans in with a smile. "I can't help but notice we're being stared at a lot. Your brother is really protective, isn't he?" If he knew the full extent of that protectiveness, I wonder if he'd still be so ballsy. But isn't this what I wanted? Someone not intimidated by my family?

"Care to walk to the bar with me for a drink?" he asks, though my glass is still half full. Then I realize he's trying to give us somewhere with a little more privacy. He offers me his arm—very gentlemanly—and I feel that sense of being watched again. I offer a smile and wrap my hand around his elbow.

Fuck Dutton, and fuck Ford. I can do what I want. I'm an adult. I'm single. And this guy seems nice enough so far.

"Your family is quite intimidating." Matthew chuckles as we reach the bar. "Though I have dealt with powerful people all my life, so I think I can handle them," he says as I pull my hand away and look at him curiously. I've never even seen this guy around my brother before.

"Would you like another one?" he asks, pointing to my drink. I decline his offer, taking a small sip from the one I already have.

"How old are you?" I ask, casually leaning on the bar. Matthew looks around my age, but I'm unsure what his actual age is. Ford is a few years older than me. "Twenty-seven. And like yourself, the baby of the family. My mother is old-school Italian and is annoyed I haven't found a nice Italian woman to settle down with yet." I smile at that, remembering my grandfather talking like that back in Italy. He's dead now, and I miss him, but he was very strict when it came to traditions. Hell, Eli had to be married before he was able to officially take over the entire mafia business. I'm lucky my brother and I were never under the same expectations.

"So, what brings you here tonight? I've never seen you around before," I say.

His drink is handed to him, and he pulls out two bar stools, offering me the first one. I sit on it, careful not to let the slit in my dress show everything I'm wearing—or, more accurately, not wearing —underneath.

Women start cheering on stage, and I laugh as Ivy swings around the pole. An older woman, who I'm assuming is the birthday girl because she's wearing a sash, is giving her pointers on her grip.

"Posie invited me, actually. I've been around, but am based in Los Angeles. I've known your brother for almost five years now, and I've done business with your family several times.

"When I met Posie, she asked if I was single." I laugh. Wow, Posie's really putting herself out there for me, and I'm kind of grateful for it. Had I known the way to get a leash on my brother was through a woman, I would've tried to find him one sooner. Then again, I don't think just any woman would've done—it was always supposed to be Posie.

I glance over at them, admiring their love. Ford's nowhere to be found, which stirs something unfamiliar within me. Disappointment maybe? I refocus on the man in front of me.

"Did my brother try to kill you because he thought she was hitting on you?" I joke.

He raises his eyebrows, and I know it might've not been too far from the truth. "Let's just say she was quick to clarify that she was asking on behalf of his younger sister. His anger didn't exactly recede even then. I felt like she'd dragged me into a field of land-mines." I laugh again. I can just imagine it. He smirks as he takes a sip. "To be honest, I didn't even know he had a younger sister. He keeps that pretty quiet. But when she showed me a photo, I knew I wanted to come and meet you. You're beautiful, and I thought it was worth the risk of getting my throat slit." I smile at him.

This Matthew guy might not be all that bad.

But he's not Ford.

I squash that thought immediately.

"So, tell me more about yourself," I say, trying to push the man I shouldn't be thinking about out of my mind and focusing on the one in front of me.

I find myself laughing with Matthew; my first impression of him is he seems funny and kind. And if he's willing to challenge my brother in any way, it's a bonus.

We probably haven't even been talking for ten minutes before we're interrupted.

"Billie." I turn to find Ford standing there. He doesn't acknowledge Matthew; his gaze is intently on me. "I have something to show you," he says, then turns and walks away. I'm actually gobsmacked that the asshole has this kind of audacity. He tells me we're nothing but sex, then pulls me away from a man who might be willing and able to offer me more.

Matthew seems confused but stands up.

"I'm sure whatever it is, it can wait," I say defiantly.

Matthew smiles. "It's okay. I think I've monopolized enough of your time. I don't want to push your brother over the edge; he looks like he's about to blow a fuse." I follow the direction of his gaze, and sure enough, Dutton's staring at him with the intensity of a lion stalking a gazelle.

"How deep is the friendship between you and Dutton?" I ask.

Matthew chuckles. "Not deep enough for him to let me have you for more than twenty minutes at a time, apparently. *Yet*." The last word is full of an intent I don't want to unpack right now. He leans in and presses a kiss to my cheek.

"It was lovely meeting you, Billie. I'll make sure to message you. We should do this again, but maybe somewhere more private. If I make it past tonight, that is."

I laugh and then notice Eli and Jewel walk in. Posie pulls her in for a hug. "Besides, I have some business with your cousin," Matthew says, then excuses himself and makes his way to Eli. I don't even want to know who Eli's targeting with a smear campaign.

I'm tempted to join Ivy since she looks like she's having the time of her life, but that nagging feeling in my stomach gnaws at me, demanding attention. I shouldn't be curious as to what Ford might have to say to me, but I am. Part of me wonders if he regrets what he said the other night. Another part of me shouldn't care. I yoyo with the sentiment, but my feet undeniably take me the direction he went, always curious and unable to control myself.

I hate the power he holds over me. But I hate my lack of control when it comes to going to him more.

Addicted, he'd said. Is that what this is? Am I no better?

Because now I know this isn't good for me since I've started developing feelings for Ford. And yet, I'm walking toward my demise once again.

Hawke comes out from the back, almost barreling me over. He beams with a goofy smile, which is such a contradiction to his blood-thirsty personality.

"Whoa there, little tornado, where you off to?"

I'm about to tell him I'm grabbing something from the back when Eli grabs his attention. Hawke bounds over, and whatever business they're discussing has them forgetting about me. I head backstage, where the dancers usually get ready, but I don't see any sign of him.

That's when the bathroom door opens, and I'm pulled inside, the door closing behind me. Ford leans into me, caging me between the door and his lean build.

He looks pissed, and it sparks my own frustration.

He has no fucking right to be mad at me because I was talking to a guy.

"What are you doing?" I ask, trying to remember to breathe because this man does all kinds of fucked-up things to my body.

"I wanted my fix," he says as his hand slides up the slit in my dress.

His fix. Like a crack addict needs their next hit.

I get what he means and I don't like it. Especially with the way he described it to me the other night. I won't just be a little fuck doll to him.

My anger boils as I shove him. I know I'm not strong enough to move him, but he takes a step back, removing his hand from my thigh.

"I'm not your plaything," I hiss. "What? Does it upset you that someone else wants me?"

Ford remains quiet that intimidating and brooding gaze staring through me. I fucking hate when he does that. Shuts me out, gives me no hint of what he's thinking, but keeps reeling me in. I grit my teeth. One of us has to have some kind of control because we're falling so deeply into an abyss neither one of us can crawl back out of.

"Well, I don't need a fix, so fuck off." I turn and grab the doorknob, but his body slams me against the door.

"Are you upset, Chaos?" he asks, his breath tickling my ear.

Of course I'm fucking upset! But I'm too proud to say that. I can't admit how much he's gotten under my skin and into my bloodstream. Not one day has passed that I haven't thought about him and the conversation that we had. He made his expectation clear, and yet here I am. Again.

"This has to end. *We* have to end. Sneaking around was fun, but I'm over it." I push back against him, which is a mistake because I feel his hard cock against my ass, and my body freezes with immediate anticipation. He bites my earlobe, and a shiver runs down my spine, goosebumps rising on my skin, the heavy pounding of anticipation heating my pussy.

"That's all for you. You can take it if you want it," he croons. I shake my head, trying to tell myself no.

But I really want it.

Fuck. I want it more than anything right now.

"This isn't smart, Ford. There are people right outside."

"I don't care. All I want is you. To be in you. Consumed by you. Use me how you want."

"That's not fair," I grit as my ass rubs against his cock, my body betraying me. *No, Billie, more willpower.*

"Nothing about you is fucking fair, Chaos." He runs his nose along my neck as if smelling me. A moan escapes me, and I chastise myself as all my anger morphs into something else.

"I need more," I whisper.

"Of this cock?"

"No. More from you. Not just sex."

He remains silent behind me, and I can see his knuckles turning white from how tightly he grips the doorframe. How typical to ask Ford for something more, and he freezes up. I build the courage again to leave, but then he says, "Like what?"

My heart falters. The first thing that comes to mind is small and sounds childish when I say it, yet for some reason, it means so much. "I don't know. Like texting me more or something."

It's so minor, so juvenile, and yet I want it. I need something more than this situation where we come and go as we please. I hold my breath, my body buzzing with the tension rippling around us. I wait for his rejection or for him to reiterate that we're nothing more than fuck buddies. The moment he says it, I'm out the door.

"Okay," he says.

I'm startled, my breath releasing in a rush because I wasn't expecting that response at all. My heart fills with what feels like victory, and it's so stupid. Irrational. And yet, my body acts of its own accord, reaching behind me. I come into contact with his leg, and my hand slides up until I reach his belt. But this angle is too awkward. He hurries to assist, unbuckling it for me, his movements desperate as he frees his cock. We're breathing heavily, our hunger insatiable despite being together only a week ago.

My hand clasps his veiny cock, and I stroke to the tip, my thumb rolling over his piercing and enjoying the feel of the bar running under the head. I let out a soft moan as he presses himself into me impatiently, then reaches for my dress and starts lifting it.

"Fuck. No panties," he growls, and I can sense the shift in him as he turns from man to beast. It fries my brain, making me feel desired. Makes me want to be claimed.

Before I can respond, he kicks my legs apart. And without warning, he adjusts himself to my height and then slams into me. I curse, trying to hold myself upright against the door as he rails me against it like a starved man. But, fuck, how I needed this.

I needed *him*.

Even against my better judgment, I need it like my next breath because it makes me feel alive.

He thrusts once, then twice, before he picks up a

perfect rhythm. I try to be quiet, not wanting everyone to hear us. But then his hand slides between my legs, and he starts rubbing my clit. I grind against him with so much need that I can't stop myself. I groan.

"See, Chaos, you want this."

"I do," I whisper, craving him more and more. I can't manage this insatiable thirst. My eyes roll into the back of my head as his cock hits my sweet spot over and over again. I already feel the climb building, shocked at how quickly this man unravels me.

I love his cock. I love the way he drives into me. I feel so fucking full that I am afraid no man will ever make me feel this good again.

I don't want any other man to make me feel this way.

He keeps thrusting, his hand on my hip as he pounds into me like a wild man, and I bite my hand, attempting to hold back the loud screams trying to rip from my throat.

"When he touches you next time, I want you to remember how it's *me* who makes you come undone. That it's my cock you crave." Then he slaps my ass hard.

It's not fair that Ford punishes me this way. That he leaves his imprint every time and has me craving more.

But, fuck me, I don't know what's right anymore as a haze overtakes my vision and rational thinking.

He slaps me again, no doubt leaving his handprint there. I yelp. The pain explodes and rips my orgasm from me. I see stars, and tears track down my face as I come.

Hard.

And everything else becomes irrelevant.

Once again, it's only me and Ford.

TWENTY-FOUR
FORD

I PULL OUT OF HER, rubbing my cock through the mix of our cum, fixated on the sight and memorizing every inch of her. I grab a paper towel and hand it to her.

I feel the moment her anger returns, it's a palpable tension around her. I can't say I had the intention of fucking her senseless in here, especially with almost everyone we know being here, but it happens so quickly every time. I internally reprimand myself because I don't want Billie to feel like I'm using her to sate my vices, but I can't control myself around her. I tried to seem unfazed by Matthew and her speaking, but the moment she seemed amused by something he said, it stomped on my last fucking nerve. He's lucky he's not leaving in a body bag and the only reason I was able to refrain was because I promised her this would be a secret. If I killed the man talking to her, then it'd be pretty fucking obvious.

She turns around and starts wiping between her legs as I take care of my own cleanup. When she finally raises those stunning eyes to me, I know she's mad.

But selfishly, I love it when she's mad. It makes me want to fuck her all over again.

"So let me get this right. You want what's between my legs but don't want me?" she says.

I want her. Of course, I want her, But not the way she wants me to want her. I can't allow myself that luxury of an alternative world where she could be mine. But, fuck, I wish I could rein in my impulses. The moment she stepped into the club in that red dress, I wanted to tear it off her. I was lucky I was able to restrain myself enough to not actually do it.

I wouldn't even give a shit as to who might notice what's going on between us. But she wants us to remain a secret. I just want her. But I can't tell her that. Can't give her hope. And I'm a selfish bastard for calling her in here. But I was fucking jealous. I either had to mark and fuck her or kill that fucker. Both are unreasonable reactions. Both were equally tempting.

"I want you," I growl, meeting her eyes as she stares me down. My response only makes her angrier. I won't let her move on, but I won't give her what she wants, either.

I'm the actual fucking worst.

The more I push her, the more I hope she'll finally end this thing. It'll be like cutting off a limb, but I'll manage... I think. I've overcome addictions before. I just don't have the self-control to stop supplying myself with this one.

She laughs, the sound menacing and vile. *That's my girl.*

I can sense it coming before she even says it. And although I knew it'd feel like a noose around my neck, it does nothing to lessen the impact of her words.

"It's over between us. This was the last fuck you'll get from me," she says, as I throw the towel in the trash and then zip my pants up. Her dress is already perfectly readjusted, the slit running up the side showing off her sexy fucking legs. Everything about her is perfect.

We're both hypocrites. She tells me she needs more. And in the next breath, she's telling me we're done. And I do everything I can to solidify her resolve for her.

I smile, and I can tell it absolutely fucking infuriates her. "Is it?" I ask cockily.

She slaps me across the face. Hard. My cock

twitches excitedly, but I make sure not to react. She's furious, tears welling in her eyes as that savage rage boils over. "Yes, it is. And forget about texting me. We're done."

She turns then and throws the towel over my head, missing the bin. She curses and pulls open the door, poking her head out first to make sure no one is there before she slips out.

A fucked-up mix of relief and nausea sets low in my stomach. I want to chase after her, but I know better than to do that. I don't deserve Billie. I never did. We only got together because she had a need. And maybe I did pity her a little at the start. I know what it's like to be trapped in a cage, not of your own making. My brother and I never deserved to be on the streets, barely surviving. And I saw the same frustration in her gaze—frustration at her brother's suffocating overprotectiveness.

I pick up her discarded towel and toss it in the trash, and then I wait a while for the red on my cheek to fade. When I exit the bathroom, one of the dancers is standing there, and she smiles at me.

"Heeey, handsome," she says, slurring a little. I've seen her before but never cared to remember her name. "Need a hand in there?" She flicks her gaze to the bathroom. I ignore her and push past her, a cold disdain radiating from me because I don't crave any woman other than the one I just purposely pushed away.

I notice Billie at the bar talking with Ivy and that Matthew prick. She looks like nothing happened, and I try my hardest to distract myself from glancing in her direction or doing something I'll regret, like killing Matthew. I liked him before, and even worked with him twice. But the moment he held out his hand to Billie in introduction was the moment I swore I'd kill him one day.

Eli is sitting on a couch, Jewel perched on his lap, as they talk with Hawke, who has a blonde sitting on his own lap. He frequents this place enough that he has a favorite dancer. I don't have the heart to tell her he has favorites everywhere.

I pull out my phone and lean against the wall. Dutton walks over, muttering something under his breath as Posie joins Billie and the others. He looks like he's about to kill me as he comes to a stop in front of me.

I wonder if this is the time. Has he finally found out about me and Billie?

Did his fiancée tell him what she stumbled across months ago?

Oddly enough, I find myself welcoming the repercussions.

"What?" I ask him.

"No one deserves her. No one," he says and throws a look Billie's way.

He doesn't know about us, then. Because if he did, he would've already tried to kill me. To him, everyone is a piece of shit, and she's his baby sister. At first, I found it weird he was so protective of her. But then I thought about Hawke and how if someone hurt him, I wouldn't hesitate to kill them.

Her being a woman in this world makes it worse. It's rough, especially when everyone knows their family name. They all know who she is. I find her shackles ironically part of her draw for a lot of people, and I can't fucking stand it. I wonder how many of them get to see the true fiery side of her.

"Then shall we tie him up tonight and carve a message into his chest?" I ask, doing my best to sound bored. We all have our "soothing" methods, and Dutton favors the blade. I'm not going to judge him for it, even if one day he uses it against me. Then again, I most likely won't ever lay another hand on his sister.

"No," Dutton growls. "If it were you out there trying to win my sister over, I would kill you. Wouldn't even second-guess it. But Posie keeps on telling me Matthew is fine, and I need to let Billie decide." He looks back in the direction he came from, and I do as well. His words sink in. I'm not scared of Dutton, but he's a man I respect. And he has given me respect in return, so I thought we were good. But it's another reminder that I'll never be viewed as anything more than that street rat. And although I'd come to terms with that a long time ago, it doesn't do anything to steer me away from the one thing I really want.

Billie laughs, and I can't fucking stand it. Can't stand that she's laughing at another man or looking in his direction.

"You good?" Dutton asks, and I snap out of my thoughts, my phone cracking under the force I was holding it with.

"Perfect," I say, trying to keep my voice calm.

"Since you're not drinking, you can drive Billie and Ivy home. I'm not letting that fucker drive her home the first night."

I go to argue, but I know doing so will make Dutton suspicious, considering I've done it so many times before. I want to leave, vanish from this place, because I know I'll only last a few more minutes before I actually break that guy's fucking neck.

"Ford." Eli is calling me over to him.

"He most likely wants to ask about the poisonings. Are you any closer to figuring that out?" Dutton asks as we walk over together.

"Not yet," I tell him. We're all on high alert because it might not just be Eli they target. Anyone associated with him could be in danger, too.

Eli and Jewel are standing close to one another, and I can tell that Eli's gone into his killer mode.

They've found something.

Or, most likely, some*one*.

"Will was able to track down someone suspicious the security guard had been in contact with days before his death."

My phone buzzes. A document has been shared to my device. It's a photo of a guy named Henry Fall. My eyebrows furrow as I read the information on him.

"He used to work for Laurence Tate," Hawke says. Our gazes meet, and we share a silent thought. Tate is the guy we killed to get Anya her ring. *Fuck.* We brought trouble for Eli.

Eli's gaze ping-pongs between us, knowing when Hawke and I are having silent conversations. Then Hawke opens his mouth and shares the missing link. The strangeness of the situation is the bouncer at Eli's club was never in association with any guys from the wharf. So, potentially, there's more than one person involved with this. The only way we'll find out is by torture, of course. Thank fuck because I need something to replace this ravenous desire.

TWENTY-FIVE
BILLIE

I don't look for him again. Fuck Ford and his assholery.

I want to leave, but if I take off too soon, it'll be suspicious. And besides, Matthew is entertaining. At least he has that going for him. Six months ago, I didn't think I was looking for any type of relationship; it's why I was happy to have my secret nights with Ford. But I think I want that now. I want someone to want me and treat me the way I deserve; send me flowers, tell me how beautiful I am. And I know I can't get that from Ford. Not only is he not that type, I don't think he's ever done that in his life. Or ever been in a rela-tionship before. The red flags are blinding, and he's a killer, for fuck's sake. Shouldn't that rattle me, even though I know my family is just as lethal? Don't I want a normal life? When did that change? When did I become so attached to him?

I notice my brother, cousin, and the twins standing in a group. Something serious looks like it's going down, but out of spite, I try not to look in their direction in case Ford thinks I'm looking for him.

"Do you have next weekend free?" Matthew asks. We're on our third drink, and he's told me stories about work and his family, peppering in questions about me as well. At least he isn't showing me stupid fucking thirst traps like the last guy I went on a date with.

"It's the weekend, so I have it off."

"Good. Would you like to go see a movie with me?"

Ivy and Posie suddenly pretend they're interested in something else.

He's so different from the man I had sex with only an hour ago, the one who can't give me anything past that. Matthew actively shows interest in more. A small pang of guilt hits my core. Am I a terrible person for fucking Ford and then organizing a date with someone else?

Then I think of what Ivy would say. She'd most likely encourage me to see both at the same time, not knowing one of the men is Ford. So, I throw caution to the wind.

I smile at him. "Like a date?"

"Sure. We can go to dinner afterward as well."

"Yes, that would be nice. But I don't do horror movies; my life is already a shit show," I tell him.

Ivy laughs and mumbles, "Isn't that the truth."

Dutton joins us, and Posie puts her drink down, concern marring her expression. "Everything okay?"

I ignore whatever Matthew is saying because whatever is happening seems pretty serious.

Posie nods at something Dutton says, and then she smiles at me and Ivy. "Ready?"

I look over to Ivy, who nods, agreeing that she's ready to go home too. We could stay if we wanted, but I'm more than happy to leave. Tonight has been eventful, to say the least.

"If you need a ride, I can take you home," Matthew offers. A guttural noise escapes my brother, and I shoot him a glare.

"It's fine; she's coming with us," Dutton says pointedly. I can tell Matthew is trying not to smirk. He's not a killer, but he might be ballsy enough to survive a few nights with Dutton and his crew. I can only imagine Dutton's reaction if he were here only a few minutes before to hear us organizing a date.

Matthew's agreeable, however, giving a curt and respectful nod to Dutton.

Eli, Jewel, Hawke, and Ford make their way to the

exit, and it infuriates me that Ford doesn't look my way. I know I was the one who ended things, but I want...

I cut that thought off. I can't keep going around in circles with this shit.

I've made up my mind, and I have to stick to it.

It was only ever sex.

Matthew hands me a card and leans over to whisper in my ear, "Text me. We'll sort details out for tomorrow."

He pulls back, and I can feel the fire at my back as my brother is basically being held back by Posie. I'd consider it comical if I didn't wish he would have this glimmer of restraint around a different man.

But I smile at Matthew and tell him I can't wait.

I need to move on from my fixation. Perhaps Ford's use of the term "addiction" is the right word.

Ivy, Dutton, Posie, and I take our leave. When we're outside, I notice the others' cars are already gone.

A sadness tugs at my stomach, and all I want to do is cry. I grit my teeth instead because Ford doesn't deserve my tears. And just like that, we're done, and I'm going on a date with another guy.

Posie moves between Ivy and me, clasping our hands. "He's good, right? I did good?" She's drunk, and my brother glares at me, most likely because Posie is giving us attention and not him.

She's so proud of herself, but it's Ivy who I notice studying me intently.

I fake a smile. "You did, but I'll be sure to take it slow."

"Good," Dutton interrupts. "Would hate to kill him already."

"Oh, stop!" Posie says and throws herself at him. I can't help but admire them and this playful nature she seems to bring out in him. I couldn't be happier for him, and yet it makes me miss something I've never had.

Ivy falls into step beside me and whispers, "Are you sure? If you're not into him, you don't have to go."

"He was nice," I say, defending Matthew.

She eyes me but doesn't say anything else. And I'm grateful for that because the last thing I want is to be pressed about the Matthew situation when my thoughts are on the man who has sworn not to give me any more than he thinks he can. And I was the fool for falling for the dangling carrot yet again.

TWENTY-SIX
FORD

Torture. Not my usual method, but today, I'm willingly participating. I want and need the release. Unfortunately for this poor bastard, he'll be my outlet.

Henry Fall is tied to a chair, his average-sized frame quivering in fear. It didn't take us long to track him down, break into his home, and drag him into the car—willingly, of course. At least that's what we made it look like in case any neighbors were awake.

"Look, man, I don't know anything," he begins. Eli is pacing back and forth, amused by the situation. The fucker always gets off on this type of work. I stand behind Henry, waiting for the order, praying for it like a well-trained dog about to be told to fetch.

"Hmm. I don't believe that," Eli says and gives me a nod.

I internally grin, the release feeding through my soul as I step to the side and tower over Henry. His eyes grow wide, and his bottom lip trembles. He begins to beg, but I ignore it. Any person who tries to hurt our boss will meet a very uncomfortable demise, and I'm more than happy to be the one to end them.

With one clean swipe, I bring down the crowbar and crush his hand. He screams, and I revel in the sound, imagining it's someone else in his place. Fucking Matthew.

I tolerated him and thought he was a decent guy before he set his sights on Billie. I know I set this up myself by forcing Billie to end things between us, but it doesn't make me hate him any less.

Blood splatters, Henry's hand an obliterated mess. Hawke is watching me carefully. He's usually the one with the bloodlust, and when I get in these moods, he's always wary of me. But I don't give a fuck. If he can use violence to satiate his cravings, then so can I.

Henry looks like he's about to pass out, but I step behind him and wrap the crowbar around his throat, jerking it up so he's forced to look at Eli. Again, like a well-trained pet, I wait until I'm allowed to bite. Our relationship with Eli makes me think much of the way River trained his dogs. We're at his beck and call, and for the longest time, I made sure not to allow myself to want anything. And I certainly wouldn't beg.

Billie is unattainable, however. She's not made for someone like me, and yet every one of my hackles rise at the thought of another man touching her. Especially fucking Matthew because I know he's probably better suited for her. But fuck that. It doesn't give him a right to her.

"You seem to be one of the few who weren't there the night Laurence Tate and his team were wiped out. You escaped the wrath of my two men here." Eli gestures to me and Hawke. "How lucky for you. Well, at the time, that is. Were you looking for vengeance?"

Henry's sobbing. I always find it interesting to cut open a man and see what his undoing is. Pain is an easy way to break someone, but sometimes, a little more is required. Some weaknesses aren't physical but emotional. Not in this case, though.

"I was only with him for a few months. I don't give a shit what happened to him. I quit working for him two nights before you got to him. I don't deserve this!" he screams.

Eli rolls his eyes, bored. "Unfortunately, I'm not the only enemy you made. It's a crime by association, you know that. You're going to die slowly and painfully unless you tell me more about the poison that seems to be circulating around my men. That might pique my interest."

Henry spits on the ground near Eli's feet, and my knuckles whiten over the crowbar at the disrespect. I don't make a move until Eli looks at me. I hook my other elbow around the crowbar and choke the man from behind, enjoying the way he struggles. I wait until he looks like he's about to pass out, his body going limp before I release my hold. He weakly gasps and is barely conscious, so I step to his side and smash the crowbar into his right knee.

He screams, startled back to life. Eli watches me carefully, and I retake my spot behind Henry. I don't look at Hawke, but I can tell he's monitoring me. I don't give a shit. I have the right to manage my shit in my own way.

"I don't know what you're talking about, I swear! Please. Please, I'll give you anything you want. I'll work for you. I'll die for you. Please, just let me go," he whimpers.

Eli is looking at his phone, most likely reviewing the profile on Henry. He hums to himself. "I wonder if your sister has anything to do with this. Are you two close?"

"My sister?" Henry blanches. "No, she's a good girl! Don't you dare drag her into this!" he screams, and

I can share his sentiment regarding his sibling. I would do anything for Hawke. I would definitely die for him.

"I'm bored with this. Maybe a few days of 'discussion' might jog your memory," Eli says as he adjusts his suit. "I will have it known I'm not a patient man, and my men aren't always obedient. Sometimes, they get carried away. Sometimes, they go on the hunt for fresh meat. I wonder if they might have to make a visit to your sister."

It's an intimidation tactic. Eli isn't above killing women, but he avoids it as much as possible and draws the line at killing children.

"Please," Henry sobs. "I don't know anything about poison."

"How about the snooping you did in my club and around my cargo ships, then?" Eli questions.

Henry turns paler, and unfortunately for him, even if he isn't associated with the poison, he tried to sway some personal deals himself. He might've thought he was smart by stepping out from Laurence Tate's shadow, but that was not at all the case. The poisonings, however, still run too high a risk, and I'm sure they are somehow connected to this man.

"Hawke, you're to watch over him tonight. I don't want him dead yet. We'll give him some time to reconsider his options."

Henry growls—a last-ditch effort to keep his dignity—and I'm impressed by his balls.

"You piece of shit. You're going to kill me anyway, aren't you? Whoever's poisoning your men, I hope they target your wife next. I hope—"

Eli's on him within seconds, holding him by the throat and raising him with one hand. He has a sadistic smile on his lips, and the monster has come alive. I take a step back, knowing too well what's about to happen. Any mention of, or threat toward, Jewel will trigger Eli. She's his everything, and her life is something he won't mess with, even when trying to gather intel.

"Stupid boy," Eli purrs as he lifts his hand to Henry's face. I sigh and turn my back, disappointed that my fun has been taken away from me. Henry's scream ricochets through the room as Eli gouges out his eye.

I walk over to Hawke as the unhinged level of torture begins, Eli dismantling the man.

"Want to tell me what's happening lately?" Hawke asks. I stand beside him, placing my crowbar on the counter next to its twin.

"What do you mean?"

"You know what I mean," Hawke growls. "You've been more distant lately. Something's up."

"Nothing is up. I just needed a release tonight, that's all."

Hawke folds his arms over his chest, and his almost black eyes, the same as mine, stare at me. We remain like that for a long time, screams echoing around us as Eli begins to laugh like a madman.

"Are you—" Hawke wets his lips. "Are you using again?" he whispers.

"Excuse me?" I growl in warning.

"I don't think you are," he's quick to clarify. "But something is up with you."

"Fuck you," I snarl, turning away. He grabs my arm, preventing my escape. I swing, clocking him in the side of the face. He stumbles only for a second before he jumps on me.

We're rolling on the floor, throwing fist for fist, my heart pounding as the adrenaline fuels me, and I finally get what I want—a release. I kick at his stomach to push him off me.

Hawke might be bigger than me, but it makes him slower. He wipes his mouth, blood trickling over his bottom lip, and a deranged smile takes over his face. I smile back.

He pounces again, tackling me back to the floor. I block his fists, his full weight pinning me down. I hook my leg around his, using momentum from one of his punches to flip him to his back and strike back.

I break through his forearm block, hitting his face again. My head is pounding, a dizzy spell rattling my head.

I go to hit him again, but the click of a gun behind my head stops me. My hands raise in the air as I sense another predator behind me.

"I think not," Eli says. "I'm all for bloodshed, but do it on your own time."

I want to punch Hawke again and again and again. But I know it's not him I'm angry with. It's not him I want hurt. I'm heaving in deep breaths, my sadism in full swing, as I lean back into the barrel of Eli's gun, relishing the thrill.

I'm exhausted. Defeated in some ways. I stare at the ceiling and smile, looking like a madman, as the realization hits me that I'm already too late. Because Billie is in my blood, and after only hours of denying myself of her, I'm nothing but a rabid dog.

"Get up, dickhead," Hawke says, calling me back into the room. I look at him, unfazed by the gun pointed at my head.

"I think perhaps you should have the rest of the night off," Eli tells me, but it's actually a command.

I spit blood on the floor, my face swelling from a

good punch Hawke got in. I stand slowly, holding out my hand. Hawke grabs it, and I pull him up as Eli lowers his gun.

Without another word, I grab my crowbars and walk out the door. I glance in the direction of the bloody mess on the floor that was once Henry Fall.

And part of me wonders if it would be bliss, being free of this world. No longer a victim to the demons that constantly gnaw at me.

The need.

The impulses.

Billie Taylor has turned into my addiction.

And I have no fucking clue how to get her out of my system.

I SEE the tattoo shop a block away. It's been refreshing to walk lately, and I've been doing *a lot* of walking. Work has been hectic this week, and every day I've been walking from the office to my apartment, which is just under an hour, to clear my thoughts. Except it feels like I'm spiraling further.

Matthew and I have exchanged a few text messages throughout the week, and our date is this evening. Yet, I can't muster the excitement I should be feeling. I finally got approval to date someone, and I'm not feeling it. If anything, I'm more furious at the fact that I even have to feel like I'm getting permission in the first place, and that has nothing to do with Matthew at all.

My thoughts and urges keep coming back to one

person, and I fucking hate how many times I've grabbed my phone to text him.

Ford.

The man I can have only in body.

I even thought of using the excuse to see Felix to drop by his house, but I've exerted all of my self-control not to.

It's not even that I was lying to my family and keeping what was happening between us a secret. My feelings were getting too heavily involved, and cutting it off felt like the closest thing to a breakup I've ever experienced. I've never felt this way for any man before. And while I've told myself over the past year there is nothing to it, I know I'm lying to myself.

It's why I booked myself an appointment to finish the tattoo he started. I learned my lesson from last time and didn't tell him about this one, so I'm relieved that it's still in one piece. It's absolutely wild to think he burned down the last shop just because I threatened to have someone else finish the tattoo. But it's not at all surprising. I've seen Dutton, and Eli do some pretty crazy shit and hardly get reprimanded for it.

The woman behind the reception desk smiles as I approach her. I reciprocate it but get an uneasy feeling. Her smile seems forced.

"Welcome, Miss Taylor. I'll just let him know you're here. Please, take a seat."

I'm a little confused. I didn't even tell her my name or who I'm here to see. I glance around, impressed by all the sketches and drawings hanging on the walls. It reminds me a little of the room Ford has in his home. Except he doesn't have so many drawings hung up. And a sinking feeling hits me as I note these aren't as good as his.

I scoff at that. That's a lie; these artists are probably better. At least they'd finish the actual job, unlike a certain asshole. It's unfair of me to think that, considering I'd been the one to get restless while he was working on me, and every time I was over after that, we were too distracted by ripping one another's clothes off.

I internally growl. *Stop thinking about him.*

It's like the longer I go without seeing him, the more stir-crazy I become, and that's so fucking crazy.

He said he can't give you anything more than sex. You ended it, so stop spiraling. I reprimand myself.

"Billie?" I look up when the lady calls my name. She waves me through to one of the rooms and holds the door open for me.

"Thank yo—" My manners die on my lips, and my feet stop at the threshold of the room. Sitting on the stool beside the tattoo bed, wearing an arrogant expression, is Ford.

"Close the door," he commands, and the lady who walked me in does just that, almost hitting me as she does. I feel like a trapped animal as my heartbeat picks up.

"Why the fuck are *you* here?" I demand, popping a hand on my hip. All the self-pity bullshit flies out the window, and I'm once again flooded by so much hurt and rage that I want to slap him across the face again.

It's like a fucking detox with this man. I'm trying to get him out of my system, and although I don't think I was making progress, this makes it harder.

"It would appear the artist you booked with suddenly fell ill, so I took over," he says smugly.

Is this guy out of his fucking mind?

"Please tell me you didn't kill the artist," I growl. This man is madness in a bottle. One that, up until now, I've been happily sipping from. But where does it stop? When does it hurt too much that I run away, even though I already have?

"No, I have no reason to kill my employees. Unless, of course, they lay a hand on you." He shoots me a devilish grin, and I want to smack it off his face.

"Since when the fuck do you own this place?"

He looks at his watch and then back to me. "Since

four hours ago. And you can run, but just so you know, I've bought every tattoo parlor in the area, and they all have your name and face, so the moment you book an appointment, I'll be notified."

"You're out of your fucking mind!"

His expression changes. I know that look well. It's the one he gets when he's about to strip away all of my clothes and inhibitions. My body freezes. I hate the way it responds to him, even when I'm at odds with myself and trying to fight it. Even when I'm trying to rationally tell myself he's crazy.

"I told you I won't let any other person mark your skin."

"You mean finish off your tattoo?"

"No. I mean, touch you."

The silence stretches between us. "We agreed to end us. You don't get to go all macho over the decisions I make with my body," I say, infuriated.

He stares at me, and the silence and tension build. I know I should walk out. I know that. I know it's the same dance without rhythm or rhyme that we've been repeating these last few months.

He's always there. Even when he's not there, I'm thinking of him. And when I'm trying to walk away, he still appears.

"You can't keep doing things like this. What if I tell Dutton?"

"Tell him," he says, his tone serious. Hearing him say that has a wave of emotions breaking over me because we know the consequences will be greater for him than for me. It was my idea to keep us a secret in the first place, and yet I'm pissed with him for following the rules I set. "Until then, jeans off and on the bed like a good girl." He taps the bed, then sits back and watches me. "Or we can play this same game every time you try to get that tattoo finished. But let me tell you now, Chaos, I'm the only one who will be finishing that piece. So either you get your ass up here, or we continue this game of yours."

"I'm not playing any games. You're the one who showed up here uninvited!"

He arches an eyebrow. Okay, so maybe I've been biting back a little, but this is different. Isn't it?

Ford is a man of his word. Which means he will absolutely show up to every tattoo parlor I ever try to go to.

"You can't possibly afford to buy every tattoo parlor in the world," I grumble in complaint as I drag my feet toward the bed.

The defiant part of me wants to turn around and walk out the door, but I really want this tattoo finished.

And he's the one who started it, so he should be the one to finish it. I just didn't think he would go to these lengths to do so.

"I'm a man with few needs, little chaos. I have more money than I know what to do with. And if I have to use it all buying every tattoo parlor to ensure no one else touches your skin, I'll do exactly that."

He begins fiddling with the gun and inks, and I hate the way he so easily commands a room. The way my heart flutters at his declarations that can so easily be taken differently by another woman. I consider myself not to be one of those foolish, lovesick girls... but maybe I am. And I hate that he has that over me. It turns out that even though my brother has been protecting me all this time, I never once had my guard up around Ford. And now I'm dealing with the consequences.

I begin undoing my jeans. "You understand what you did was crazy, right?"

"How so?" he asks, his gaze pinned to where I fiddle with my zipper.

"No. We're not having sex. I won't be your hit or fix, or whatever the fuck you think I am to you," I firmly state.

His gaze darkens, but then he looks away as if ashamed. My stomach drops at the harshness of my words for poking at his demons and using them as a weapon. But if it's the only thing to protect my heart from this monster who so easily stole it, then I'll do it.

The palpable tension sits with us in this room like an insufferable weight, and I can't stand it. Hate how much we're both hurting when we never set out with that intention, so I extend a slight peace offering by changing the subject. "How did you manage to purchase this place so quickly? Aren't there contracts and waiting periods?"

"When you have money, you don't really have to wait for anything, do you, little chaos?" I can't argue with his logic because I know he's right. I've seen my family members buy many things, not in the legal way. So I shouldn't really expect anything less from him, considering who his family is. But Ford's right about something else, too. Besides his modest home, I don't often see him spending his money. He wears plain, affordable clothes and lives a humble enough life. He's not lavish like Hawke, who spends most of his money on women and partying.

"Now, drop the pants." He nods to my jeans, this time without the smoldering gaze he had on them before. I remove my jeans and toss them on a chair in the corner. I actually wore panties today in an attempt at modesty. I was just planning to slip them to the side so the artist could finish my tattoo. He eyes the silky garment but says nothing.

I climb up onto the bed and get situated on my stomach. After a moment, I feel his hand on my ass, and then he adjusts my panties so he can see the cheek with the half-done tattoo.

"Are you starting?" I ask nervously. When I look over my shoulder, he's smirking. "Shut up. Tell me when you're starting," I grumble and lay my head back down. I was the same the first time, and although I know what I'm in for now, it doesn't lessen the apprehension. I can understand why some people get addicted to it. The rush and anticipation. The thrill in the subtle pain.

I'm relieved when his callused hand leaves my ass; it's as if my tension has been sucked away with the removal of his touch. Noises begin as he prepares the ink gun. I brought headphones today, hoping they'd help me to forget about the pain. The first half of the tattoo wasn't the most painful thing I've ever felt, but I can't say that I loved it either. I'm sure this will be my one and only tattoo, and I'm not even sure why I asked him to do it in the first place. He'd just shown me his tattoo room for the first time, and it felt like I was seeing a part of him not many got to see. The fact that he was marking me felt special, and I left the design up to him.

"Stay still," he warns.

"Wait. Count to three."

He chuckles as he cleans my skin, and then the gun starts buzzing. He counts down from three. It's the same as last time. I fall into a semi-relaxed state, trusting him entirely.

I give in to the experience but angle my head so I can't see what he's doing.

I usually like watching him work, and he's gifted. There's no denying that. I've seen him add to Hawke's tattoos, but I don't want to watch as it happens to me.

I've also heard he's very gifted with a set of crow-bars, but that's not something I ever want to see. He has a set of crowbars tattooed on his chest, so they must mean something to him at, least. I've overheard Hawke sharing stories about how Ford crushes peoples' heads in with them, and I always cringed at the thought. I understand that Ford is dangerous, but to me, he never has been. The buzzing stops, and he turns the machine off. Then I feel coldness on my ass.

"Is it done?" I ask, not yet ready to look, even though I can't properly see it from this angle.

"It is. You can look now."

I move my gaze from him to my ass and see a

perfect heart. Half of it is red, and the other half is black—two halves meeting together to make a perfect whole. I love the unique beauty of it. The curve on the red side has a Q representing a queen card, and in the curve of the new half, he added a K, which I assume is for a king card. I don't know if it means anything beyond that. I've been driving myself crazy by over-thinking everything lately, and this can't be another thing that monopolizes my mind. So, I accept it for the beautiful piece of art it is. And in a way, it kind of helps me accept the beauty of what Ford and I are. Or were.

I'm smiling as I face him, genuinely grateful for how beautiful it is. But the moment our eyes meet, my heart stutters at the intensity of his gaze.

TWENTY-EIGHT
FORD

It takes her a moment to get off the bed, and when she does, she steps over to the mirror and turns around so she can properly see the tattoo. I considered tattooing my initials on her ass, but I figured she might kill me for it. Though if I died, I guess I'll always be remembered by anyone who looked at her ass.

"I need to cover it," I tell her.

Her golden eyes meet mine, and her silence fills the room.

When my family finds out that I purchased not one tattoo parlor but several of them, I'm sure they won't be surprised. They all know how much I love to tattoo. I've done most of my father's and brother's ink since the moment River bought me my first tattoo gun. It was a weird present to give a teenager. I remember when he placed it in front of me for the first time, then rolled up his sleeve and told me to practice on him. Hawke and I had been with him and Anya for just shy of two years at that point, and it was then I realized how much I trusted them and how I'd be willing to die for them. No one has ever made a point to care about what my brother or I cared about. And despite how ruthless both River and Anya are, they treat those they care for well.

"I love it," she finally says, then turns to grab her jeans from the chair. Bending over to put them on, she gives me a clear view of her ass, and I fight the urge to bite it. It's fucking torture as my fingers dig into my palms to physically restrain myself.

Fuck, this woman does all kinds of crazy shit to me.

She stands back up, and my hand is already stretching out for her. It pauses midair when she asks, "Do you think it's fine to sit on it for a few hours? I'm going to the movies."

A dangerous sound escapes my throat, but it's not loud enough for her to hear. "With who?"

"Matthew," she answers without hesitation, then steps into my space as I grab the wrap. My teeth grind as she averts her gaze. I know she's doing it to intentionally piss me off. And, dammit, it's working. Her wrist dangles close to my face, and I notice she's wearing a bracelet she's fond of.

I slowly cover the tattoo, my focus locked on the task at hand because I'm certain if she looked into my eyes right now, they would be anything but friendly.

"You should cancel," I suggest.

"No, I shouldn't," she says defiantly. "I just want to know it's fine to sit on. I didn't ask for your opinion on whether or not I should keep my date."

"He's a dickhead," I growl as I finish securing the wrap.

"He's someone who can provide me with the things I want from a man."

I laugh, and it's nothing short of sinister. "And what is it that you think you want, Chaos? Do you think he'll take kindly to when you take a blowtorch to his front lawn?"

"I don't think he'd be the type to piss me off so much."

"Or give you any type of stimulation," I mutter.

Her eyes narrow. "No, I think he'll find other ways to spoil me. With nice gifts, dates, and text messages. He'll shower me with attention like a normal fucking man who can express himself."

"I bet he has a tiny dick," I grumble.

"At least he's not wasting my time and doesn't treat me like a damn hit," she snaps.

That one hits home, and I immediately retreat into myself because she's right. I don't even know why I came here in the first place. Granted, no one else but me was going to finish that tattoo, but we're running around in circles. I'm repeating the same fucking pattern just because I want to *see* her.

"Doesn't matter anyway," she says as she slides her jeans the rest of the way on. She looks over her shoulder at me. "How much do I owe you?"

"I'll have a taste as payment." I nod to her pussy.

She scoffs, affronted, and I can't help but smile at the fire that rages in her gaze. That pencil dick will never see this side of Billie, and part of me feels triumphant about that, even if I can only keep it as a memory.

"Money, Ford. How much?"

"I don't want money. The choice is yours if you want to make the payment I requested."

"You are such a dickhead, you know that?" She rummages in her purse and then pulls out a lollipop. She places it on the bed without so much as looking back at me. "Thanks for the ink. Taste this instead."

I silently watch as she slips on her shoes, opens the door, and then strides out with an air of superiority. I grab the lollipop and pop it in my mouth, unable to stop myself. I always thought that her honey cakes were my favorite dessert. But I've come to realize that my favorite dessert just walked out the door to go get ready for a date with a man who isn't me.

I want her and only her. I want our arrangement to be like it was. But I'm beginning to question if that's all I want from her. I know I want more and can't so easily walk away. And that makes me an asshole.

Life has kicked me in the ass more times than I can count. There's no way in hell it's going to be nice to me now. Then again, why has it ever had reason to?

I want the best for Billie, but I know it's not me. I refuse to weigh her down.

I uncurl my hand and dangle her bracelet from my fingers, staring at it, mesmerized. I couldn't help myself. If I can't have her, I need something of hers instead.

TWENTY-NINE
BILLIE

I'M lucky the walk home is long enough for me to get my emotions under control. I was so close to breaking Ford's nose. The balls of that asshole. The mixed signals. The hot and cold. The everything. He's fucking infuriating.

Half way home, I realize I dropped the bracelet my mother bought me for my graduation, which pisses me off even more. Today's already shit.

I get to my apartment, flop onto the couch on my stomach, then try to numb my brain by watching TV. All I can think about is Ford, though. Every time he pops into my head, I swear and think up creative ways to get back at him.

I regularly check the time, reminding myself to

prepare for my date tonight. I contemplated canceling, but then that would mean that Ford wins, and I'm not going to let another man dictate who I date. Especially Ford. He doesn't get to have that kind of power over me anymore. I already have enough men in my life who think they can tell me what to do. I don't bother changing my clothes, but I do swap out my sneakers for a pair of heels, then fix my hair before I walk out the door.

Matthew messaged me what restaurant to meet him at, and luckily, it's not too far from where I live. When I arrive, I find him standing outside, speaking on his phone. He's dressed similarly to how he was last weekend when I met him. Except today his suit is a nice blue that matches his eyes. When he notices me, he hangs up.

"Perfect timing." He offers me his elbow and then guides us into the restaurant. He tells the hostess his name, and we're led to a private area at the back. He pulls out my chair like a gentleman, and I thank him as I sit.

When he takes a seat, he orders a bottle of their finest wine. Despite not being a big wine drinker, I don't bother to mention it as the waitress walks away.

"Did you get up too much today?" he asks,

adjusting his tie. He's attractive, but it feels like there's something missing, and I can't quite put my finger on it. Maybe it's the man with the haunting, almost black eyes that I would prefer to be sitting across from me.

Fuck. Stop it. I chastise myself.

"I did, actually. I got a tattoo," I say proudly. He scrunches up his nose before smoothing his expression. "You don't like tattoos?"

He nervously chuckles as if he hadn't meant to show his distaste. "Not particularly. I was raised with the belief that you don't damage perfect skin."

The waitress comes back with the wine, and I smile as she pours it for us. Then I take a sip of the bitter liquid.

"I was raised that it's your body, your choice," I reply.

"Yes, of course." He doesn't ask me what I got or where I got it. He actually changes the subject and then starts talking about the movie that we'll be seeing after dinner. The meal is nice, and thankfully, the company isn't too bad either. As the night goes on and the wine goes to my head, I stop thinking about Ford.

That is until Matthew finally asks me what tattoo I got. It pulls me straight back to the tattoo parlor. Straight back to Ford's hands all over me. In true Ford fashion, he's interrupting my one experience of what seems like an ordinary date. And he's not even here.

"Sorry, what?" I ask as he offers me his hand when we stand to leave.

"You said earlier you got a tattoo, but you didn't say what it was."

"Oh, yeah. Sorry. It's just a small heart."

"Nice. And where on your body did you get it?" He looks me over. "I don't see it."

I wait until he pays for the meal, and we're outside to tell him. "That's because you would have to remove my clothes to see it." He stops in his tracks.

"Remove your clothes?" he questions. I nod, smiling at the way he says it like it's an option. "Well, that just made the night more interesting. Now I'm going to be wondering where I can find a small heart." He winks.

The night air is cool, and we walk to the cinema, which is only a few blocks away. He pays for our tickets, and we get popcorn and chocolate to share before we head into the theater. It's the most ordinary date, and it's kind of nice.

The movie is a romantic comedy, and at one stage, he reaches over and clasps my hand in his.

It's sweet. Not what I'm used to, that's for sure.

When the movie is over, he doesn't let go of my hand as we leave. I'm wondering if he's going to kiss me when we get outside. *Do I want him to?* The few times Ford ever kissed me, I had to ask him to do it, and I hate that I'm once again comparing Matthew with him.

"Did you drive? I can walk you back to your car," Matthew offers.

"No, I walked," I tell him. "But I'm not far." I point down the road, wanting to walk. It's become a ritual lately.

"I'll walk you, then." I go to decline, so used to doing things independently, but I accept the offer, curious as to whether he'll try to come upstairs. I don't think he's that type of guy, but who knows. And I don't know if I'd let him up if he does ask.

He doesn't let go of my hand as we walk to my apartment. We talk about his work, which I find fascinating in a dramatic way. I can definitely see how my cousin and brother use him for business.

When we're only a few doors from my apartment building, he casually asks, "So, can I see you again?"

"You want a second date?" I ask, somewhat charmed. I'm obviously a good date, then.

"Yes, I do." I smile at his words. When we reach my apartment, I try to pull my hand free, but he leans in so close our bodies are almost touching. He smells different. Feels different. Everything about him is different. And I'm not entirely sure if I want it, but I definitely want to try.

His hand releases mine to raise and touch my face, ever so gently holding me still. "A second date?" he asks again.

"I think I can arrange that," I reply. But there's no butterflies. I push past it because I should be focusing on someone like Matthew. He's nice, driven, normal. He smiles as I stare up at him, then he leans down. His lips lower to mine. It's soft and tender. I open my mouth just as he pulls back.

"I'll call you tomorrow," he says, stepping back with a smile.

"Okay." And I watch as he walks away. My smile falters as I realize my heart didn't flutter when he kissed me. It's gnawing at me, knowing I should like a guy like him, wanting to, but it feels no different than if I were hanging with a friend. But it's more than that with Matthew, right? We get along so well.

"Remind me why I shouldn't kill him." A low growl comes from over my shoulder, and I gasp, turning and swinging my fist. I hit Ford straight in the nose, but he barely flinches.

"Oh fuck me! Don't sneak up on me like that. Where the fuck did you come from?" I blurt, steadying my breathing as the adrenaline starts to recede. I go to ask him if he's okay, but then it hits me. *How long has he been here?* "You've got to be kidding me. Ford, what the actual fuck? You can't keep showing up like this. We're done, remember?" I throw my hands in the air.

His jaw tics as he glares over my shoulder in the direction that Matthew went. "I think he's the least of your concerns, wouldn't you say? What if someone else saw you?" I ask.

"I never cared about who found out about us. *You* did."

I blanch. "You can't be serious right now. You were the one who made it clear you didn't want anything but sex."

"You were the one who made it clear you wanted it to be a secret," he responds sharply.

I'm gobsmacked. I can't keep dealing with this head fuckery. He says he doesn't want anything more with me but then won't leave me alone. And I can't deny the fact that I might've given mixed signals of my own in the past, but what good is any kind of relationship if we can't even have an honest conversation? It feels like trying to pull blood out of a stone.

Fuck this. Matthew is at least kind of normal.

Ford's like a fucking phantom popping out of

nowhere. *A phantom I'm deeply attracted to.* I internally growl. *Ah, shut the fuck up.*

"It's a little too late now, wouldn't you say?" I go to walk into the building, and he reaches into his pocket and pulls out a bracelet.

My jaw drops. "My bracelet. Where was it?" I ask, reaching for it. He pulls it away from my grasp. Fury pumps in my veins. Is this all just a game to him? "Did you take it?" I accuse because I know I was wearing it at the tattoo shop.

"Did you want to fuck him?" he asks as he dangles the bracelet in front of me. I try to grab it, but he's taller than me and easily holds it out of my reach. "Did you want to fuck him?" he repeats.

"No," I growl, infuriated. He considers me for a moment longer before lowering the bracelet. I snatch it out of his hand. "You can leave now."

"I can't stop thinking about you."

I'm shocked by the admission, and my mouth opens and closes a few times before I finally find words. "What kind of game are you playing?"

"I'm not playing any game. I'm just telling you the truth."

"But you won't date me? Just sex, right?"

"Is that what you want? Dating?" He squirms at the thought, and it's clear as day that Ford has never dated anyone in his life. And while I might not be the most experienced when it comes to dating, at least I know it's not a death sentence, the way he's treating it as.

"I want a man who will claim me without hesitation, Ford."

"I claim you all the time."

"Not like that, and you know it," I bite back.

"Yet you're the one who wants us to remain as a secret. So you want me to what? Shower you with gifts and dates but remain in the shadows? Sounds like *you're* using *me*, Billie, not the other way around."

My hands shake because of how furious I am.

"Seems like you're fine with dishing it but don't like when you're called out on your own shit," he says, his gaze hard.

"Have you met you? You know exactly what it would do to our families if they found out. It might damage everything you've built with Eli. My brother will kill you. I'm *protecting* you."

He scoffs. "I never asked for your protection, Chaos. The only thing I needed protection from, it would appear, is you. I can't get you out of my fucking system."

Now it's my time to scoff. "Why, because I'm just

some kind of addiction? Some kind of entertainment for you to be amused by until you find something else?"

He growls, and a cold warning tingles down my spine. "I told you that to explain why I'm not good for you. You don't know what you're signing up for with me."

"Well, maybe I should've asked the right questions before we started anything. This is hopeless, and you need to find something else to entertain you."

He looks like he's about to say something, but then Ivy's voice interrupts us. I was so wrapped up in my argument with Ford that I hadn't even noticed her pull over to the curb and approach us.

"Damn. Shit looks tense here. Did someone die?" she asks as she looks around. "Is Hawke not with you? It's weird when you two aren't up each other's asses," she says to Ford.

I take a step back, trying to put all my effort into reining in my anger so Ivy doesn't think too hard about why we might be out here arguing. But then the silence stretches. I don't know why I expect Ford to say something because he doesn't. Instead, he shoves his hands in his pockets and stalks away. Of course he just takes off.

We're just going around in circles at this point. Aren't we? Did he think any of that would convince me to sleep with him again? Then again, maybe he has a point about me hating that he calls me on my shit. I wanted us to be a secret because it wasn't anything more than just sex. But as I watch him walk away, I wonder what something more with Ford might look like. But just as quickly, I think about the fallout with our families.

"What was that about?" Ivy asks, staring after him.

"Nothing." I shake my head and turn for the door. "My brother just asked him to check up on me after the date with Matthew."

Ivy whistles. "I'm surprised Dutton wasn't waiting out here with a bat to check on you himself."

When I don't laugh, she grabs me by the arm. "Hey, is everything okay with you lately? I don't know if I'm reading into it too much, but there seems to be some weird tension between you and Ford. Has something happened?"

I stare at my best friend. I know I can tell her anything. She'll take it to the grave if I ask her to. I also know if I choose to remain silent, she won't dig into my personal affairs even when she's equipped to. Ivy's always respected our privacy, and I'm just too tired to tell her. Too exhausted to catch her up on the last year and a half that's turned into a fumbled mess. It just has to stop.

"No. I'm just mad at my brother. That's all," I say, placing my hand over hers. "But I'm sure I'll feel better soon. When Hope's back, let's have a spa day."

Ivy doesn't seem to believe me but smiles anyway, nodding in agreement. She asks me about my date with Matthew, and I describe the very ordinary date I went on. A date that I'd been begging for as long as I can remember. And yet, in all of those hours with Matthew, my heart didn't flutter, and my stomach didn't drop, not until the one man I've sworn myself from showed up on my doorstep.

It doesn't make any sense. I accused him of using me, but I know I've done the same to him. He has a right to be mad, but it doesn't change the circumstances. Ford and I were never meant to be more, even if I want it.

Even if we hurt one another with our rejection of the other.

We're just not meant to be together in that way.

It's not until after I have a shower to calm down that I crawl into bed and cocoon myself in my blankets. I just want to hide from these spiraling, confusing thoughts. It feels like I don't know left from right, right now, and it's so fucking distracting. No matter how much I swore myself off him, I only keep thinking about *him*.

I stare at the bracelet on my side table and wonder if he took it so he had a reason to speak to me again. But that feels foolish. Ford isn't the type to do something so juvenile. Then again, he bought me numerous jackets without so much as a card to let me know it was him.

My eyebrows furrow when I notice the bracelet looks different. Picking it up and inspecting it, I discover it's not just a plain, dainty chain anymore. Attached are two charms: the tiniest little black heart and a small cat.

My heart sinks, and I want to cry.

Why is he doing this? Does his cruelty have no bounds?

I can't keep going back and forth like this, and yet I know I'm part of the problem.

I might've forced his hand into wanting nothing to do with me, but deep down, I wanted him to fight for us. *And then what?*

Aren't I the one being unfair since I'm not willing to take the risk and tell everyone about us?

Hadn't he been the honest one all along while I pushed and demanded more than he was able to give me and more than I was willing to actually accept?

I close my eyes and release the bracelet back onto the side table, refusing to cry. I feel like all the fight has been sucked out of me. I don't even know what I want anymore. It's unreasonable to blame Ford when I had as much a part to play, but it's so much easier pointing the finger at him than myself.

I'm coming to learn that falling for someone isn't always a great thing. Sometimes it fucking hurts. And I'm not sure if I've hit rock bottom yet. And I don't know how to climb out of this abyss.

THIRTY
BILLIE

"So, how did the date with Matthew go?" Posie asks. I just finished work and thought I'd drop by their house for a few hours. It's only four weeks until the wedding, and Posie seems as cool as they come; however, my brother appears high-strung, even when she tells him everything is going to be perfect.

"It went well. He said he'll be in town next weekend and wants another date, but I can't because we have Aunty Rya's birthday."

"Invite him," she's quick to say as we lounge in the living room. Bentley is playing in his bedroom with a new Lego set Dutton bought him. That kid is so spoiled now—in the best kind of way. He's such a sweet kid and is still grateful for everything he's given.

"Umm, no. I think I'll be fine." I wave her off.

"Do it. It'd be fun."

I'm not sure how to tell her I'm not really comfortable bringing men around the family. Yes, Matthew met some of them at the last party, but he wasn't there as my date. Bringing him to a family event would be a little bit weird and would involve a lot of explaining that I don't really want to deal with.

My job has been a little stressful, and while I enjoy learning, I'm also exhausted almost every single day when I finish. I'd intended to leave work at five o'clock every evening, but I haven't been getting out until closer to seven. So I'm basically working twelve-hour days, and the last thing I want to do is deal with questions from the family about the first man I've ever brought to meet them.

"It doesn't mean you're walking down the aisle with the guy. Are you sure you're not using Rya's birthday as an excuse not to see him?"

I look at her then, really hating her insight. I mean, Matthews is nice, but I'm still not sure about trying to start a relationship with him. And then there's Ford. If anything, I think I should step away from guys for a bit. I feel like it's a good example of the idiom "Be careful what you wish for." All I wanted was a normal dating life, and now I'm torn between two men: one who offers that normalcy and one who lives in the shadows and kills people for a living. And, of course, the latter is the one my heart yearns and sings for. It's ridiculous since I don't even know Matthew that well. And I have to decide whether I'm truly able to let Ford go, even though I know moving on from him is the right thing for me.

"Does this have something to do with Ford?" she whispers.

My head snaps in her direction.

"No." My voice rises a fraction, and her expression softens.

"Have you two continued seeing each other?"

Posie and I never spoke about what she saw that night at my parents' house. I still can't help being on high alert in my brother's home, even when he's not here.

"No, we stopped," I confess.

She nods, and I can tell she's torn as to whether she should ask more about it but yet she doesn't want to know the incriminating details. Besides, there's nothing more to tell.

"I'll think about asking Matthew to come to the party with me," I tell her with a smile as I stand to leave. "Maybe I need to throw him to the wolves and hope for the best."

The front door opens, and Dutton enters with Eli,

Ford, and Hawke closely behind him. I freeze as if I've been caught doing something wrong.

Dutton walks over to us, giving me a hug and kiss on the cheek before moving on to Posie, kissing her on the lips. "You heading off?" he asks me, and I try my hardest not to make eye contact with the others. I haven't seen or heard from Ford since the night I went out with Matthew, and I just can't face him.

"Yep. Starting a new project tomorrow at work, so don't want to be out too late."

"Billie is thinking about bringing a date to your mother's birthday," Posie says to Eli.

"Date?" Dutton snaps to attention. "Over my dead body. Who is this fucker, so we can dismantle him?"

"Calm down. Seriously," Posie warns him. "You already know him. It's Matthew. Their date went well the other night."

Dutton's jaw clenches as he asks, "Did he touch you?"

"Oh my God." I roll my eyes. "You'll be crazed to know there was hand holding."

"Don't tease the man too much. He looks like he's going to blow an artery," Eli says, far too amused by the situation.

I sigh. "I haven't asked him yet, but I might."

"And we're okay with that, aren't we, Dutton?" Posie asks, staring pointedly at her fiancé.

His jaw tics, and he looks like he's choking on his own words as he grits out, "Yes."

I hold in my laughter because I know he's trying his hardest. My brother is anything but normal, but it's nice to see the subtle changes in him due to Posie's influence.

"Do you need a lift home?" Eli asks.

"Nah, I was just going to catch the subway," I tell him.

"Over my dead body," Dutton growls. "You don't take your safety seriously enough."

"I'll take you," Ford cuts in. It's the first time I glance in the direction of the twins. Hawke raises an eyebrow, then just walks to the kitchen, most likely to steal food.

"It's fine," I tell him.

"You're going with him," Dutton demands.

"Anyone thought to ask me since I'm his boss?" Eli interrupts, but he nods his permission to Ford anyway.

Posie is biting her bottom lip, most likely because she thinks there's more going on with Ford and me than what I expressed. I try to harden my resolve, reminding myself that Ford and I were just too warm bodies looking to fill each other's beds. The conversation with him the other night doesn't change anything. The bracelet doesn't change anything. I can't let whatever this thing between us was devour my every thought and interfere with my life. It's pathetic.

"Let's go," Ford commands, then walks straight back out the door.

I throw my hands in the air as I turn on Dutton. "You'll let me go on a date but not catch the subway?"

"One step at a time," he growls in warning.

I shake my head. These guys are so unreasonable. I'd make for the subway if I didn't know one of these oafs would literally come after me and throw me over their shoulder.

"Whatever," I grumble as I grab my handbag.

Ford's already waiting outside, holding the passenger door open. I'm sure if my brother had so much as the tiniest suspicion that there was something going on between me and Ford, he wouldn't so easily trust him. Wouldn't so quickly demand for him to take me home. And part of me really wishes Dutton hadn't done it.

I silently slide onto the passenger seat and set my bag on my lap like it's a weighted restraint that will keep me from doing something I'll regret, like crawling into Ford's lap.

It's fucking torture being in his car. It smells like

him. Feels like him. And I've fucked him so often in this car that my inner thighs begin to tingle with anticipation like I've been conditioned to the response.

My nostrils flare as I watch him stalk around the car and get in beside me.

"Put on your seat belt," he instructs, not looking in my direction. I sigh, ever irritated by the bossy men in my life, but do as he says.

Silence fills the car for the first five minutes of the drive. I stare out the window, hating how his presence alone can so easily grate on me. Like a gentle caress without so much as any other physical or verbal interaction. This thing between us creates a palpable tension, and the longer we ignore it and try to step away from it, the stickier it feels, wanting to drag us back together. At least it has that effect on me.

I finally turn to face him at the same time, he looks at me and says, "You're dating him?" His knuckles whiten from his tight grip on the steering wheel.

"You already knew that," I say cooly. I won't change my mind. No going back. Only forward. If dating Matthew is the thing that helps me step away from Ford altogether, and has the potential to be something more, then why shouldn't I throw myself into it?

"More than one date?" he asks, looking for confirmation.

"There will be. Are you seeing anyone?" I question casually as if we're just two friends talking, but the intensity between us is anything but casual.

"Like real dating or hallucinations?"

I can't help the smirk that touches my lips at his words, the tension obliterating in a heartbeat. I hate that he can fucking do that.

He smirks, too, and it saddens me how natural it feels to be with him like this. How good it used to feel between us before our hearts and demands started getting in the way.

"You know I'm not dating anyone," he answers.

"Why? You could have anyone you want," I say, looking out the window. As fucked up as Ford is, a lot of women won't care to look past his physique and personality. And although a pretty face doesn't hide the crazy underneath, deep down, Ford is a good man, even for a killer. One day, someone other than me will see that if he'd let himself be seen in that way. The thought shrivels my heart.

"I don't want just anyone. I only want *you.*"

I close my eyes, trying to push away the impact of those words. Trying to solidify the narrative in my head that we're done. Because I've recently discovered that my greatest weakness is denying my urges and needs for Ford.

And I'm certain if I can get through this hurt for a man I can't have because he's incapable of giving his all to me, then I can get through anything.

So I rub my lips together and refuse to speak for the rest of the drive.

There is no us.

Addiction be damned.

We both need to come up for air.

I just hope that's sometime soon.

THIRTY-ONE
BILLIE

I INVITED Matthew to the party, and he accepted. Not that I thought he would decline, but I expected some kind of hesitation at the very least. He offered to pick me up and drive us there, and I agreed. I would usually call for a driver or just catch a cab, but since this is my first time bringing a date to a family event, I figured we better arrive together.

I run my hands down my red leather dress. It's mid-length, so it stops just above my knees and has a small slit up the side. It fits me beautifully. I actually haven't worn it yet, so I was excited to have an event to wear it to.

I pull my hair back in a nice tight bun and then put on some big earrings while I wait for Matthew to arrive. I know Ford will be at the party and that I'll have to deal with him either ignoring me or eyeing me all night. Which one it will be, I'm not sure, but I've promised myself I'll try my best to only have eyes for Matthew.

Just as I slip my heels on, a knock comes on my apartment door. When I answer it, I find Matthew standing there holding a bouquet of lily's. I take them from his outstretched hand, and he leans in to kiss my cheek. I can't say I've had a man buy me flowers before. It's a nice gesture. "You didn't have to bring me flowers," I say as I invite him inside.

"I did. Every woman deserves flowers."

I put them in some water, rearrange them quickly, then grab my bag.

"Are you nervous?" I ask.

"No, should I be?"

I want to laugh at his confidence because most sane men would be nervous about entering this party, knowing who will be in attendance. I'm not sure how much he knows about my family, but I know he knows exactly who they are.

"No, but you're the first date I'm bringing to meet them."

He smiles and places a hand over his heart. "I'm honored. That's a big step."

Matthew is easy to get along with. He's kind and

thoughtful. But I still have that nagging feeling that something is missing.

He guides me to his car and opens the passenger door for me. He ticks all the boxes: never been married, has no children, isn't afraid of my family. Actually, that last one probably deserves a question mark.

He may have worked with my uncle before, but my uncle has retired. And now the new generation is in charge, and they'll drop him the moment he no longer holds any value.

We talk about his week in the office and a smear campaign he's currently working on. Then he changes the conversation.

"So, I won't run into any old boyfriends at this party, right?"

I laugh. I've never been in a serious relationship. And unless you count Ford, which I'm sure Ford wouldn't even count himself, I haven't been in anything close to a relationship.

"No, you're safe from that situation," I tell him, though I can't guarantee Ford or the other men will be friendly. One date was a fluke; a second date might be what breaks him.

We continue talking casually, and he asks me if it's okay for him to text me a little more often. I'm surprised by the question because he didn't text me at all this week, and I kind of felt unsure about what was happening between us. I now understand he has boundaries, and I'm not quite sure if I like them. I don't want to have to tell a man to text me. I want him to just think of me and do it. Is that really too much to ask? I know that's something Ford wouldn't have done. Another pang of frustration echoes through me because my mind, yet again, so naturally turns to Ford.

When we arrive at the rooftop bar, the valet opens my door, but Matthew is waiting for me. I slide my hand into his and, trying not to laugh, ask, "Are you ready?"

He gives my hand a squeeze as he answers, "Yes."

And I think this man is out of his mind. Had someone told me a year ago I'd be able to hold a man's hand in front of my brother, I would've called them insane. It's what I've always wanted, though, so I try not to let my thoughts stray to anything but embracing this experience for what it is.

He leads me to the elevator. Pressing the button for the rooftop bar, we ascend quickly. The moment the doors open and we step out, we're greeted with the sight of leather and diamond-accented decor, which I find rather fitting for my family.

I spot my parents straight away and take a deep breath as I guide Matthew over to introduce him. My father offers a polite enough smile and his hand, and I remember then that they've worked together before. I'm not the least bit surprised. What does catch me off guard is my mother, who hasn't met Matthew before and is studying him intently. Her usual welcoming nature is nowhere to be found. Her gaze dips to our intertwined hands, and I swear, for the first time ever, my mother looks at me disapprovingly. It's only for a second, and I wonder if I read her wrong. Her gaze then snaps up to meet Matthew's.

"Eli mentioned you were dating my daughter. I hope you're treating her like the princess she is," my father says with a smile, but his eyes hint at something else. It's not a joking matter at all. It's an obvious threat, and Matthew gives my hand a gentle squeeze as if to reassure *me*.

"Yes, of course," Matthew replies. He turns to my mother then and offers his hand. "Lovely to meet you. I can see where Billie gets her beauty from." She doesn't seem flattered, though she offers a polite enough smile.

I know my mother too well. She's acting cold toward Matthew, and a sickening feeling swirls in my stomach. *Do they hate him? Did I choose wrong?* My mother is one of the sweetest people in this room, and for her to act this way makes me second-guess everything.

A clipped "Thank you" is the only response she gives him.

I lean against Matthew. "Can you go grab us a drink? I just want to speak with my mother for a moment."

"Yes, of course. Wine?"

"She hates wine," my mother is quick to say. I've never seen this side of her.

He looks confused and like he's about to mention the bottle he bought at the restaurant, but I offer a smile. I mean, I would've told him eventually, right?

"Vodka soda, please," I tell him.

Once he's gone, I turn on my mother. She was the last person I was expecting this from.

"Why are you being rude?" I demand. My mother and I have hardly ever fought, even when I was a teenager.

"You don't like him," she states.

My jaw drops. "I obviously do, or he wouldn't be here with me." I point at her. "So be nice. I bet you weren't like this to Posie when Dutton introduced her, so don't have double standards."

Her lips press into a thin line. It makes her uncomfortable when we have any type of disagreement. My mother has always been my everything. I'd even consider her as one of my best friends. She taught me everything I know about being a woman, so it's startling to see this side of her. She doesn't often dislike someone.

"We like him if you do," my father interjects, trying to smooth things over, but my mother looks hurt, not offering to even consider changing her opinion.

Okay. I don't even want to dive into that right now.

I turn and head to the bar to join Matthew. If my own mother is giving him the cold shoulder, I'm too terrified to leave him alone, where the rest of the family will tear him apart like a pack of animals.

But that's when I notice he's talking with Ivy. At least I know he's okay with her.

"Billie." My aunt Rya calls out to me.

"Aunt Rya." I smile and hug her. "Happy Birthday."

"I was just telling a friend of mine how good at piano you are." She glances at the piano. "Are you willing to play for us?"

"Oh." A blush streaks across my cheeks. "Sure."

My agreement was immediate, but I'm actually nervous. It's been years since I played, though it was something I always loved. I stopped when I went to college. It just didn't seem like a practical career path. I'm sure I'll be rusty, but a small part of me is excited to play again.

I glance back over to Matthew, who seems to be thoroughly entertained by something Ivy said.

I scan the room anxiously. I get a small boost of confidence when I notice Hope sitting beside the piano, a drink in her hand, looking like she's suffocating with the number of people here.

I chuckle, and an obvious wave of relief washes through her when she sees me approaching.

"You look like you're being tortured," I tease as I slide onto the piano stool.

"More than you can imagine. You going to play?" she asks, leaning in. She always used to listen to me play, and suddenly, it doesn't feel so daunting.

"I'm about to humiliate myself by how rusty I am, but sure, why not." I shrug.

She places her drink on top of the piano.

"At least this way, you can pretend you're drunk." She chuckles. "Oh, this must be the loner area, then," she says as someone comes up behind me. I don't even have to look to know who it is. I can sense his presence before his scent drifts toward me.

"Is this seat taken?" Ford asks, already sitting down beside me. "It's been a while since you've played."

I roll my shoulders. "Well, some things don't change," I say pointedly as I place my fingers on the keyboard. I press down on one of the keys, and it pulls a string in me. Then I play a second note. My fingers slowly but surely find a rhythm, like a story I've read many times in the past, rewriting itself. The melody rings through the room, and it brings me a sense of serenity.

I glance at Hope, who has a small smile on her lips. Nothing seems complicated at the moment, and it's nice. It's funny how old things find ways to come back.

Ford's hand, the one with the sun tattooed on it, reaches toward the keyboard. I shoot him a glare.

"Care to share?" he asks.

"You don't know how to play the piano," I scoff.

He actually has the audacity to smile smugly as he forces me to move as he invades my space. "Don't be so sure you know everything about me, Chaos." His finger presses down on a key, and I narrow my gaze at him in silent challenge. "Try to keep up," he says as he begins to play a classical piece.

I'm shocked, absolutely floored. My eyebrows furrow in confusion as I watch this beast of a man play something so beautiful. And it's a song I know well. It's the one I performed solo at my high school graduation ceremony. But I've never played it with someone else.

I follow his lead, an easy harmony flowing between us. A few people have surrounded us now, and I can tell Ford is uncomfortable with the attention. He's used to being in the shadows, under the radar, where no one notices him. Yet he's willing to put himself in the spotlight now. I have no idea why that is, but my heart races excitedly at how perfect this moment is.

It feels so out of this world, and I embrace all of it, my shoulders sagging as I let the tension of the last few weeks ripple away... and I simply be. In this space. In this now. Remembering why I loved piano so much in the first place.

I'd forgotten the things that brought me joy as I focused on what everyone did or didn't want of me.

No one ever put pressure on me except for me.

The song comes to a close, and I look at Ford, who's still staring at the piano as if numbing out the small crowd we've gathered.

"How?" I ask quietly as we finish a few slow and careful notes as if the second the song truly ends, we'll be taken away from this serene moment. It's the first time in a long time I haven't looked at Ford in anger or despised him for everything that's happened in the past.

His voice is so quiet, I know only I can hear him. "Addictive personality, remember? I have many useless skills I learned in order to distract me."

My eyebrows furrow again. So he skips from one thing to another to keep him entertained? I don't even know how to interpret that. Seeing this kind of softness in Ford, a man who seeks punishments and seclusion, shakes my hatred for him. Not that I ever really hated him. But it reminds me how complicated this man is, and I soften to the thoughts of when he opens up to me little by little. I don't expect him to have feelings that mirror mine, but simply being here right now, shoulder to shoulder? It's... nice.

It's peaceful.

It's *right*.

A few people clap, and we're suddenly taken from our peace, the world around us coming back into play. A world that doesn't favor me and Ford together.

One question plays on my mind, and I ask it. "I played for so many years. Why didn't you ever join me?"

"Because I enjoyed watching you," he says matter-of-factly.

I try not to let it slip past my defenses, but it's hard when it comes to this man. The bittersweetness of the lingering feeling that we're not entirely done. The reality that is we're not good for one another. And not just because of Ford's fixation and addiction, but because of my own as well.

"Wow. I didn't know you could play," Matthew says from over my shoulder. I turn my back to Ford, my heart pounding as if I've done something wrong. I see he's holding what I assume to be a vodka and soda.

Ivy joins Hope, and they watch us carefully. I feel like I have nowhere to run with the man I desire at my back, and the one I know I should want in front of me.

"You didn't like the wine I ordered on our date, did you?" Matthew asks.

"Of course, she didn't," Ford grumbles.

Matthew seems to have not heard him.

"I tried to like it." I blush, trying to block out Ford's voice.

What I said isn't a lie. I did try to like it. But wine just isn't for me.

"Okay, noted. No wine for you." He winks. "Ford, I never took you as the piano-playing type. Nice, dude." He turns and says, "Good to see you, Hawke."

I shift, spotting Hawke standing behind his brother, arms folded over his chest. Tension ripples through the room, and I have no fucking idea what is happening.

But from the way Hawke is looking at me, he clearly suspects something or is particularly sensitive to his brother lately. The two have always seemed weirdly in tune with one another. I guess it's a twin thing.

"So, they actually let you date, little tornado?"

Hawke asks, sounding anything but friendly, which is so unlike him. He has no reason not to like Matthew... unless Ford told him something. I flick my gaze to Ford to find him standing up from the bench.

"Well, considering I'm a grown woman, yes," I reply, getting to my feet.

Ford clicks his tongue, and my jaw grinds at his dismissal, the bubble we were in bursting.

Eli and Jewel join the group, and I wish I were anywhere but here right now.

"Wow. I didn't know you two could play the piano. That's amazing!" Jewel says.

"We all have our own talents, wouldn't you say, wife?" Eli gives her a pointed glare, probably referring to her ability with a gun. I didn't know Jewel was a hitwoman when I first met her, but after I found out, it made so much sense as to why she always kicked our ass when we played shooting games on Eli's gaming console. Come to think of it, that's something we haven't done in some time now.

"Matthew," Eli says, holding out his hand. "I'm actually surprised you got the approval for a second date."

I narrow my eyes at him. Fuck this family and them giving me so much shit for having an overprotective dickhead for a brother. It's not like I asked for that.

The men in my family are assholes.

"So it would seem," Matthew interjects.

Jewel tries to save me from the humiliation and overdose of testosterone by changing the subject. "Oh, Ivy told me you got a tattoo. Did it hurt?" Every pair of eyes flicks from Jewel to me.

"Her heart one?" Matthew says, and Ford's posture noticeably stiffens.

"You got a tattoo, little tornado? Dang, I knew you were a badass," Hawke jokes.

"Do your parents know?" Eli asks, and I see the moment Jewel understands it was meant to be a secret.

"Let's go get a drink, Eli," she says, then leans forward and touches my arm as she whispers, "I'll make sure he doesn't say anything to your brother." I nod as she straightens and pulls Eli away.

Hawke continues to stare at me with approval, and Ford basically glares at Matthew.

"You know about her tattoo?" Ford asks Matthew, and I'm certain he's about to kill him.

Matthew looks down at me and smiles, unaware of the train wreck that's most likely about to happen.

"I do," he replies, and I can feel the lethal aura come off Ford in waves.

He is beyond pissed.

I step in front of Matthew as if shielding him from Ford, who at any point might snap.

"Ford does tattoos. You should have had him do it." Hawke smacks him on the back, and it's then Ford relaxes his hands, which were bunched up into fists.

"That's cool. Do you do it professionally?" Matthew asks him, having no idea how mad Ford is right now. Hawke seems to notice, though and smacks him on the back again.

I glance down at my drink and make the executive decision to just down the entire fucking thing. Because the situation is so fucking awkward. And to make it even worse, Anya and River come over and flank their sons, staring at us. This usually wouldn't be a problem, but Anya hates new people. I'm pretty sure she even hated me when I was a child. Fuck, she probably still hates me. But I think that's just her personality. She doesn't even seem to soften much around the twins, but we all know that if anyone hurt her children, she would be the first one to slit their throats.

"And who are you?" Anya asks Matthew, and I wonder how attuned she is to her son's emotions. Did they walk over here because they could sense the killer intent rolling off Ford?

"Mother, would you like a drink?" Hawke asks as if trying to find any excuse to lead her away. It's well known that Anya doesn't drink alcohol. Anya ignores Hawke, giving Ford a quick once-over before she pins me with a stare.

"Yes, a drink. Billie will take me to the bar, won't you?" she says without so much as a smile. Most people don't say no to Anya Ivanov, and for good reason. She doesn't even wait for me to answer as she steps away from the group and expects me to follow. I do precisely that because I value my fucking life.

Her long, red nails tap on the bar impatiently as I move to stand beside her. She's a regal woman who barely looks any older than a woman half her age, and she's terrifying. She turns to me, a scowl on her face. Her Russian accent comes out thicker than normal when she asks, "What's going on with you and my son?"

I feel the blood drain from my face. "Excuse me?"

She waves her perfectly manicured hand.

"Don't deny it. I know my sons well enough to tell when they're acting abnormally... well, more abnormally than usual." It's great to know she's aware that her kids aren't totally sane. "I know Ford. I watched him practice piano religiously for a year, mastering it like so many other things, but I never understood why until now. The way he was back there is not like him. So, tell me, what is going on with you two?"

My mouth opens and then closes. Is she implying that Ford learned how to play piano because of me? But that would mean he felt something for me years before we ever hooked up. And I certainly didn't suspect his mother, of all people, to catch on to our addictive lies.

I glance over my shoulder at where they're all still standing, my eyes widening when I see Ford.

He's a beautiful savage.

But his mother is fucking terrifying.

He seems to understand my silent plea because he pushes past Hawke and stalks toward us. But the moment he's standing in front of me, I forget how to speak.

THIRTY-TWO
FORD

PANIC FILLS Billie's eyes as her gaze meets mine, and I just know that somehow, my mother worked out exactly what she is to me without either of us having to say a single word. That's one of the reasons I avoid being around Billie in public because people like my mother are clued in to everything.

"Come to explain, son?" she asks when I step up next to Billie. The bartender stops across the shiny counter from us, and Mother demands a glass of water, then turns back to me and Billie with an expectant expression. I feel like a teenager again when she would pin Hawke and me with her scrutinizing gaze and reprimand us for doing something she didn't approve of. "You didn't have to rescue her, you know. I don't bite... hard." Her attempt at teasing falls flat. We're similar in that regard, both having a very dry sense of humor.

"There is nothing to explain," I say adamantly.

"Oh, really?" She arches a perfectly waxed eyebrow. "Nothing? Do we lie to each other now? Is that our new thing?" Her Russian accent is getting thicker, giving away her rising anger. Anya Ivanov is a woman who acts on her anger quickly. It's unlike anything I've ever seen before. And trying to reason with her is often futile.

"I'm not lying. There is nothing going on and nothing to discuss. Especially at Rya Monti's birthday party," I warn her. I know she doesn't give a shit where we are and who is around us; it's one of the reasons I respect her. She doesn't give a flying shit what anyone else thinks. But I counter her glare, a tendril of warning in my gaze.

She takes the water from the bar and stares at Billie.

"He must really like you if he's willing to lie to his mother." She turns and starts back toward my father. "We'll discuss this later," she shoots over her shoulder to me.

I eye her warily, waiting until she's out of earshot. She might be my mother, but she's unpredictable. And it's not my safety I fear for but Billie's. Because Anya is protective of me and my brother, and if she suspects anything and comes to her own conclusions, it might be a similar reaction to the one Billie fears her brother would have.

I guess both of our families are fucked up in that regard.

I notice Matthew curiously looking in our direction and feel rather smug that I'm standing here with her instead of him. I'm also seriously fucking pissed off that he's here in the first place. When I turn to face Billie, my breathing falters. The moment she walked into the room in that dress, I was thinking of all the ways I could rip it off her.

And then I saw his hand wrapped around hers, and I was thinking about all the ways I could detach that hand from his body so he could never touch her again.

"That was awkward. I don't ever want to do that again." Billie heaves out a deep breath as she turns to the bar and waves the bartender down to order another drink. I try not to smirk at how entertaining she is. I don't drink alcohol, but I imagine any sane person would be begging for a drink after being cornered by my mother.

I casually shrug. "Could have been worse. She could have found us fucking," I whisper so only she can hear. Goosebumps appear all over her skin, and it fills me with satisfaction that she still reacts to me in the same way that I do her.

"Stop that," she chides, fixing her gaze over my shoulder. I move so she has no choice but to look at me. "Ford," she growls.

"Yes, Chaos?"

"Stop it."

"I have to check the tattoo. Meet me in the closet?"

"You're insufferable." She shakes her head. "The moment I start thinking you have a decent bone in your body, you go and ruin it."

I don't know why I gravitated to her the moment I saw her playing the piano, but it was something I'd always wanted to do. I used to watch her practice, mesmerized by how at ease she was when she played. Before I knew it, I was playing the piano every morning and every night, memorizing every stroke and key played.

My addiction for her started long before I wanted to admit it.

"It's not a bone, but there's a particular part of my body that you like," I remind her with a wink.

"You're so infuriating." She rolls her eyes. "No, I am not going into a closet with you." The bartender places her drink on the bar. "Now, if you'll excuse me, I need to return to my date."

"You should leave him."

Her blue eyes narrow at me, and I know I'm about two seconds away from feeling her wrath.

"And why would I do such a thing?"

"So I can fuck you." I grin at her, and her eyes go wide. She shakes her head in disbelief. It's the only way I can express to her how alive she makes me feel, yet I know immediately it's not what she wanted to hear.

"No. That's not how this works. By the way, your mother is watching us." She goes to push past me, but I can't help myself. I step in her way and block her path.

"I wouldn't let him kiss you again. If he does..." I deliberately trail off.

"You will do nothing. And he can kiss me anytime," she hisses.

"That wouldn't be a smart thing to do."

"Move. Now."

"Hmm. I like it when you talk dirty to me."

She huffs and pushes past me. I turn to watch her go, only to see my mother staring at me. She walks back over, and I know she saw our interaction. I wait for her because I don't want others to hear what she has to say.

"You lied to me," she accuses.

"I didn't. At this current time, nothing is happening between us," I tell her honestly.

"So there was something going on between you?"

"It was nothing serious."

"So you were sneaking around," she guesses. "For how long?" She pushes harder. And I know I can't lie to her again.

"For almost a year and a half."

She seems to think on my words as she looks over her shoulder.

"I can kill him for you if you want," she offers.

I lean down and kiss her cheek. I love how ruthless she is. "No, Mother, it was my choice to let her go."

"You don't sound like you're doing a very good job of it. You sound just like me. Your brother is more like your father," she comments. "Make no mistake, your father was the best thing to happen to me. And then you and Hawke came along."

I know Anya's sentimental side is not something she shows freely... or often.

"I know."

"Don't think you can't have anyone you want," she tells me, then nods before she walks away.

Our tender moment is over, and we both move through the room in our usual predatory manor.

THIRTY-THREE
BILLIE

Matthew's arm slides around my waist when I reach him. Jewel whispers something into Eli's ear, and then they leave us. At the same time, Ivy drags Hope away. Matthew then turns, and both of his hands slip around my waist. He pulls me to him, his front pressing into mine. I force a smile, placing one of my hands awkwardly on his chest, the other hand still holding my drink, as I look up at him.

"Do you have plans after this?" he asks, gripping me a little tighter.

"No."

"Good. I want you to know I don't expect anything, but I'd like to invite you back to my place."

"For?"

"Dessert." He smiles at me. He doesn't know that's

my favorite thing to make. I can't say I've had anyone other than my mother makes me dessert besides a restaurant. But the double entendre isn't lost on me. I've had a certain someone else demand his weight in sweets and dessert, and yet when Ford does it, it makes me feel an entirely different way. But with Matthew... there's nothing.

I stare at him, thinking of how to respond, when someone bumps into me from behind, and my drink spills all over Matthew.

"Shit, I'm so sorry." I attempt to wipe at his shirt, noticing it's also spilled down his pants.

"Fuck. Maybe you shouldn't be drinking." He steps back, wiping at the spot himself as if I'm only making it worse. I'm shocked at his outburst, and I immediately know how I feel about him. He seemed too sweet, too perfect. And maybe that's why I was doubting it.

"I think I'll decline your invite for tonight." He raises his head, his hands pausing on his clothes.

"Why? I'm sorry. I was just shocked, that's all. It won't happen again." He tries to step forward and grab me again, but I back away from his reach.

"I'm just not sure this will work," I tell him honestly.

I've been trying so hard to force it. Wanting to believe that someone so normal would be everything I need, but this man is not it. The clarity hits me like a sledge hammer, and I'm not even remorseful for it.

"And you think this is the place to tell me?" he quietly seethes. "Are you trying to humiliate me?"

My jaw drops and then snaps closed as I see him for what he really is. And perhaps I should've seen it sooner. He's most likely only dating me for name recognition or the connections he could've made via my family.

"I don't really care about your ego. I was just communicating how I felt."

He scoffs, but before he can reply, a voice carries over my shoulder.

"Billie, dear. I think your date should leave." I turn to find Anya standing next to me. When I don't say anything, she turns to him. "If you don't leave, I'll have someone break your leg. And let me assure you, that's me acting on my best behavior."

Matthew looks at me in shock, but I don't say anything. It's not like anyone overheard me gently letting him down; he's the one who started making a big deal about it. It takes me a moment to recover, but I outright refuse to have any man speak to me that way. Not even Ford, unless he's making me come, that is.

"I'm sorry, Matthew. Really, I am. Do you want me to walk you out?" He looks stunned.

"No, I can see myself out." He turns and storms off without saying another word to me, cursing about his expensive shirt.

"He isn't meant for this world anyway. It was silly of you to think he was," Anya says snidely. I understand it's probably for her son's sake, but though she intimidates me, I won't have anyone challenge my decisions.

"That may be true, but I didn't ask for your opinion," I say to her, and someone close by gasps. Perhaps it was River. But it's her I'm watching because disrespecting Anya Ivanov is deadly.

"You didn't have to. I'll always give it freely. But it's good to see the little Taylor princess has a backbone after all," she replies with a slight smirk.

"Billie." Hawke slides his arm around my shoulders, and I know he's trying to protect me from his mother. The tension is palpable. "Where did your date run off to?" He eyes Anya as he says, "Mother. Father is waiting for you."

"Both of my sons seem to be turning on their own mother today. How interesting." Anya offers me a smile before she turns and walks off.

The moment she's gone, Hawke taps my forehead and shakes his head. "Going head-to-head with Anya? You have some balls on you, little tornado. Tell me, when did you grow them? Was it when you became a little baddie with a new tattoo?"

"Shut up, Hawke." I push his hand away and make my way to the exit. Fuck today. Everyone was so sure I should bring Matthew to this party, and it turned out to be a giant fail. Besides, I'm not exactly in the partying mood anymore.

I need to get out of here, go for a walk, and get some air. When the elevator doors open in the lobby, I see Matthew waiting at the curb. I wait until he gets into his car and drives off before I exit the building. I don't want any more confrontations tonight.

"Running off?" I turn to find Ford wearing a black trench coat with a cigarette in his hand. He usually only smokes when he's stressed about something.

"Disgusting habit," I state, nodding to the cigarette. He smirks and takes another puff before dropping it to the ground and stepping on it.

"I'll take you home."

"No, you won't. I can't keep doing this. You need to leave me alone," I say as I step to the curb to hail a cab.

"But what if I can't leave you alone?" he asks just as a cab pulls up.

"Billie." I refuse to look at him as I open the cab door. He grabs it, holding it open for me. "Look at me." I don't.

"Just stop, Ford. Close the door and let me go."

I yank on the handle once. He doesn't budge. The cab driver is staring at me through the rearview mirror. "I mean it this time, Ford. I'm not anyone's property, especially not yours since we only fucked."

I can feel the intensity of his gaze, and eventually, he releases the door, and I slam it shut.

I hold my head high. It has to come to an end. This back and forth is too painful.

THIRTY-FOUR
FORD

I'm waiting for him to leave the hotel room. I've watched him since the moment he first arrived in Manhattan and showed an interest in Billie. Now that she's openly rejected him, I can finally take matters into my own hands.

He often frequents a bar only a few blocks away from his hotel, a bar that's known for its shady dealings, which is exactly the type of place I expect a man like Matthew to go. For someone who is used to classy establishments and prestige to fuel his ego, I love that he chooses such a low-class establishment.

He walks a short distance down the sidewalk and then steps into an alleyway. I kick off my car and silently follow him; the hood of my sweatshirt pulled up over my head, and my small backpack slung over my shoulder. Just before I enter the alley, I put a mask on and slip the two crowbars out of my backpack.

He's smoking, whistling a tune as he walks down the narrow passage. He frequents this hotel because every night, he hires a woman to visit him and then afterward goes out to the same bar. I know this because Eli owns the bar. And every time, he purchases the same amount of drugs.

I'm not going to judge someone for their habits, but what I won't excuse is him touching another woman while giving Billie the idea that she's something special to him.

Besides, I'm wildly pissed off that he ever touched her in the first place.

I'm unreasonable.

I'm spiteful.

And I'm entirely addicted to her, so I'm not in a place to share.

I drag a crowbar along the row of trash cans as steam creeps from the manhole covers.

He spins, finally noticing he's not alone.

Sheer horror mars his features as he turns and quickens his pace. I match him step for step, with cool control, still dragging my crowbar.

Suddenly, he turns and holds his hands up. "I don't know what this is about. I don't want any trouble."

I've never wanted anything for myself, and I've never ignored the restrictions and rules laid down by my family and Eli Monti.

But Billie Taylor has become a poison I can't help but ingest, and I've learned that I'm not entirely a sane man when it comes to her. Now I just need to make sure this asshole never reaches out to her again.

It's not my style to hide behind a mask. But it feels like the more I spiral in my need for Billie, the more addictive lies I'm willing to create for her.

That, and I don't want my little visit getting back to Eli or Dutton.

Again, I've never done anything for myself, and even now, I feel like I'm betraying Eli. But I'll do anything for *her*. It's not her older brother she has to worry about anymore.

"Do you know who my family is?" he says nervously. "What do you want? Money? Is this about the recent smear campaign?"

I shake my head, taking great pleasure in the way his hand shakes.

Killing him will complicate things, and Eli will most certainly dig into the person behind it. So I choose to remain a faceless demon, terrifying enough to spook him and run him off from my woman.

He looks confused as he licks his lips. "Is this about the hooker?"

I shake my head slowly again.

His eyebrows dip, and I rub my crowbars against one another as if to warn him of my impatience. I can't risk him recognizing my voice.

"Wait!" he shouts as I take a step forward. "Is this about the Monti family?"

I tilt my head to the side. He's close. The dumbass sparks with a thought. "No? The Taylors? Billie Taylor?!"

I offer one curt nod, then place the tip of my crowbar at my throat and drag it along the skin as if slitting it—a clear warning.

His body trembles and his knees go weak and give out. He falls into a puddle. I stare down at him, wanting to put this fucker out of his misery. I can't believe they actually thought this man was a good choice for her. He's all talk, but when faced by a demon, he'll throw anything or anyone out as a sacrifice. He's the worst type of man and certainly not good enough to be by her side.

"You don't want me near her?" he inquires quietly.

I nod again. Fucking idiot has some brain cells after

all. The cigarette that fell out of his mouth smolders on the ground.

I imagine all the things I could do to this pitiful man. They called him powerful, but he's nothing but a sheep in wolf's skin, trying to play in a world he was never meant to be a part of. Sure, he can ruin someone's reputation, but that means nothing to someone like me, who doesn't give a fuck what others think.

But Billie has too much to lose, and I'm not willing to leave it to chance that he isn't bold enough to target her after she so publicly rejected him.

"I won't go near her, I swear." He whimpers. "Please, just let me go."

Let him go. My lip curls at the thought. I've never been good at catch and release. I hunt my prey, and I bring it back to my master. Then again, I've never acted of my own accord before. Not until now.

I care about her more than I'm able to express in words.

And I've never had much restraint when it came to my addictions.

But I force myself to take one step backward.

And then another, slowly backing down the alley, only turning away from the sniveling asshole when I'm a few feet from the street.

I may lack in restraint most of the time, but I can

force it when I need to. To protect her. To not bring questions about her or our relationship.

But it doesn't mean I'm done with her.

I can't be.

I can't let go.

Even when she asks me to.

THIRTY-FIVE
BILLIE

He knocks on my door.

I don't answer it.

He knocks again the following day.

I still don't answer.

I know it's him. He's the only person who would knock and not call my name.

So when Monday comes along, and I open the door, I don't expect to find him standing there. But here he is, coffee in hand, dark gaze locked on me.

"It's my birthday," he says, offering me the coffee.

"I'm late," I tell him, not accepting it. "Happy birthday," I add just as he holds the cup out to me again. I ignore the coffee, shut, and lock the door, and walk past him. He follows. Because of course he does.

"Will you come over tonight?" he asks.

"No," I reply without hesitation.

"Tomorrow night?"

"No," I repeat.

We step out onto the street, and I pass his parked car. He keeps following me.

"The day after?" He's persistent. I'll give him that.

Sucking in a breath, I turn to face him.

"Stop," I tell him. "Stop and go home."

He smiles at me as he steps closer. "I lied. My birthday is next week. But I was hoping it would work."

Huffing, I continue walking. This time, he doesn't follow.

I manage to get to work on time, his words playing on my mind the whole time.

Tuesday, I once again find him waiting in the hall-way. I close and lock the door behind me and don't accept the coffee.

Wednesday is the same thing. He doesn't speak, and I'm thankful for that. I feel like I might give in if he does. I can only take so much of this back and forth. And whenever I try to push him out of my mind, he's there.

Thursday, he isn't there, though.

Friday, he isn't either.

By Saturday, I've checked my phone multiple

times, expecting a text, even though that's never really been our style, but there's nothing.

I bake. I bake so fucking much that my apartment is overflowing with food.

And then I cry.

I wipe at the tears, not able to stop them. *Why won't they stop?*

Fuck my life.

My phone rings, and I ignore it.

How did it even get to this point?

I pushed back so much. So why do I feel so fucking miserable with everything, even when I'm sticking to my guns and not buying into his games? I want to romanticize it. I want to think he's trying because he wants me. But I don't think Ford is capable of that. Even when he lets me in a little, it just doesn't feel like it's enough.

Or maybe it's my own reservations about giving my heart fully to a man I think is incapable of handling it with the love and care it deserves, which is ridiculous. I have so many people who love and care about me, but this feels entirely different. I'm coming to realize that love is a shitty thing. I begged, kicked, and screamed for my brother to get out of my way and let me date, and now I'm not sure why.

I got lost in a secret relationship that was only sex.

I'm not that girl. I've always wanted commitment. I want a man to want me for *me*—every part of me, not just my body. And don't want him to look at another woman the same way he looks at me.

I want what my parents have.

Yet, here I am, single, alone, and baking in my kitchen. Crying over a man who tells me sweet nothings but can't back them up. And I know it's an excuse because I'm somewhat the same. What a mindfuck.

Glancing around, I decide I need to get rid of all of this food. There's no way Ivy and I can eat all this. And I know someone who would, but I don't want to see him.

Picking up my phone, I see two missed calls from Jewel. I like her a lot. She's a total badass who knows what she wants. But I can't say we're particularly close. Calling her back, I wipe at my face, knowing I probably have cake batter over it. I lick my lips and can taste the buttercream icing I put on the cupcakes.

"Oh, hey. I know it's late, but I desperately need help," she says, sounding frustrated.

"Yeah?"

"Well, Eli said you can bake?"

"Yes...?" I hedge, looking at the counter and all the shit I baked today. I did way too much, but like my mother, I find it soothing.

"Eli took on a big job, and well, I tried to bake him something to celebrate. And let's just say, I can't bake," she admits, defeated.

My eyebrows shoot to my hairline. I don't necessarily think my cousin would care for baked goods, but I know for a fact if it comes from Jewel, he'll fucking freeze it for life, not letting anyone touch the treasure that his wife made. And I think it's cute that she's trying. It's nice to see they have these types of moments. Like a normal relationship would.

I didn't plan on leaving the apartment today but considering Ivy's away in Ibiza for a week and all I've been doing is baking, I might as well do it constructively.

"I'm coming right over."

"Oh my God, really?"

I need to get out of here. Stop thinking about him.

"I can pay you. I mean, I know you have a job, but I can pay you for it. You're saving my ass right now."

"It's fine. You don't need to pay me. I'll be there soon." I hang up and start putting everything into containers. At least now, my efforts won't go to waste.

They might be sad baked goods, but the sugar will always override any inner turmoil.

THIRTY-SIX
FORD

I smell her baking before I see her in the kitchen with Jewel, covered in icing. The counter is filled with all the sweets and treats that taste like her. And then she laughs, and I can't stop my feet from walking into the kitchen, lured like a moth to a flame, ready to be burned if only permitted one more glimpse.

She's avoided me for two weeks. I've risked being caught entering her building just to see her, smell her, and be close to her. I don't seem to know what to say or how to say it. All I can do is be there. But I didn't go the last few days, and I've felt like I've gone through the motions of my day-to-day, unable to sleep. Only able to work and sketch as I listen to screaming music, wishing and praying that I'll hear her light footsteps down the hallway of my home.

Every time I see my front lawn, I think of her. Every time Felix jumps through the kitchen window after a day of adventure, demanding to be fed, I think of her. The cat and I tolerate each other at best. It's when Hawke comes around that the traitorous little thing shows any affection. But I'm okay with that.

Eli is in the kitchen with his arm around Jewel's waist as she tries to feed him cake. The sight of it is sickening; my killer of a boss acting in such a normal human way.

But I feel the loss, the desire, the moment I see Billie. Wishing in a different life that, perhaps we could do the same. She's cutting a cake when she raises her head and gives me a hard look. Jewel turns and says something to her, and that's when her gaze leaves mine.

"Sorry, what?"

"Eli said I did great," Jewel repeats with a wink.

"She did. You should try the cake." Billie plays along, encouraging Eli to eat more of the cake.

"I'm still not above the idea of my wife poisoning me by baking," Eli growls.

"Shut up. It's edible," Jewel chastises.

I know without even tasting that Billie baked it. I've walked in on her baking so many times and know the distinctive smell her mother's bakery has.

"I'll try the cake," I say.

Eli shakes his head. "What a shock—you eating a cake. But care to explain to me why the fuck you're in my house?"

"Of course you want some," Jewel smirks and then slaps Eli on the shoulder. "Be nice. I invited everyone around for the afternoon. It's been a while since we've all been together."

Eli's gaze turns lethal, the way it does when he realizes he's not going to be alone with his wife for the next few hours. She often does this without his knowing, but he takes it out on us instead. Once, we didn't show up, and he threatened to beat the shit out of us if we ever denied his wife again.

I move closer to Billie, brushing my arm against hers as I check out all the baked goods. I just need to touch her, smell her, be beside her. If that's all I can have, I'll take it. "Which one should I try first?"

Her gaze falls to my arm, but she doesn't move as she answers. "Any of them. Jewel baked them, so I'm sure they all taste amazing." I turn then and pick up a cookie. Lifting it to my mouth, I take a bite.

"Any good?" Eli asks.

"Of course, assuming it's made with love," I mumble around a mouthful, and Jewel bites her bottom lip.

"See? Made with love!" She points at Eli, clearly

upset he hasn't trusted her cooking before now. Even though I know she didn't make a damn one of these items.

I lean in closer to Billie. "Tastes just like yours," I whisper. She looks away and starts arranging the cakes.

"I just have to move this to the table. I'll be back." She lifts a tray full of cupcakes and walks out, giving me the back view of one of her silky sundresses.

When she's gone, Eli begins pressing kisses down his wife's neck. He's certainly hungry for something, but it's not cake.

Swallowing the last bite of the cookie, I wipe my hands and then follow the little bundle of chaos. She's arranging the table with her sweets as I walk around it, so I'm directly in front of her.

I've missed the pink on her cheeks when she's flustered, and I can tell she certainly wasn't prepared to see me today. It's obvious by the way she tries to ignore me. Again.

Fuck. I've missed her.

"Chaos?" She shakes her head and fixes her attention on the cookies that really don't have to be rearranged. "Do you plan to ignore me forever?"

"Forever sounds pleasant. Even when we're in hell," she says with an insincere smile, still staring at the table.

"There's my girl." I'm proud of her for being unable to hold her vicious viper tongue.

Her hand pauses at my use of *my girl.*

"Is there something you needed?" She finally meets my gaze, and I can't fight the smirk that slowly grows on my lips. She has icing above her lip, and the only thing I can think about is how I want to lick it off.

"Little tornado!" Hawke bounces into the room and throws an arm over her shoulders. Ivy enters directly behind him, and the girls look at one another, confused.

"I thought you were in Ibiza," Billie says.

"I was. I had this feral animal pick me up from the airport because I decided to come back a day early." She points at Hawke.

"Is it all sweet?" Hawke asks, sounding judgmental.

Billie hooks a thumb over her shoulder. "There's more in the kitchen." Her tone is nicer for him than it is for me.

Hawke smiles wide, like he just won the lottery, and makes for the kitchen.

"I need a drink. An hour in the car with that asshole will drive anyone insane," Ivy says, giving Billie a hug. She then nods to me. "I still have no idea how the two of you can be related. Like chalk and cheese."

"Not by choice," I reply, and she laughs as she follows Hawke. Billie seems even more pissed now that I've made Ivy laugh.

I move so I'm standing next to her again, and she turns to face me. She doesn't pull back as my thumb rubs above her top lip, wiping away the icing. I'm past the point of caring who sees us. I don't give a flying fuck anymore. I'll take whatever I can from her.

I *need* her.

"You've been avoiding me." I lean in, my mouth moving closer to hers. Touching the side of her face, I lick the top of her lip as she takes a sharp inhale. Hawke calls out my name, and I pull back. "All gone." I smile at her stunned expression.

I can tell the moment her shields start to lower. She's letting me in slowly, and I've been working on them for the better part of a month. "Do you want me to stop touching you?" I ask.

Please, God, do not say no.

She says nothing.

"Billie." Her eyes find mine. "I really miss touching you." I put my hand on her hip, and her eyelids flutter like she's in a trance. I slide it up her side, admiring the smooth feel of her dress and everything I know is beneath it. But it's not just her body. It's *her*.

And I'm so starved that I'll eat any crumbs she'll give me.

If I were a better man, I'd actually let her go.

But I'm not.

"Ford!" my brother yells. I drop my hand, knowing I'll do something I might regret if I don't step away. Not that I'd ever regret touching or kissing her, but I would if she didn't want it.

And the idea of her not wanting me kills me. Even though I assumed it was bound to happen.

It's kept me up at night, but even I need to learn when to cut off my own air supply. Right?

But I'm a glutton for punishment.

I somehow got stuck here for dinner... and, of course, dessert, which I baked. I'm pretty sure most know that, but for Eli's sake, we're pretending it was Jewel.

Ford is sitting across from me because I purposely took the seat beside Hawke instead, not trusting myself to sit so close to him. Everyone's discussing random bits about their week, but mostly, Ivy is monopolizing the conversation about her recent sexual conquests that Jewel seems invested in. Which only makes Eli jealous. Hawke then starts comparing his recent conquests, and it turns into this overtly sexual conversation about positions that then leads to the blood play my cousin and his wife favor. Eli doesn't seem at all okay with her discussing their sex life, but he doesn't stop her, a very male pride oozing off him.

The conversation then somehow turns to guns, and Jewel can't stop talking about her favorites.

Someone asks Ford a question. He hasn't spoken the entire time. His head is bent, and he's playing on his phone, which is a usual thing. It's not until recently that I concluded it's one of the things he does to occupy himself.

My eyebrows dip when my phone vibrates. When I check it, there's a text from Ford.

Ford: I really want to be up that dress right about now.

I PUT the phone down without replying.

And then it vibrates again.

Ford: Excuse yourself. Now.

I LOOK UP and find him watching me. I put down the phone again and turn to Hawke, listening to whatever he's discussing. Something about fighting with his bare hands, I think.

"Billie, I need vanilla extract. Show me what it looks like," Ford says, cutting across the conversation like a sharpened blade. Everyone looks at him, and Hawke starts laughing.

"Man, you don't even know how to turn on an oven." And I know that's the truth because when I've baked at his house, he seems baffled, like I'm using some kind of witchcraft. But with what I recently learned about him, I think he was most likely making notes. He could probably perfect some of the hardest recipes within a year with his apparent addictive personality.

"I was attempting to make our parents a cake for their anniversary. Maybe you should fucking help," he snaps at Hawke, who raises his hand in defense.

"No fucking thank you. That woman's poisoned us so much with her cooking that I think if I were to return the favor, she'd put a bullet in my head."

"Or a stiletto," Ivy says casually as she takes a sip of her drink.

"Ooh. I heard about that. Is it true? Did Anya kill a man with her stiletto?" Jewel asks.

"Yep," Hawke says proudly.

"Maybe you should just pay Billie to do it," Eli suggests, and Jewel smirks. "We all know none of us can bake for shit compared to her."

He ignores everyone else, his focus solely on me.

"Vanilla extract?" he asks again, then turns to Jewel. "I can take yours, right?"

Jewel nods, but she probably doesn't even know what it looks like either. That's confirmed when she says to me, "You'll show him, right?"

That simmering fire stokes in my stomach because, of course, Ford is conniving enough to figure out how to get me alone when I'm trying my hardest to ignore him.

"Of course." I stand at the same time Ford does. I excuse myself and walk through the door into the kitchen. The minute the door shuts, a set of hands are on me and pushing me forward.

"What are you—" My words cut off when his hands slide around my ass and lift me. My legs wrap around his waist as he carries me to the pantry and closes us in the dark. The only light available is from the small crack at the bottom of the door.

I feel his length pushing against me as his lips waste no time finding mine. I'm overstimulated as he consumes me, my hands bunching in his shirt to pull him closer and deepen the kiss. I feel starved and deprived from all the times he wouldn't kiss me before. And now he's eating at my mouth without restraint. And, fuck me, I've missed this. I've missed *us*.

I can't think straight as my body reacts naturally to his, so certain in my desire for him.

He holds me up with one arm as he undoes his trousers, then I feel his cock pushing against my underwear. My hips grind against him, a small whimper crawling up my throat as all my inhibitions fade, and I'm dragged back into a world where he was all I knew, where he was all I wanted.

"You taste so fucking good. You're my favorite sweet," he says between kisses, and I believe him. Even if I don't know what we are or what we will ever become... I believe him. My body trusts him. And it's just my heart that falters. And that's what hurts because of how desperately I want this.

Of how desperately I fight against the undeniable need to have it.

To have *him*.

I slide my hand into the neck of his shirt and dig my nails into his back as he trails worshipping kisses down my neck.

He lifts me a little higher, and his cock at my

entrance, only a scrap of thin fabric keeping him out. He slides my panties to the side, and his lips pause on my neck.

"Have you missed me?" he murmurs.

I don't reply. Fuck him and his magnificent cock.

"Tell me, Chaos." His cock is teasing me, the head pressed against me so I can feel him but can't have him.

I lean back and glare at him, furious that he's dangling the bait in front of me. I can't say it. I can't tell him how much I've missed him. It's not fair to either of us. But all this restraint has been killing me inside every day. And now it's bubbling over and pouring into me as I rip at his clothes.

"Do you want to hit me?" he asks, and I nod. It's not sane, and it's intensely fierce. But I would rather hit the man I love than tell him I miss him. Because that's our twisted language, and I know it gets him off.

"Hit me," he orders. I'm hesitant, but he bites my bottom lip, dragging with his teeth. When he releases my lip, he growls, "I like it rough. Now, fucking hit me." He bites my lip again, harsher this time, and I swear I taste blood. I react, slapping him across the face. A deadly smirk appears as he shoves me forcefully onto his cock.

"Fucking perfect." He groans as I gasp, trying to

adjust to his size. Then he starts moving, and I forget about everything and anything we ever fought about. I can only feel us in this moment. This thing that I've begged for and cried over for months now. It's in the palms of my hands, where it should always be.

"Go on, Chaos, scar me with those fucking perfect nails." I hold on to him as he pulls our bodies flush with each other and moves me like he's done so many times before.

But this time, it's desperate. Unhinged.

Shaking me at my core as we hate, kiss, and torture one another after months of deprivation and frustration.

But why does it feel so good?

I dig my nails into his back, breaking his skin and carving it with my nails. And I know that he fucking loves it. And it's never felt more right.

"Tell me you missed me," he pleads.

I can feel myself about to come already. He thrusts in harder, and as I start to cry out, he kisses me again. We're biting, sucking, and marking as he rips his lips from mine. "Say it!" he demands, gripping my ass painfully tight.

"I-I missed you." I pant out the confession. I can't help it. It's true. And he knows it. I come, and he follows right behind me, jerking inside me, kissing me gently through the aftershocks as if he can't get enough. He strokes my hair from my face, his tongue dominating mine, as I melt into him, overstimulated by the harshness of his claiming and the gentleness of his kiss.

A kiss that I always had to ask for.

Always demanding that he give me more.

And now he's giving it to me when we've already decided we're done.

I'm shaking and panting as I shove him, reality setting in that everyone is literally a room over from us. *Fuck.* We're out of our goddamn minds. I try to unwrap my legs, but he grips me to him.

"Come home with me tonight."

"No," I tell him as my feet touch the floor. Fixing my dress, I don't even bother looking at him as I open the door and slip out. I need to run away from this situation because I just betrayed my own resolve.

"Ummm." I startle at the sound of Jewel's voice. "Did you find the vanilla extract?"

Just then, the pantry door opens, and Ford steps out, doing his pants up with one hand and holding a bottle of vanilla extract in the other.

"Got it."

Jewel bites her bottom lip, nods once, then leaves.

There's no fucking way she doesn't know. We're so bad at this. We might be addicted to lying and sneaking around, but the bigger this secret is, the worse we become at hiding it.

I turn back to find him staring at me as if he's bracing for what I'm about to say or do. His cheek is a stark red from where I slapped it, and a part of me feels a little guilty. That is until the voice of my brother rings out through the house. Both of our gazes snap in the direction of the door.

"He can know," Ford says.

"Know what?" Dutton asks as he pushes through the door.

I school my features, giving him a fake smile as I lean up to give him a hug.

"I ended things with Matthew," I tell him. He releases me and meets my eyes.

"Good." He nods to Ford and then notices the handprint on his cheek.

He looks between us. "Why do you have a handprint on your face?"

"I slapped him because he slept with one of my friends." I lie with such ease that I almost believe it myself.

"Oh," Dutton says, and I'm not sure if he's taking the bait. "It's not Ivy, is it?"

"Ew," Ford and I both say at the same time. And I know she would share the sentiment. "No, a college friend."

Ford's clenching his jaw, probably pissed that I've lied yet again. But what does he expect me to do in a roomful of knives, which just so happen to be my brothers' favorite weapon?

"Is Posie with you?" I ask Dutton as he reaches into the fridge and pulls out a bottle of water.

"No, she's working, and said under no circumstances am I to interrupt her," he grumbles. I follow behind him when he leaves the kitchen, not wanting to be left in the same room with Ford again because look what just happened even though I told myself it would never happen again.

I have no self-control around him.

I'd become cocky over the last month, thinking I could deny myself what I know he has to offer.

I feel weak.

Careless.

And like this thing between us has taken on a life of its own.

My brother takes a seat, then grabs a slice of cake and takes a bite. He turns and looks at me just as Ford comes through the door.

"Jewel made it," Eli says, and Dutton raises a brow at me.

"You made this. It's Mom's recipe." Dutton states the obvious. Everyone's attention turns to me, and I look at Jewel, who is sitting there chewing her lip.

It's ridiculous how I've become addicted to lying lately.

"Nope, I helped. That's all," I chirp.

Ford takes the seat opposite me. He's furious, I can tell. He doesn't even glance at me as he picks up his phone and ignores the conversation around him. Just as I think how rude he's being, my phone lights up, and I see that he's texted me yet again.

I lean into the conversation circulating the room, trying to ignore my phone. It's distracting every time it lights up. I know it's him. I can also feel him looking in my direction every time I speak. I'm so hyperaware of everything he does.

"He can know."

Ford said it, but I immediately denied anything happening between us. And as much as I've hated on him these last few months, I realize he has a point. He's been my dirty little secret. I always thought it was because I was too scared of how my brother would react, but Ford's been willing to hit that head-on. I've just been too scared to give my heart over to him entirely.

I'm a fucking coward.

But sometimes, we run away from the precise thing that we've been asking for.

After sitting in the tension and self-flagellation for another thirty minutes, I decide to take my leave. Ivy says she's going to stay, most likely because she's four drinks in with Jewel, but I'm not exactly feeling social tonight.

I make up an excuse that I have some work to finish and say my goodbyes. Jewel follows me out.

"Thank you for helping today. I know no one believes I baked any of that stuff, but it's the thought that counts, right?" she says with a shrug. I like that she makes these excuses up so that everyone can come and spend time together. My understanding is she doesn't really have any family of her own, and I'm glad she's starting to accept that she's now part of ours. I never thought Eli would find love, but I'm glad he has it.

I give her a hug, surprised when she pulls me in tighter. "Your secret is safe with me. But if you two continue to do that, the others will find out. You were sloppy today." My heart stalls at that because I know exactly what she's talking about, and part of me wonders if she's always known.

Does everyone know? Are we that bad at keeping it a secret?

But it's only me who still wants to keep it that way.

"Thank you," I whisper as my stomach drops to the floor, truly considering if it would be so bad if my brother found out. But my heart squeezes, terrified by how he'll react because I don't want him to hurt the only man I've ever loved.

Eli tries to stop me on my way out, but I push past him. I need to know why she's still ignoring me. She tells me she wants more from me, and the moment I try to give it to her, she shoves me away. She's as much of a fucked-up contradiction as I am.

I manage to catch her before she gets into the cab, and I slip my arms around her waist, pulling her backward.

"What are you doing?" she squeaks, trying to wriggle free of my grip. She's probably concerned that Dutton might see us, but I'm over caring who finds out. I'm over living for only them. If I ask for anything in this lifetime, it will be for her. Consequences be damned.

Even if her brother kills me for it, I want to know that she chose me, too.

And then I'll simply haunt her for all of eternity.

I hold on to her tightly because if the only way I'll keep her is by catching her, then we can play this game over and over again. "Come back to mine. I want you to do something for me," I whisper into her ear.

"Ford, what if they see us!" she argues.

"I don't care who sees us. I only agreed to keep us a secret to protect you." Her body stills under my grip. "Stop running away."

Something in that statement strikes her because she looks over her shoulder at me, her eyes wide and frightened. She's scared. I let her go immediately. Is she scared of us? What could be us?

"Why are you doing this?" she asks quietly.

"Just come back to mine," I plead. "Please."

My *please* seems to surprise her. She swallows hard, glancing at the house where most of our loved ones are still gathered.

"Fine," she agrees.

I open the passenger door of the cab and throw him a hundred bucks. "I'll take her home."

He smiles at the cash and nods. I never understood why Billie prefers cabs and subways over the drivers her parents happily supply. But I suspect it's her desire for what she might consider an ordinary life.

I don't look behind me to see if anyone notices us leaving because I don't fucking care anymore. She's quiet on the drive back to my house. I'm so used to the giggly and smiley Billie that I wonder if I'm doing the right thing. Am I what frightens her? Am I just as undeserving of her as I've told myself all this time? But I reach for her, always with the possessiveness of a man who will take no other as his.

I want her to be all mine, and I know that's fucking selfish as all fuck.

But I won't deny myself any longer.

When we arrive at my place, I notice the small smirk on her face as she looks at the front lawn. When I open the door, she immediately explodes with excitement when she sees Felix, and for once, I'm grateful for the little fucker who has brightened her mood.

My impatience grows, though, as she fawns over Felix, but I focus on the fact that she's here at all. I finally have her back in my home, where she belongs.

Eventually, she looks up at me. Those beautiful blue eyes striking against the honey color of her hair. It's so strange that I feel like she's the color in my life. And having her not be in it for so long seemed to drain everything from me. "What did you want to show me?"

"Come with me." I lead her into the back room where I do my tattoos and start setting everything up. She looks confused, and I ask her to sit in the spot that I'd usually take.

"Why?"

"I want you to tattoo me. I can't reach."

"Can't reach?" she asks. "You want me to tattoo you? That's not my job. I don't know what to do. What if I fuck it up?"

"You're more than likely going to fuck it up," I smirk but grab her by her hand and gently pull her in. "I'll show you," I tell her. I explain how the gun works, how to use the ink, and how to clean my skin, and she listens and takes it all in. She doesn't ask any questions, but I always knew she was a quick learner.

She pauses as she's putting on a pair of gloves when she notices me removing my pants.

"What are you doing?"

"I told you I can't reach." I lie on my stomach on the bed in nothing but a shirt. She's watching my every move, gripping the tattoo gun tightly, hyperawareness fueling the both of us. I want to rip her clothes off, but I expend what little restraint I have because I want her to permanently mark me first.

Whether she'll have me or not, I want to always have her markings on my skin.

"What am I doing?" she asks breathlessly, apparently still in disbelief that she agreed to this. Not that I gave her much choice.

I motion to my ass. "I want the exact same one as yours."

"My heart?"

"Yes."

She bites her bottom lip. "What if it's bad?"

"What if it's great?" I counter. "Besides, it's on my ass. Even if you fuck it up, I'm not wearing any bikinis anytime soon, so no one else will see it." I wink, and she laughs, the sound of it drawing away any tension I was holding on to.

Her eyes narrow, as if she's suddenly serious about the task at hand. It's the same expression she showed when learning new songs on the piano or when her mother would teach her new recipes. I've been silently watching her whenever I could ever since I met her. I was just in denial from the start, but not anymore. I couldn't deny it anymore if I tried.

Lying here, I try to tell myself that she's an ugly duckling so my cock doesn't get hard as I watch her. But it doesn't work because I know she's the most beautiful girl in the fucking world, and her hands are about to be on my ass.

"Any second thoughts?" she asks, looking at my ass.

"Not about this," I reply, then instruct her how to start.

She nods and bites her lip as she listens, then she leans forward. I lie there, completely captivated. I can see her hands are shaking, but she quickly gets the hang of it. When I tell her to add a little bit more pressure, she does. And by the time she's done with the first half, I barely have to guide her at all.

The minute the tattoo is completed, she puts the gun down and takes off the gloves. Then she studies her handiwork with a small smile, seemingly satisfied.

"It's actually not bad," she says, meeting my gaze.

I get up from the bed, go to the mirror, and have a look myself. She's actually did a pretty good job. When I turn back around, my focus locks on her face. She's no longer looking at the ink on my ass. Her gaze is trained on my cock, pressing against my boxers. It twitches as if aware of her attention.

Her blue eyes meet mine again, and I've never seen anything more beautiful—my girl smiling up at me, cheeks flushed with pride and gaze filled with desire.

But what hits me the hardest is the fact that this house doesn't feel like a home without her in it.

And my heart—not to mention my cock—is led by the leash she's put on me. I'm insatiable when it comes to her, but not just for her body; I need all of her all the time. And I'm starved when she's not near.

I CAN'T BELIEVE I just tattooed him. Ford is amazing at what he does. His brother's skin is a testament to that. I love the tattoo he gave me, and I stare at it often when I get in and out of the shower. And now he has a matching one, which is a little weird but also flattering. And it makes me want to believe that, although he can't say it in words, that deep down, he feels the same as me.

He makes his way back across the room, not bothering to grab his jeans. Instead, he comes over and stops directly in front of me, his crotch almost eye level with my face.

"Stay tonight?" he asks. And I'm too tired to tell him no. So when he holds out his hand to me, I take it.

Here in his home, it always feels like it's just the two of us.

Like I'm in a dream.

It feels right.

It's when I step back out into the world that reality sinks in.

But right now, I wonder if it's really possible to merge those two things.

Can Ford and I really be something more?

Am I allowed to be carried away by this?

I take his hand, accepting all the consequences that might ensue.

He walks me to his room, and when we enter, he climbs onto the bed with me and wraps his arms around my middle, pulling me to him.

"Why am I here, Ford?"

"Because you should always be here. In my bed. In my arms. No more running away."

"What does that mean?"

"You know exactly what it means," he growls. "I can't be a normal boyfriend or show you all the flowery shit. But I can try to be enough for you if you'll let me."

My heart fills, and tears spill over my cheeks as all of my wishes and craziness feel like they're finally aligning.

He gently wipes away the wetness as I sob. "I didn't think you wanted me."

"I've always wanted you. I tried to stay away, but I can't anymore, Chaos. You're in my blood now. I need you. I don't know what this might look like for us. I'll be obsessive. Intense. Probably all the things you don't want in a man, but I can't let you go again."

This is what I've wanted to hear him confess for so long, but it's terrifying because I don't know how my brother or parents will react. But right now, I'm overjoyed. I want Ford. I don't want the push and pull of this dance anymore. I know I'm a lot to handle. I'm hot and cold and don't always react rationally, but I'm certain that's why we might work. I need someone who can handle me as well. I'm finally relieved that Ford, despite the walls surrounding his heart, is finally letting me in.

I hate the tears that continue to fall as I kiss him softly. "You let me decide that. I can handle you."

"Is that a threat?" he asks, and I chuckle.

"No more of a threat than your cock currently digging into my ass."

"Then we agree on something. You and my cock are just as damning and damaging."

I sigh, a sense of relief passing through me. "Definitely. But always a very good time." I bite his bottom lip, and he smiles.

He turns me so my back is against the mattress, and it is like being at home.

"Do you remember when we first started this?" I ask, thinking of where it all began.

"Of course I do."

"And what did you think back then?" I'd never been daring enough to outright ask him.

He seems to think it over, momentarily prioritizing restraint, which I think is rather cute because I can tell it's taking all of his control and willpower. "To be honest, I was always charmed by you, but I never allowed myself to get carried away with improper thoughts. It wasn't until that night that I really jumped on the opportunity. You were my friend's little sister, not someone I should have wanted to crawl between their legs to see what she tasted like." He pauses. "That night in the club changed everything, even the way I view you. You were a girl willing to take risks and barrel through obstacles to get what you wanted and damn the consequences. I can't even express how beautiful you are, it's why I tried to push you away. I wasn't raised like you, Billie. I'm scared I'll taint you, make you dirty in some way."

My eyebrows furrow. All this time, he was holding

back, thinking of himself as something less than, and I never knew. I never want him to feel that way again.

"Ford, you make me happy. Well, most of the time." I chuckle. "You are more incredible than you give yourself credit for. Not once did I think you were less than me. I want you to truly know that."

His smile is small as he stares into my eyes. "Thank you, Chaos, but some things we will disagree on. I thought you'd get sick of me eventually. But then I became addicted to our lies. I didn't think when we started that this would be an issue. I was happy to service your needs and benefit in the process."

I agree with him because I didn't think this would go on for as long as it has, either. And neither of us seem to know how to cut it off. It's like we're drawn to each other without us actually understanding how or why it happened. I'm not complaining about having him in my life, even though he thinks he makes every-thing darker. He doesn't dim any of my light. If anything, he embraces the crazy inside me that's willing to scorch messages in his front lawn and bend me over his knee as punishment for it. Heat starts pounding at my core at the thought, and my gaze lowers to his sizable cock again.

I don't think I'll ever truly understand what's going on in his head, and he may never share that with me, but I won't force it out of him, even if it kills me on the inside not to know.

"Kiss me," I command, and without hesitation, he takes me as I am, his hands cupping my face and drawing my lips to his. I taste and bite at him, savoring this moment as he devours me. I never want this to stop. Never want us to end.

I grab his cock—my favorite toy and anticipate his every touch.

FORTY
BILLIE

Ford's still sleeping peacefully a few hours later. I only ever stayed here for the full night once when I was drunk and brought Felix back, but I wonder, had I stayed any of the other nights, maybe I would've found enjoyment in watching this killer sleep peacefully. He's beautiful, and I see the vulnerability in him now like it's something I have to protect.

I manage to crawl out of his arms, which have had me in a stranglehold, wanting to keep me close. I take in his sleeping form, noting the new tattoo I inked on him, smiling at the crooked lines of the heart. I guess it matches mine, kind of like our feelings toward one another.

I quietly make my way to the door. When I pull it

open, I see Hawke on the other side. I quickly step into the hall and shut the door behind me. Hawke stares at me, his usual smile absent. Instead, he looks mad.

This is so different from the Hawke I know. It's like getting a glimpse of the killer he really is.

I step away from the door in case he wants to say something. I don't want him to wake Ford as I'm sneaking out.

I laid awake next to Ford for at least an hour, trying to decide what I'm going to do about the conversation we had. He's ready to take the leap, and I think I am too, but there's still a part of me that remains terrified of what truly falling means, even if I'm already there.

Hawke points down the hall, indicating that I follow him. *Fuck.* He leads me to the kitchen, and I pick up Felix, using him to soothe me because I know this conversation isn't going to be a smooth one.

"I would say I'm surprised to find you here, but I'm not," Hawke says, crossing his arms. I've never been afraid of Hawke, not that he isn't scary or intimidating —he's both of those things. To me, he's always been a family friend who eats everything in the house. But the man currently standing in front of me doesn't look like the man I know. "I thought you two had stopped after I caught you at Bentley's birthday party."

"We did...for a bit," I say quietly, as if being scolded.

He tsks, and it makes me bristle. Who is he to judge who we sleep with? He'll fuck anything that moves.

As if reading my angry expression, he says, "My brother may be a badass killer, but I still look out for him, and I will do anything for him. He is my twin, after all. And I fucking knew something was up with him; I just couldn't put my finger on it. He dove in like he would with any other addiction. I don't think you realize how much your back and forth impacts him."

"I didn't know about his addictions and vices until recently."

Hawke doesn't seem surprised that I know, or he wouldn't have spoken about it so openly.

"I was fucking there for all of it, and I can't watch him relapse and be hurt again."

"I tried to walk away," I grit.

"You did a pretty shitty job of it if you ask me."

I'm not even sure what to say to that. Is he angry at me? Is he angry at his brother?

He steps back and nods at the door. "I like you, little tornado, but I don't like you for my brother."

"I—"

"You're too normal for him. While you may come

from the same world we do, you're a sheltered princess. The moment Dutton finds out about you two, he'll try to kill Ford. And then I'll get involved, and all that Ford's built over the last few years will be ruined. He's loyal to Eli as much as I am. You complicate that. I get it. You've been shielded for most of your life and wanted to have some fun. But my brother is not to be used by you anymore. Find someone else."

I'm taken aback by what he's saying. Why the fuck does he assume I'm the one doing the hurting? Why does it all have to come crumbling down the moment Ford and I finally find peace with the situation?

But were you ever all in? A tiny voice in the back of my head asks.

Yes.

So why haven't you taken the plunge?

I swallow hard, the internal fight ripping me apart.

What is holding me back?

Hawke just looks at me as if he's waiting for me to say something, but I don't know what to say in this situation. I know everything he said is valid, and he has a right to kick me out. But why does it feel like every time Ford and I take a step forward, we're shoved back onto our asses by reality?

"You're a real asshole, you know that?" I bite out, setting Felix down.

"Maybe. But at least I'm willing to fight for my brother."

I snap, rage and fury blurring my vision as tears begin to stream down my cheeks. How fucking dare he?

But his knowing expression crumbles my resolve because how have I fought *for* Ford? I've only fought against him. Hawke's penetrating glare unravels me like he sees how weak I truly am, and I can't stand it. It's like he's heard all of my inner thoughts and doubts.

Keeping Ford a secret never had anything to do with Dutton.

I was running away all this time from the one thing I wanted. Never willing to take the leap, too scared of how it might break me.

Hawke gave me the reminder that it's not just my feelings on the line. I might've convinced myself Ford was incapable of having feelings or emotions, but I know better than that. If anything, he has more reason to want someone to love him, considering everything he's been through. And I'm still only thinking of myself.

I don't deserve this, I realize with startling clarity, shocked by the impact.

Ford is willing to bring all of our secrets to the light and risk everything he's built for me.

And the intensity of that terrifies me. I know in my gut I want to be with him. But what if I'm wrong about us? What if it implodes, and I don't know how to pick up the pieces?

Love isn't what I thought it'd be.

I turn and head for the door. He says nothing else, but I can feel his gaze until I finally shut the door behind me.

A cab conveniently drives around the corner, and I hail it down. I get into the back seat and breathe in and out, trying to keep the tears at bay.

"Rough morning?" the woman asks, looking at me through the rearview mirror.

I chuckle weakly. "Something like that."

Silence fills the car as she awkwardly twists and offers me a coffee. "I got a spare coffee for free this morning. I was going to throw it out, but it looks like you need it. Sometimes I think everything happens for a reason, you know?"

"Thank you." I awkwardly laugh at the irony as I take the cup from her. Because maybe that's exactly what I need—a boost of coffee to figure out what the fuck I'm doing. I take a sip and swirl it in my mouth. Shit, this really has a kick to it. "Does this have a syrup in it?" I ask, staring at the cup.

The woman shrugs. "I'm not sure. It's not supposed to taste sweet."

My eyebrows furrow in confusion as a sudden drowsiness comes over me.

"Poison, that is," the woman says, looking over her shoulder with a smile. "Poison's not often sweet."

FORTY-ONE
FORD

SHE'S NOT beside me in the bed when I wake up but I hear noises in the kitchen. But when I walk down there, expecting to find her, I see my brother instead, cooking bacon and not looking the slightest bit happy.

That's not fucking good.

"I kept my mouth shut even though I knew it was happening. I stayed silent in hopes that you would end it yourself," Hawke says furiously. "I fucking knew something was up with you. Eli and Dutton are cousins. So when Dutton wants to kill you, Eli will have his back." I say nothing. "Which means I will have to kill my only friend."

Everyone thinks Hawke has a lot of friends because he seems so outgoing and friendly. But the truth is, other than myself, he only really respects Eli and Dutton. We're the only ones who really know him, and I know I'm being selfish by potentially destroying that for us.

"It won't come to that," I tell him, even though I don't know if it's true, as I pull the milk out of the fridge and drink it straight from the carton. I'll still put Billie first. And that hits me with an alarming feeling of anguish. I never thought I'd put anyone before my brother. I'd die for him, but I'd do the same for her.

"You say that now, but we both know Dutton would never approve of you being with his baby sister. He knows where we come from. And while you might think they accept us, we weren't raised the same as them."

A knock comes on the door, and I don't ask if it's Billie because I know it's not. With the way Hawke's looking at me, I can tell he said something to her that made her leave.

"Let's stop talking about this," I say as I walk to the door. I adjust my loose PJ pants, a slight sting on my ass reminding me of the new tattoo.

When I open the door, I find our cousin standing there. Hope pushes her glasses up her nose and looks at me. She's an unusual visitor, considering she prefers to keep to herself when she's in town.

"This letter was on your front porch," she says,

handing me an envelope. "I need to talk to both of you." She pushes past me, welcoming herself in.

I flick the envelope back and forth, confused by the sealed note without a stamp.

"This is important. I need your help," Hope says quickly. I close the door and follow her to the kitchen, not at all surprised that she expected to find Hawke here, too.

She isn't our blood cousin, but we've been around her since Anya and River adopted us. Considering her father and my mother are twins—and bat shit crazy themselves—we immediately had things to bond over.

Hope is only twenty-two, four years younger than us, so Alex was especially guarded about bringing her around when we were all teenagers. But he soon came to realize she's like the little sister we never had. He also trusts Anya's instincts, which somehow gave us a pass directly into his very limited circle of trust.

She drops into town from time to time when she's not touring the world for her sculptures. And although we don't see her often, she's another person we will do anything for.

She's very guarded, much like her father, and I respect that because I'm the same. But she also has a softer side, which I think is thanks to her mother. Lena Love has always accepted Hawke and me. In fact, I'm certain we almost got killed the first time we met her because she gave us a hug, which flared Alek's jealousy. But she never once judged us as delinquents. She was also the first person to ever take us to see a movie in the cinema, which is weird when you think about it because that's something children do with their parents. But we didn't have a normal childhood. And Anya Ivanov wouldn't be caught dead doing something so mundane.

Hawke grabs a third plate and starts serving her food. She thanks him softly.

"Is everything okay?" I ask.

She swallows and nervously fiddles with her thumbs for a moment, then seems to find some resolve as she meets our eyes.

"I want you to teach me how to kill someone."

We both stare at her in shock.

"Sorry, what did you say?" Hawke blurts.

"Oh, yes, little red, we totally can. As long as Uncle Alek won't remove our balls because of it," I say.

She looks down at the food—greasy bacon and eggs—and starts pushing it around with her fork. This is not something I expected at all from Hope.

I open the envelope with a knife as we wait for her to continue.

"I don't want my father to find out," she says with a smile, and it looks half-crazed considering the request.

"Not find out?" I scoff. "You know who your father is, right?"

She pushes her glasses up her nose. "If we can keep it between us, that would be great."

"Okay, so who are we helping you kill?" Hawke asks excitedly.

"*I* want to be the one to kill him. Just teach me how," she insists.

"Who knew there was a little bit of devil in there," Hawke jokes as I pull out the thick sheet of paper.

"Who pissed you off? And why do you want to kill him?" Hawke asks, stuffing bacon into his mouth like a caveman.

"He's a detective. And he lied to me about who he is."

"You want to kill a police officer?" I ask.

"Yep." She nods. "Dead."

Hawke whistles, impressed. He looks at his arms. "I actually have goosebumps because of how proud I am."

I shake my head disapprovingly. And when I turn my attention to the contents of the letter, my entire world stops, and everything I've ever known turns to ash.

You took something from me.
Now it's my turn to take from you.
You have two hours to be at the below address.
Come alone, or she dies.

A LOCK of honey-colored hair spills out of the envelope, and every shackle that's bound me to be a man breaks free, and I become one with the predator. If there's no Billie Taylor in this world, there's no me. I'll do anything to save her.

FORTY-TWO
BILLIE

My head is fucking pounding. I moan, trying my hardest to push past the fog in my brain, but it feels like I'm not waking up fast enough.

Groggily, I open my eyes. I blink once and then twice, trying to clear my hazy vision. Ow. Fuck me, my head really hurts.

"It's about time you woke up." I turn my head in the direction of the voice to find the woman from the cab sitting in the corner.

"Who the fuck are you?" I say, slowly pushing myself up from the cold cement floor.

I scan my surroundings. I'm in what looks like a cell. There's a small single bed to my left and a sink in the corner that's stained with mold.

"That's not a polite way to ask, considering I'm offering you such fine hospitality," the woman says. "Didn't think you'd actually fall for the coffee trick. I was going to use chloroform as a backup, but you took that coffee without question."

I squint at her. She doesn't look familiar. Should I know her?

"And who I am is irrelevant. It's not you I want, but you make good bait for the one I'm after." She glances up the stairs, where I can see a door. We must be in some kind of basement or bunker.

Bait? What is she talking about?

I blink rapidly as I try to stand, but my body isn't cooperating.

"I used to have a lover too, you know. He was very handsome, and we were bound to get married and have kids and live happily ever," she singsongs. "He'd just gotten a really high paying job, and he promised to take me around the world. But then your boyfriend and his brother swept in, killing everyone."

She giggles, the erratic movement making her shoulders twitch. Blisters bubble up her fingers and arms. "He let me go, you know. Your well-trained demon. Most people might have been grateful, but I thought he was mocking me. He took everything from me, and I was left all by myself again."

She laughs hysterically. "Kids called me weird in school, but I always enjoyed experimenting with different potions. Kind of like a witch, you know? Or a scientist? Sometimes they hurt, though." She pouts, looking at the blisters on her arms.

This woman is not fucking sane, I realize. She jumps from one trauma to another, and I'd be so fucking terrified for myself if I didn't already know I was being used to lure in Ford.

"He would never kill a woman," I grit. "And whatever business you have with him, you can take it up with me."

She laughs. "And what? Ruin the fun? It's rather poetic, isn't it?" She squeezes the stool she's sitting on and puts her hand to her lips. "Or wouldn't it be crazy if he didn't come? What if he doesn't actually care? Ooof. I don't know if I'd survive that. I'd probably want to kill myself."

She looks pointedly at a bottle that's propped on a stool in the middle of the room. It seems to glow against the dim light.

The steady sound of water dripping breaks some of the tension in the room.

The woman angles her head strangely, as if listening in on something, and then she points a gun in my direction. "Looks like he's a hero after all. How sweet," she purrs as the wooden door at the top of the stairs is flung open.

"I wouldn't if I were you. I have a perfect shot," she warns.

"No," I squeak quietly. I see his feet before his face as he comes down the steps.

"Be a darling and close the door. Things are about to get interesting in here," she says to Ford as he prowls into the room.

I try to stand again, but my legs feel like jelly.

His gaze lands on me, and without so much as being told, he lowers his crowbars.

"She has nothing to do with this," he growls. "Take me and let her go."

She laughs, swinging her legs joyfully. "On the contrary. You took something precious from me, so I'm going to do the same to you."

His eyebrows furrow in confusion, and she throws her hands in the air. "Isn't it funny how no one ever notices you when you're a woman? You went after my brother but never considered me, huh?"

Understanding dawns in Ford's eyes. "You're Emily Fall. Henry Fall's sister."

"Bingo!" she shouts, pretending to shoot him. "Now, get in the cage with your beloved."

Although the cell door isn't locked, I'm incapable

of standing, no matter how hard I try, so I couldn't have escaped even if I'd had an opportunity.

He doesn't hesitate slipping into the cell with me. She's smug as she crosses the room and padlocks the door.

Ford rushes over to me, desperately scooping me into his arms. "I'm so sorry. I'm so sorry. I'm so sorry," he repeats, and my eyebrows knit together.

I weakly place my hand on his cheek. "This isn't your fault. It was bound to happen one day, considering what our families do."

He presses his forehead to mine, and I'm overwhelmed by the knowledge that this man will find me no matter what. I'm terrified of what's going to happen to us, but right now, I have all the confidence of a grim reaper, even if I can't physically stand up. It seems less scary by his side. Though I wish he wasn't in here with me like some sacrificial lamb.

"Aww, how cute!" the deranged woman gushes, and Ford snaps on her.

"You'll let her out, or so help me, others will come after you. You can do whatever you want with me, but she goes free."

Emily looks shocked for a moment and then smiles, clearly out of her fucking mind. "I'll be long gone before anyone comes here. But I can't say for sure how many days or weeks you'll be here for." She taps the edge of the gun against her chin. "But let me tell you how this little game works. I've been working on my concoctions, you see." She motions to the small bottle on the stool. "This one should be stronger. The other ones took too long for me to get instant gratification." An evil glint flashes in her eyes before she says, "One of you is going to drink that before I let the other one go."

"What?" I blurt, trying to stand again. Ford blocks my view of the crazy woman. I understand he's protecting me, but every hair on my body rises in terror at how things are shifting.

"And if I drink this, you'll let her go?" he asks without hesitation.

"No," I growl, pushing myself as hard as possible to stand on my wobbly legs.

"Of course," Emily says, looking into the barrel of the gun, like she might shoot herself.

I wish she would. I hate that the thought crosses my mind, but I'm willing to put that gun to her head myself if it means we'll make it out of this alive.

We have to make it out alive.

I'm infuriated by my own inability to stand. All those years I took self-defense classes. Honing skills to use if I ever found myself in a worst-case scenario. Yet

I'd somehow so easily fallen for a trick like that. I wasn't thinking clearly, and my brother's words of not taking my safety seriously come back to me. Had I been more cautious in the first place, Ford and I wouldn't be here right now.

"You're lying. You'll just kill us both," I sneer. Emily tilts her head, leaning to the side so she can see me. My silk dress from the previous day is all dirty now, and I imagine I look like a fucking mess. But her eyes sparkle like I'm the most magnificent thing in the room. I shudder at her crazed fixation.

Ford once again moves to block me from her line of sight.

"Motivation is key, I see." She pulls the trigger, and I scream, the jolt of adrenaline and fear forcing me to close my eyes. But when I don't feel pain, they burst open, and a dread fills me.

Ford grunts but doesn't move as his hand goes to his leg. "My, my. Even a demon bleeds red. Just like my boyfriend and just like my brother," Emily seethes. "Drink what's in the bottle, or the next one goes into your head, and then I'll shoot her."

"Ford, don't do it. We can figure this out," I squeak, trying to drag myself to him.

He turns then, those dark-brown eyes the lightest I've ever seen them, which is ridiculous considering the dim lighting in here. Blood runs down his leg, and he smiles, beautiful and stoic, unfiltered from all the things that once weighed us down as if he always knew it might come to this.

I know immediately, and my heart squeezes. "Don't you fucking dare!" I scream.

"It's been fun, Chaos. Thank you for loving me even when you couldn't say it out loud." He smirks playfully. And I throw myself weakly in his direction.

He's too quick. All of it happens in a blink of an eye. Emily leans forward on the edge of her stool in anticipation, waiting excitedly, her breath held. I can't stand or chase him or drag him to me as he grabs the bottle and gulps down the contents.

His face scrunches up as he wipes his mouth. "Definitely not sweet." It's almost instantly his body lurches backward, and I barely have time to catch him as he falls. His weight slams into me, and I smack the back of my head against the brick wall, but I don't even feel it.

"Ford," I squeak as I stare down at his unconscious, pale face. "Ford!" I cry. "Ford! Wake up right fucking now!" I scream violently. My hands are shaking as I slap him. I slap him again as hard as I can. I wait for his devilish smirk or the telltale sign that he's bated me into arguing with him. I wait for him, but there's nothing.

Emily whistles a tune as she scoots off the stool. "My Peter would've died for me as well," she says as she rests the gun over her shoulder, dangling it casually with a loose wrist. "Oh well, now you can die in here together."

"Let us out!" I scream. "Ford. Oh God. Ford, please." I put my fingers to his throat, trying to find a pulse. It's barely there. But it's there. He's still with me. "Don't you fucking leave me, you asshole!"

"Well, toodaloo!" Emily says as she moves toward the staircase.

"Why didn't you kill me too?" I scream violently, desperately trying to tap Ford back to consciousness. I don't know what to do. I don't know how to fix this.

Please, let me fix this.

Her gaze is cold and distant as she looks back over her shoulder at me. "Because that would be too easy. You and I will forever live with the same pain, knowing what it's like to have someone we love taken from us and being left behind in an abyss."

I realize then with startling clarity that she most likely wants to be caught, wants to be killed. I wonder if she was ever a normal woman or if the trauma fucked her up so badly she became this wraith of a creature. I can't empathize with any of it as I scream, unhinged, chaotically, wanting it to tear everything around us down.

"Oooh, a trophy," she coos, picking up one of Ford's crowbars.

"Leave that there!" I yell.

"Why?" she asks daringly. "It's not like anyone is going to find you two. Besides, he's already a dead man. And a dead man doesn't need such an uncivilized weapon."

"Says the bitch who poisons people. You're a coward!" I bite out.

She shrugs, unaffected by my words, as she reaches for the door. "I'm a woman living in a man's world. I found the tools that work for me. Not all of us are handed everything, princess."

Without so much as another glance, she opens the door. Bright light filters in and blinds me as she steps out and closes the door behind her. My heart is rattling in my chest, and I think I'm about to have a panic attack. My eyes adjust to the gloom again as I stare down at his thick eyelashes.

What the fuck do I do?

"Ford?" My voice cracks.

Fuck. Fuck. Fuck.

Stop.

I slap myself across the face, hoping it wakes up my

slow moving body and reins in my focus. I taste blood, and it's enough to drag me back to my senses. I need to get us out of here.

I kiss his forehead. "I'll get us out. I promise."

I drag myself across the cement and onto the bed. My legs are still wobbly as I stretch my arm through the bars toward the remaining crowbar. I can't reach it, so I try to jump, and my ankle gives out. I scream, feeling a sharp, shooting pain as I crumple to the aged mattress.

I take a deep breath and then two more, staring at the crowbar dangling above my head. I dig my nails into the cement wall, determined I will get us out no matter what.

With a steely resolve, I get back to my feet. It's not until the fourth jump that my fingers brush the edge of the crowbar. By the sixth, it clatters off the step, and I barely catch it, terrified it'll fall in the opposite direction.

The smooth metal is cold in my hands, and I inhale, knowing this is the weapon Ford chooses to kill with. Even though it's irrelevant at the moment, I wonder how many people he's murdered. I accepted the fact that he was a killer from the start. But if anyone should live, it's him.

"Stop being a drama queen and wake up," I shout

with my back to him, as I'm not daring enough to look back at him, terrified I might not see the rise and fall of his chest. I talk to him like he's awake, reprimanding him like I always do, because it's the only thing pushing me through. I hold the crowbar outside the bars and angle it down, then strike at the padlock again and again and again.

My hands slip, and I smash my arms. But I ignore it. I strike, and I strike, infuriated by my own weakness.

"I should've never gotten in that cab," I curse, tears streaming down my face.

With bruised, bleeding, and battered arms, the padlock breaks. I'm so shocked that my tears turn into a savage determination I've never known.

I drop to my knees, finally looking at him again.

I will not cry.

We are not done.

"Come on, baby. Wake up. *Please*."

He doesn't respond. I awkwardly try to lift him. I try a few times, my knees dropping to the hard cement under his weight. I drag myself across the bars with his weight crushing me. Slowly, I drag him up the stairs, his crowbar shoved into the back of his pants, convincing myself he'll be sad when he wakes up if he doesn't have it.

Because he *will* wake up.

He has too.

I shove at the door, but it doesn't budge.

"Come on, Billie," I groan as I try again.

It swings open, and bright light takes away my sight. I immediately twist myself around Ford, trying to protect him as I sob, knowing the woman's come back to finish the job.

"Little Tornado!" I hear the voice before I see him, and tears well in my eyes as I look up.

"Hawke." My voice quivers. "She poisoned him. Please, help."

When my vision finally clears, I see the sheer horror and panic on Hawke's face. He pulls Ford from my arms without so much as a strain and grabs my hand to pull me to my feet.

We're in the middle of nowhere, trees surrounding us. In the distance, I see Hawke's car.

He half drags me across the grass as he carries his brother over his shoulder. I've never seen him in a panic like this. He is fast moving, laser focused and looks like he's in total control. He's usually so playful, but even his alter demeanor terrifies me, the reality of how bad the situation is sinking in.

"I'm sorry," I say on a sob, but he doesn't seem to hear me. He's laser focused on getting us out of here.

My legs buckle, but I push through, still affected by whatever the fuck she gave me.

When we reach the car, bile fills my stomach. Hawke's and Ford's cars are beside one another. But there's a third car, which I assume to be Emily's. Beside the open door, I see her lying on the ground, her mouth open, a gunshot wound to her head. Hawke must've tracked Ford's car and found her when she was escaping.

Hawke throws his brother into the back seat, and I crawl in behind him, placing his head on my lap, sobbing as I comb my fingers through his hair.

"Wake up, you asshole," I cry. "Please. *Please.*"

I've never known fear like this, a vise around my throat painfully closing in on me as I begin to realize his breathing has slowed.

Hawke throws the two crowbars into the passenger seat, obviously sharing the same thought as me, expecting Ford to come back to us and carry on with his life.

"Please, please, please," I beg. "Hawke, I don't know what to do," I cry as he hits the gas.

His gaze flicks to me, and it's the most lethal I've ever seen him. I startle at the intensity and imminent guarantee of death. "You've done enough, little tornado."

Every hair on my body rises as I realize I've become the threat.

An obvious weakness for a man who's considered more demon.

But he still bleeds...for me.

And it's cost him his life.

And me with it.

FORTY-THREE
BILLIE

I STARE at Ford's lifeless form lying in the hospital bed. It's been chaos as doctors and nurses hook him to different machines and insert a tube down his throat. I stare, stunned by how he can look like this now when, only twelve hours ago, he was smirking and holding me.

My palms are still sweaty as the poison runs its course through my system.

Hawke and I haven't spoken since we arrived at the hospital. He's standing across from me in the room now, arms folded over his chest as I sit by Ford's side. I have no right to be here. It's my fault. I did this.

"Show me to my son!" I hear the Russian accent echo down the hall toward us before Anya bursts into the room, her gaze immediately landing on Ford. For the first time ever, Anya looks stunned. River pushes her into the room, and she quickly collects herself as she storms up to Hawke. She slaps him across the face. Hard. Hawke barely flinches but looks away, ashamed.

"Where were you? How did you let this happen!" she shouts.

"Anya." River tries to pull her away.

I burst out of my chair, and it screeches across the floor. "It was me!"

She turns to me then as if only just noticing me. Her violent gaze narrows on me. "*You?*"

Hawke looks up at me through thick lashes, his expression unreadable. I'm almost certain he blames me as well.

Now that I have Anya's full attention, I shrink into myself. She's going to kill me.

"A woman kidnapped me and Ford." My bottom lip wobbles because the reality of everything is sinking in. "He drank poison."

"And what, you're too good for him that you couldn't drink it instead?" she demands.

"Anya!" River snaps, pulling her back. "We don't understand the circumstances," he reminds her.

I welcome her anger.

I welcome her to tear me into two.

A dark presence fills the doorway as Eli walks in.

He quickly assesses the situation and gravitates toward me, his full height and mass filling the space as he pointedly stands beside me. He doesn't say anything, and Anya isn't at all deterred by him. But it brings a clear divide to the room.

Eli looks down at his loyal man in the bed and then focuses on Hawke. "Update?"

Hawke clears his throat as if coming back to reality for the first time. He blinks a few times, clearly paralyzed in the same way I am. I sink into my chair, doing everything to fight the tears.

I deserve this, not Ford.

"It appears Emily Fall was behind the poisonings. I dealt with her. Apparently, her lover was part of Laurence Tate's crew, and she was one of the women we let go that night when we killed them."

Anya blinks as if a startling understanding hits her.

"Hmm." Eli hums as he glances back down at Ford, clearly pissed at himself for missing a vital clue before it was too late. I don't know exactly who the people they're referring to are or what business they had with them, but it appears everyone else in the room is fully aware of something I am not. "Do I want to ask how you got involved?"

Eli's penetrating glare turns to me, and I look up at him, tears in my eyes as I wring my hands in my lap.

"Ah," is all he says right before all hell breaks loose.

"I'm going to fucking kill him!" Dutton shouts as he bursts into the room. The information would've trickled to my brother, who would've been able to put pieces of the puzzle together. Eli moves in front of him as Hawke stands at the end of his brothers' bed protectively. "You fucking touched my sister!" Dutton is a wild, savage animal on the hunt for blood.

I jump to my feet and shout, "Stop!" He doesn't hear me. He never does.

Dutton is struggling against Eli. A few punches are exchanged before Anya pulls out a gun and points it at his head. I reach for one of Ford's crowbars, using whatever I have to make sure my brother doesn't actually kill the man I love.

"She would be so lucky to have someone like my son. I don't give a shit who you are. I'll put a bullet in your brain if you try to touch my son," Anya seethes. I'm surprised she hasn't already pulled the trigger.

I shove past Hawke and Eli to stand in front of my brother. He doesn't even look like himself right now, his blue eyes dilated as he glares at me, and it's the angriest I've ever seen him, almost disgusted. How did I fuck this up so badly? I realize that this is simply another thing he couldn't control. He could no longer control me, and I think *that* has more to do with it than who I choose to have by my side.

Not that I have that right anymore.

"Outside," I growl, and when he doesn't move, I point the crowbar at him. "Or I'll point that gun at *your* head instead."

He seems stunned at my outburst, and Eli looks between us, an uncertain expression on his face. But whatever Dutton sees, he doesn't challenge me. He shoves Eli off and storms out of the room. I turn to face the others. "I'm sorry for all the problems I've caused." I put the crowbar down on my way out the door. I don't deserve to hold onto this item.

"You didn't cause this," Hawke says quietly from the corner. Even if they have information I'm not yet aware of, I welcome his hate because I will never not feel responsible for this. I offer him a sad smile because I know I very much led us here. Even if something else was the catalyst for bringing a psychotic woman to prey on us, there were many things I had to apologize for. Many things I can't unsee. Things I can't undo.

I step into the hallway and find my brother pacing.

"How long?" he growls. "How long have you been fucking that street rat?"

Slap! The sound is loud and sharp as I smack my brother across the face. "That *street rat* gave his life for mine." My hands are fisted in pure rage. "Enough of this bullshit! You do not own me. You do not control me. And you cannot hate the man I love!"

His mouth opens slightly and he frowns as if seeing me for the first time. His jaw begins to grind as I see the shift in my brother, evaluating me in an entirely different light... as if, for the first time he is taking me seriously.

"It's not fair that you get to have your happily ever after with Posie while you still watch my every move, preventing me from living my life. I'm not a child, and I swear to God, if you try to interfere anymore, I'll never speak to you again."

"I don't care about that. I want you to be safe and with someone who is worthy—"

"Worthy?" I gasp wildly. "No one will ever measure up to your unrealistic expectations. You were the one who always complained about the expectations placed on you, but you forced your own prejudices onto *me*!"

His eyebrows furrow as he says, "I only ever tried to protect you."

"Instead, you made me fearful of love. You made me want something I thought I couldn't have. And when faced with it, I ran because it scared me. He might die because of me, Dutton. I don't know what further proof you need of a man's worth."

Silence fills the hallway, and doctors avoid coming down the corridor. Most likely paid off for their discretion.

"He's your friend. This has nothing to do with Ford and everything to do with *your* inability to see me as an adult who doesn't need or want your protection. Let me make my own decisions. Let me stumble and fall. Let me make mistakes, Dutton. Just please stop because your *protection* feels like a noose around my neck. No more."

I see my mother and father round the corner, and they pause at the end of the hall.

"He's your friend, and he needs you," I remind him. "He would give his life for yours as much as he would mine. You don't care where he came from or how he was raised. Because right now, you only care about yourself."

But how am I any different from my brother? Adrenaline is pumping through my veins, and I want to fight for my love for Ford as much as I don't feel worthy of it. But deeply rooted amongst all of it is a gripping fear and realization that loving Ford might always be like this. He could die at any moment in his line of work. The deeper I fall for him, the harder it will be to survive. I don't even know if I can manage now.

Tears well in my eyes, and my brother seems unsure as to what to do. I always blamed Ford for not wanting to give me more, but I just sheltered myself from this kind of love, not realizing how much it would hurt.

I did this.

I hurt Ford.

If this is what love is, maybe I don't want it because fuck it hurts so much.

I'm blaming everyone else again and yet the reality is, I'm a coward.

Run. Run. Run

I'm not welcome back in that room.

I'm not welcome out here.

I can't even face my own rollercoaster of emotions, and I know without a doubt I'm about to break down. I refuse to do that in front of anyone else. I don't want to be a burden on anyone else anymore.

It just hurts so much.

I shove past him, his mouth opening and closing in shock.

"Billie," my mother calls out. She tries to grab me, but I shake my head at her, the walls crashing in around me as I try not to hyperventilate.

The one place I want to be is by Ford's side. But how can I face him? How can I love him when this hurts so much? Because love is not guaranteed. And Ford risks his life every day. I can't do this again. I can't be crippled by this fear of losing him.

So I do the only thing I know that's best for both of us.

I run.

I know even that's a lie. I'm only trying to protect myself.

But if I don't, I'll break under the pressure. Maybe I really am just the princess everyone has described me as.

Maybe I'm not as ready as I thought.

Love isn't a fairytale.

FORTY-FOUR
FORD

I HAVE A POUNDING FUCKING HEADACHE, and something's crushing my hand. Slowly, I peel my eyes open and look to my right. My brother is leaning against the wall, his arms folded, and it looks like he's sleeping. I turn my head to the left, where I find my mother, her hand crushing mine as she stares at me like she's willing away the grim reaper himself. My father stands behind her, massaging her shoulders.

The moment she sees my eyes, a relieved sigh rushes out of her. "You fucking took long enough. I was about to kill you myself."

I can't produce a smirk, but she seems to understand. Fuck, I hurt. My body feels like it's on fire.

Everything slowly starts coming back to me, and I try to jerk into action. But restraints keep me in place.

Not restraints...but tubes, IVs, wires, and the like. I'm in a hospital.

"Don't push yourself," My father says, trying to gently shove me back down.

"You fucking idiot!" Hawke says, no longer asleep. He bounds over and pulls me in for a big hug. "I actually thought you were dead. Don't you ever fucking do that to me again."

My head spins as I try to recall everything. "Billie. Where is she?"

My mother clicks her tongue and looks away. "Who cares."

"Where. Is. She?" I growl.

"She's safe," My father confirms.

"Yeah, but she ran like a fucking coward," Hawke seethes.

I lean back, relieved to hear she's safe. "How long have I been out?" *How much have I missed?*

My mother looks at her perfectly manicured nails. "Three days. They only removed the tube from your throat this morning. The doctors say you're lucky to be alive, but I knew you'd pull through. Everyone told me I was crazy for making you both microdose on poisons. But, well, look at us now."

And I know that means my mother cares. *But three days?*

I stare at Hawke. "Where is she?" It's the only thing I need to know. I didn't think twice about drinking that poison. And, to be honest, although we'd built immunity to poisons over the years, there was no guarantee I'd survive. In fact, I'd made peace with the possibility I wouldn't.

As long as she was safe.

"We don't know. She did a runner after everything blew up," Hawke says. When I stare at him, waiting for more, he clarifies, "Dutton found out."

Oh. I'm assuming by the response, it didn't go well. Not that I give a shit.

"Eli?" I ask because I do care about him. I don't want us to have to start over. I don't want to take this from Hawke and me, even though I've been selfish all this time.

"You still have a job if that's what you're asking. But I think it'll be some time until you're up for a challenge."

I smirk. "That, in itself, sounds like a challenge."

An uneasy feeling runs through me.

She ran.

Although I love my mother and my family deeply, if I was going to wake up again, she was the first person I wanted to see. She was terrified in that room, and maybe it was selfish to ignore her pleas, but I was never going to risk her like that.

I move slightly, and my leg begins to throb, reminding me that I've also been shot.

Fuck me, my body's a mess.

"Where is she?" I ask again.

Hawke and Anya share a look.

"No one knows," Hawke says.

"Someone always knows where little chaos is," I reply.

"Not if she chooses to run. Good riddance." my mother scoffs.

"No, Mother," I say, trying to soften my tone.

Her forever-etched scowl deepens, and River rests his hands on her shoulders. "They're not going to be your little boys forever, Anya. You have to let them make their own decisions," he says softly.

She clicks her tongue. "First, it's girlfriends, then it's babies. Then it's not coming over every week and having dinner." She begins to spiral, and I squeeze her hand.

"It's okay. I'll still come over for dinner. And don't worry, Hawke will be single forever."

"Hey!" Hawke says, but it relieves the tension in the room.

"He's the one I'm most worried about bringing me

unexpected babies. Being a grandmother would not look good on me."

My father chuckles as he kisses her cheek. "Everything looks good on you, Red."

A shadow looms on the other side of the closed door, pacing back and forth, but doesn't enter. Hawke raises an eyebrow and opens it to reveal Dutton.

His blue eyes, so similar to Billie's, find me, and I'm certain he's about to kill me. That's until I notice the hand slipped into his. Posie stands behind him, stroking his arm as if to calm him down. I can only imagine how he reacted. He most likely tried to kill me even when I was on my deathbed. I should probably pat down my chest just to make sure he didn't carve a message into my chest while I was out.

Dutton clears his throat. "I'd like to speak to Ford."

"You have a lot of balls walking back into this room." My mother sizes him up.

"Mother, it's okay," I say, barely holding her back with my words.

"I'm not leaving you alone in here," Hawke says stubbornly and leans against the wall with his arms crossed over his chest.

Dutton seems okay with that. My mother eyes him, and my father places a hand on his shoulder as they follow Posie back outside.

Dutton's jaw clenches as he tilts his head back and looks at the ceiling. Hawke stares at him, prepared for anything. And although the others have become our family, it's a reminder that, no matter what, it'll always be Hawke and me. I wonder if part of the reason he can't accept Billie is because he thinks that will change things between us. And in some ways, it will.

"You touched my sister," Dutton grits out.

"Among other things," I reply dryly. His gaze slides to me, and that lethal edge is so close to snapping, but I won't stand down on this, even if I'm chained to a hospital bed.

For once, I want something for myself. And I'll get it even if I have to chase after her time and time again.

Dutton stares at me for some time, licking his lips as his knuckles turn white from how tightly clenched his fists are. "If you hurt her, I'll kill you."

"Obviously," I say.

"And I'm not happy about it."

"Clearly."

He licks his lips again. "And she's the only woman you'll ever be with for the rest of your life," he warns.

"Always." I feel that truth in my bones. In my heart. I will always give her all of me, even when she doesn't want even a portion. Billie's my addiction, but she's also my woman. And I will fight heaven and hell to be by her side.

Dutton's teeth are grinding as he curtly nods, then turns to walk out.

"Wait. Are we good?" Hawke asks, shocked.

Dutton looks over his shoulder at the both of us. "I don't fucking like it, but you're already family."

And then he slips out the door.

"Are you sure about this?" Hawke asks. "I'd be pissed if she bailed on me on my deathbed."

I smirk because it couldn't be more Billie, even if she tried. One more cat and mouse game it is.

"I've never been any more certain of something in my life."

This time, I won't push her away or let her slip through my fingers.

I'll claim her as mine, not letting her run anywhere else but to me.

FORTY-FIVE
BILLIE

The next available flight was to Mexico. I can work remotely, but Rya forced me to take some leave. I actually thought she'd be wildly pissed, considering she warned me not to let outside factors impact my work. But it turns out that when you're kidnapped and almost killed, exceptions are made.

The thought of going to Mexico would normally excite me. I automatically think of sitting on the beach, drinking margaritas, and having tacos every day. But this time it's not fun. I'm spiraling. I hate myself for leaving his side, but my heart hurts so much at the reality that Ford will forever be in danger. And I don't know if I can handle him being hurt again.

I didn't leave Manhattan until I knew he was stable. The moment they took the tubes out, and there were signs of him waking, I fled. I wanted him to be surrounded by his family. Not me, who put him in that hospital in the first place.

Eli filled me in with the details of who the woman was and the connection, but it was irrelevant to me. I felt ashamed and guilty. So helpless in that moment as he almost died in my arms.

I'm a coward, I know. Especially when he messages or calls me. It's such a relief to see his name pop up on my screen, but I've ignored him every time, always fighting my urge to lunge at the phone to answer just so I can hear his voice.

My parents know where I am, and I messaged them the minute I landed safely. My mother told me to call her if I need her and she'll be on the first flight out. Maybe I should tell her everything that's going on. Maybe she's the voice of reason I need. But I'd like to work this out by myself. Everyone's aware of my relationship with Ford now. Our addictive lies are exposed for the entire world to see and judge. And I don't care anymore. I'm just so exhausted.

On the third day, Ford calls again. I stare at the phone. When I don't answer it, my phone starts dinging, indicating text messages coming through, all with his name.

I'm lying in my hotel bed, curled under the blankets. I haven't left the room since I arrived, only ordering room service.

I don't usually spend my parents' money, but in a situation like this, I was more than happy to use a small amount just so I can hide away from our world for a while. I'd always been on the fence as to how much I wanted to embrace the life my family lived, but this feels entirely different. Ford is deeply immersed in this world. His risks run even higher than my father's and brother's involvement because he is actively sent out to risk his life almost on the daily.

An hour later, my mother calls to check in on me, and I answer as I promised.

"Hey, sweetie," she says in that soft tone that immediately makes me want to cry.

Just as I go to reply, I hear a commotion in the background and then Ford's voice floods my ear.

"Are you hiding from me, Chaos?"

To say I'm shocked is an understatement. Not once did I think he would be around my parents when I'm not there.

I curl into myself, contemplating whether I should hang up, but I want to hear his voice. It's been the only sense of relief I've felt since being here.

"Why are you on my mother's phone?" I ask quietly.

"She kindly informed me that she would not tell me where you were, and the only way I was going to find out was if you told me yourself."

Silence stretches, and I pick at my pink toenail polish.

"You're okay?" I finally ask.

"No, I'm not, because my woman's decided to go on a little holiday without me. And to say I'm the jealous type is an understatement," he growls.

I can't speak. Apparently, my parents already had suspicions about our relationship. It explains why she reacted badly toward Matthew at the party. We were clumsier at keeping this secret than I realized. Or maybe I was in denial about the bond that kept pulling us back together.

"Come on, baby, tell me where you are," he pleads. I know it's only a matter of time until he finds me. And the reality is I can only stay away for so long. I was just hoping by the time he found me or I had to head home, that my thoughts would be clearer. Because right now, I can't make sense of anything I want. My heart and head are at war. I want to be with him, but I want to protect myself in the process, and I can't seem to find middle ground.

Yet here he is, on the phone, seeking me out yet again.

We really can't stay away from one another.

Even when I try.

"Mexico," I reply quietly, and my heart picks up, my mind screaming at me that if I reopen this, there's no going back. That if I let him in again, I'm a goner, and I don't know if I can handle the risk and pain. I never knew I was such a coward.

"Where in Mexico?"

"Please hand the phone back to my mother."

"Not until you tell me," he grits.

"I think you already know." My voice is hardly audible. The phone is shuffled around, and I'm not sure what's happening until my mother's voice comes back on the other end.

"He just left," she tells me.

I'm still picking at the nail polish as if unable to lift my head. I don't know why I feel like this. And I don't know how to get out of this funk. I don't know how I'll react when I see him. When I confront him and what happened in that bunker. I don't know how I'll confront the memory of the moment I thought he was dying right in front of my eyes. It haunts me.

"Does Dad know?" I ask.

"Yes."

"And what do you think?" I ask, anxious to hear her answer.

"It's not what about I think, sweetie. This decision, you have to make on your own. But for what it's worth your father and I like Ford. And any man who is willing to die for our daughter is accepted into our family, even if he wasn't already before. But you have to put that man out of his misery. He was pacing my carpet."

"It's scary," I admit, my hand going to my heart. I feel so deeply for him. Care far more than I ever thought possible. And the way he dictates my mood, for better or worse, can't be a good thing. Right?

"Love is a scary thing. It's not guaranteed unless you speak to one another honestly. But, sweetie, imagine your life both with and without Ford. That will be your answer. If you can let him go, then you never loved him enough. And that's okay, too. But if you're willing to risk the hurt and the fall, then some-times that's when the most beautiful thing can arise. Trust in what your heart is already telling you."

"Thanks, Mom. I need to think."

"Or maybe you simply need to *be*. Go for a walk or something."

I laugh as I wipe away tears. "That sounds good too. Bye, Mom." I hang up the phone.

For the first time since being at the hotel, I put on my bikini and walk to the beach. I sit in the sand, watching the crashing waves, wondering what my life would be like without him in it. I could move away; I've done it before. But if I came back to visit family and I saw him with another woman... The thought makes me want to be sick. But worse is the thought of not laughing with him, of not pushing each other's buttons, and not embracing the wild, chaotic love we have.

I DECIDE to return to the hotel for a nap. It feels like the sun has sapped the last of my energy. Five hours later, I'm woken by someone knocking on my door. I sit up in my bed and look to it, my heart racing.

I didn't expect for him to get here until tomorrow at the earliest. Then again, knowing Ford, he most likely hopped on his family's private jet the moment he figured out my location.

I'm still terrified at the idea of facing reality with him. I'm also ashamed for running away. But despite that, part of me is so grateful he gave chase one more time.

They say even if you run from love, it will find you. And I ran. And my guess is that it's him on the other side of that door. Could I possibly make him run by telling him how terrified I am by loving him so deeply? Would that be the last and final straw for him? I doubt it.

I don't know if he's ever been in love. I have a feeling the answer is no. I've never been in love before, either, so it took me a while to work out what these feelings were. And I had to do that all by myself because we were a secret for so long.

The knocking grows more insistent, and I finally muster the strength to get out of bed and make my way to the door. Pulling it open, I see him there, one hand on the doorjamb and the other raised as if he's ready to start knocking again. His hand drops, and he stands tall. His dark eyes soak me in from head to toe. I'm waiting for him to speak because I don't know what to say. He reaches out and pulls me into a hug. I'm so startled that tears start streaming down my face.

Whenever he touches me, I lose myself in him. But I'm so scared. This goes beyond just sex and addiction.

"Hello, Chaos." He takes a step into the room and shuts the door behind him, all while keeping me in his embrace, even though I try my hardest to push him away. He grunts, and I realize he's obviously not at full health. He has a slight limp, and guilt floods me all over again.

Once he lets me go, I put distance between us

because the power he has over me when he's close is terrifying.

He prowls toward me until my legs hit the bed, and I'm forced to sit. He looms over me like a demon, his dark gaze penetrating.

"Why are you here?" I squeak. I know why he's here. Deep down, I know why he flew all this way to recapture me. But I'm so fucking scared of taking that final plunge. I mean, at least I hope that's why he's here.

"For you," he says, dropping to his knees and laying his head in my lap.

I'm stunned, unsure of how to touch him as he hugs me. Slowly, my fingers feather through his hair, and I'm reminded all over again of being in the back seat of the car, focusing on his every breath like it was my own because the moment it would've stopped... I couldn't handle the thought.

"I thought you were going to die," I say quietly.

I heard after the fact about the twins microdosing poison over the years, but it didn't guarantee anything that day. In fact, that she let me go was a miracle. But not once did I care about that. If he was gone, so was I. Having that type of leverage over me is a terrifying thing.

"I didn't," he replies.

"Ford, I held you while you were dying, and I thought—" Tears stream over my cheeks. "It scared me. Your job puts you in danger every day. You could leave me any day."

He looks up then, a small smile curving his lips, as he reaches for me. "Yep" is his only response, and it makes me so mad. His smile grows wider. "I missed the fire in your eyes."

"This is serious," I reprimand.

"I'll win you back."

"Win me back?" I ask, confused. "Am I a toy?"

"No, you're the woman I've fallen for, and I can't make it stop."

His admission shocks me. I've never heard him be so truthful about his feelings for me before, and I can't say I don't enjoy hearing them because I really do. Butterflies take off in my stomach.

"Does that scare you?" I ask. Is he as terrified about this as I am, or am I the only one feeling all of this?

"You have no fucking idea how much," he mutters, pulling me into his chest so his arms can wrap around my body.

"I love you, Ford, and it scares me so much." I squeak.

And before I can stop myself, I'm crying.

"I know. That's why I came here myself to hand deliver the message," he says, leaning back so he can see my face. "I love you, Billie Taylor. More than an addiction. More than my job. More than my brother."

I gasp because I know how close the two of them are. They would die for one another, and I don't feel like I deserve that intensity. I want it, but that type of devotion is terrifying, and I know when I accept it, there's no going back.

"I love you so fucking much I was willing to let my world crumble around me if you would even consider giving me a chance. I'm sick of thinking I'm not good enough for you. *You* are what I want, and *you* are what I will have. So, to answer your question once again as to why I'm here, I'm here for you, Chaos. And for me."

That last bit is what sends me over the edge.

"Promise me you won't die on me," I beg.

A slow smile stretches his lips. "Only by your hands, Chaos. I'm sure I'll piss you off enough one day."

"Shut up," I choke out as I thread my fingers through his hair.

"But I can't promise you that. There's no guarantee for either of us. But I know for me, a life without you is not worth living."

I laugh at the stupidity of how perfect all of his words are when, for months, we could hardly see eye to eye or express ourselves. He looks at me, confused, because the moment it bubbles to the surface, I feel like I'm free like it's the normal us again. I realize then that maybe relationships are about the good outweighing the bad. That it's not always meant to be easy, but if the love is strong enough, then any obstacle can be overcome. "And you said you weren't a romantic."

He grumbles as he places his head back in my lap. "Just don't be expecting any normal dates from me, okay? Because there's no way I'll be able to go even a few minutes sitting across from you without wanting to rip your clothes off."

Heat swarms to my core. "I don't think I was signing up for normal when I dragged you into the back of your car and let you eat me out with a lollipop."

He grins. "Just make sure that no matter how mad you are with me, you'll still carry around sweets in your bag."

I fold my body over his, pressing my lips to his forehead. "Always. But I have one request for you and one date."

He growls. "You already sound so demanding."

I chuckle as I pepper him with kisses. I realize now how tired he still looks, how sickly pale he is compared to usual. Yet he flew all this way for me. "I love you, Ford Ivanov. And I want you to be my date for a wedding."

FORTY-SIX
FORD

We've been here now for two days, and I'm getting messages asking me where I am. But there's no other place I would rather be, and it's the best type of recovery. I'm not one for holidays or adventures. I usually stick to my routine but watching Billie in a bathing suit lounging by the ocean, happily drinking margaritas, is something I could very much get used to. She's beautiful and everything I've ever wanted.

When it comes time to leave, to head back to our new reality and go to the wedding, it's bittersweet that we have to leave this place. I know we have to move past some things. What we went through that day in the cellar terrified hete4xtr to the bone. But together, we'll work through it.

I expected her to sleep on the plane ride back, but

she watched a movie, chewing her nails and bouncing her leg. She's nervous about facing everyone after everything that happened, but we'll get through it. We always have. Somehow, someway, as long as I have her fueling me, I know I'll die a happy man.

"Are you ready?" I ask, grabbing her hand as we walk off the plane. I smile to myself when she doesn't pull away. Instead, she leans into me. A car is already waiting for us, and it takes us straight to the wedding venue. I can't help but find her nervousness cute as we make our debut at her brother's wedding. And hopefully, this time, no one is pointing guns at each other's heads.

THE CEREMONY IS BEAUTIFUL, and I can't help but smile when Bentley walks down the aisle in his little suit. And I swear, I fucking swear, there's a tear in Dutton's eye when he sees Posie in her dress, and I'm sure as shit going to make sure I never let him live it down.

Hawke laughs as she walks down the aisle, and I have to nudge him to stop. Billie stands across from me, trying her hardest not to laugh. I wonder if she and I will do this someday. I know there's no other woman for me, but I think we're both content with the boyfriend-girlfriend title for now. The thought feels so foreign that I want to gag. But for her, I'm willing to subscribe to "normal" titles.

THE PARTY IS in full swing and Hawke's nowhere to be found, most likely fucking God knows who. I just hope she's not married to anyone here, because with this type of crowd, someone will definitely kill him for it.

Billie's sipping a vodka soda. She looks beautiful in her deep-red bridesmaid dress. I smirk when I notice the bracelet with the charms I got her. It's true that I'm not a man who needs much, but I'm happy I can spoil her because of it.

Ivy comes to a stop in front of us. "Well, a killer and an accountant. I never thought that would be a pairing I'd ever see."

"I'm sorry I didn't tell you sooner," Billie says quietly, almost ashamed.

"Oh." Ivy looks between us. "You thought you two were good at keeping that a secret? I knew a year ago."

"What?" Billie snaps.

Ivy laughs.

"Was it Hawke?" Billie asks, because my brother does have the reputation of having the biggest mouth. But I don't think he would share something like this.

Ivy arches a suggestive eyebrow. "I have my ways. Besides, I'm happy for you two. But I swear, if you hurt her, I'll kill you myself." She directs the last part at me. "That's a promise."

"I seem to be getting a lot of those threats lately," I say, adjusting my uncomfortable suit.

She chuckles, then wanders off as Billie leans in. "Should we sneak out and head to your place?"

I arch an eyebrow, surprised. "I thought you'd want to stay longer."

"We've taken the family photos already. Besides, I miss Felix."

"It has nothing to do with my bed?" I whisper into her ear.

She chuckles, raising to her tippy-toes and pressing a kiss to the corner of my lips. "Well, it always has something to do with that, doesn't it?"

My cock twitches, and I'm already leading us toward the door. We sneak out, certain no one sees us, and wait for the driver to bring my car around. As the car comes to a stop, a voice calls out from behind us.

"Hi, excuse me. You're Billie Taylor, right?" a guy almost the same size as my brother asks.

I immediately shove Billie behind me and square up with him. I don't know who the fuck this guy is, but he oozes complications. And he looks like a fucking cop.

"You don't have to feel threatened by me," he says, trying to sound nonthreatening but failing.

"Says the man who approached us from behind. What do you want with my woman?" I growl.

"I just have a few questions about Hope Ivanov. You're close with her, aren't you?"

"What are you, a detective or something?" Billie bites back, stepping to my side.

"Sure am." The man shows us a badge. "I have a few questions about Ms. Ivanov and her potential connection to a recent murder."

"That's nice. But we're on our way home," she tells him.

"Your cooperation would be appreciated," he says, trying to throw on the charm.

"And so would a warrant," I say, opening the door and helping Billie in first. "But we don't all get what we want, huh?"

He's pissed, and I make a point to memorize his features. I don't know what trouble my cousin's found herself in, but this man is bad news. Anyone who starts sniffing around our business is.

I get into the car, and the driver takes off. I have a woman to please, one who has an insatiable appetite.

"Don't let it bother you," I tell her as I pull her against me in the back seat, though I know it will. Hope is one of her best friends. So I'm surprised when she turns to me and slams her lips to mine, the thread of her control snapping. I fall into rhythm with her, devouring her, the driver be damned.

I will never get enough of this woman.

No matter how many hits of her I have, she will forever be my addiction.

And I will die a happy man.

ALSO BY T.L. SMITH

Black (Black #1)

Red (Black #2)

White (Black #3)

Green (Black #4)

Kandiland

Pure Punishment (Standalone)

Antagonize Me (Standalone)

Degrade (Flawed #1)

Twisted (Flawed #2)

Distrust (Smirnov Bratva #1) FREE

Disbelief (Smirnov Bratva #2)

Defiance (Smirnov Bratva #3)

Dismissed (Smirnov Bratva #4)

Lovesick (Standalone)

Lotus (Standalone)

Savage Collision (A Savage Love Duet book 1)

Savage Reckoning (A Savage Love Duet book 2)

Buried in Lies

Distorted Love (Dark Intentions Duet 1)

Sinister Love (Dark Intentions Duet 2)

Cavalier (Crimson Elite #1)

Anguished (Crimson Elite #2)

Conceited (Crimson Elite #3)

Insolent (Crimson Elite #4)

Playette

Love Drunk

Hate Sober

Heartbreak Me (Duet #1)

Heartbreak You (Duet #2)

My Beautiful Poison

My Wicked Heart

My Cruel Lover

Chained Hands

Locked Hearts

Sinful Hands

Shackled Hearts

Reckless Hands

Arranged Hearts

Unlikely Queen

A Villain's Kiss

Connect with T.L Smith by tlsmithauthor.com

T.L. SMITH

USA Today Best Selling Author T.L. Smith loves to write her characters with flaws so beautiful and dark you can't turn away. Her books have been translated into several languages. If you don't catch up with her in her home state of Queensland, Australia you can usually find her travelling the world, either sitting on a beach in Bali or exploring Alcatraz in San Francisco or walking the streets of New York.

Connect with me tlsmithauthor.com

KIA CARRINGTON-RUSSELL

Australian Author, Kia Carrington-Russell is known for her recognizable style of kick a$$ heroines, fast-paced action, enemies to lovers and romance that dances from light to dark in multiple genres including Fantasy, Dark and Contemporary Romance.

Obsessed with all things coffee, food and travel, Kia is always seeking out her next adventure internationally. Now back in her home country of Australia, she takes her Cavoodle, Sia along morning walks on beautiful coastline beaches, building worlds in the sea breezes and contemplating which deliciously haunting story to write next.

www.ingramcontent.com/pod-product-compliance
Lightning Source LLC
Chambersburg PA
CBHW072036190726
48294CB00005B/1281